The Dreams of the Eternal City

The Dreams of the Eternal City

Mark Reece

Matador
9 Priory Business Park,
Wistow Road, Kibworth Beauchamp,
Leicestershire. LE8 0RX
Tel: 0116 279 2299
Email: books@troubador.co.uk
Web: www.troubador.co.uk/matador
Twitter: @matadorbooks

ISBN 978 1789015 577

British Library Cataloguing in Publication Data.
A catalogue record for this book is available from the British Library.

Printed and bound in Great Britain by 4edge Limited
Typeset in 11pt Adobe Garamond Pro by Troubador Publishing Ltd, Leicester, UK

Matador is an imprint of Troubador Publishing Ltd

Everything Burns

The Eternal City, 2040

THE AIRPORT BURNED SURPRISINGLY QUICKLY, transformed in a moment by deft hands and hidden purposes. Ethan Thomas stood when feeling smoke in his nose, the smell a solid lump, as if he had inhaled coal dust. He followed his self-defence training, which had taught him to never stay still in an emergency. He knew what to do; civic duty had compelled him to violence before.

As he turned a corner into the area between the departure lounges, feedback echoed over the public address system, sounding like the screech of a dying eagle. He stumbled back and jammed his hands over his ears, imagining that blood was pouring from them. A woman bumped into him as she ran the opposite way carrying a baby. Other commuters looked around silently, trying to comprehend, or else screamed, screamed. Black tarpaulins fell over shop fronts, covering the brand logos with stitched 'I's, the ends of which were looped. Ethan felt a wisp of breeze on his cheek that suddenly melted his flesh. He rubbed his face and his skin pulled. With a painful tear, he removed a burnt piece of paper. He recognised a few words that told him that it had been torn from a copy of the Sleep Code. He looked up to see shreds of flaming pages fluttering from the roof.

He wanted to spit out smoke as he stumbled along but his tongue was too scorched. A thick red cloud emerged from benches before him. Ethan realised that he had reached the area where he had sat with his girlfriend, Aislin, only an hour before. He stumbled forward and stepped on something that pressed into the ground, making his feet slide. He broke his fall by pushing out with his left hand, as per his training, but still hit the floor hard on the small of his back. He groaned as he felt pieces of smashed plant pot stick into his ears. Dazed, he tried to stand, to see a figure on some sort of raised dais, illuminated by a series of flashes, wearing loose black trousers and a t-shirt with the same 'I' symbol that hung over the shops.

"Your civilisation shakes, men of the Sleep Code! You have forgotten that what is made by men always burns! You've fooled yourselves into thinking that the weight you place on your rules has made them part of the nature of things! But everything burns, you are one match away from total loss!"

Ethan navigated around the benches by holding his arms out like a blind man. His heart leapt when a security guard appeared – he must have been hiding in the smoke – and shone a torch in the preacher's face. The violent light made him squint. From his angle, Ethan saw him pull his arm back. The preacher grabbed the guard by the shoulders and pulled him aside. Ethan was dazzled by the glimmer from the shard of glass he clutched, which made blood drip from his palm. He moved to the side too slowly, and the preacher drove the point into his shoulder. He felt no pain, nothing at all, but could not move his arm and dropped to his knees.

The preacher stood over him, muttering furiously, his face distorted into a blur. Ethan held out his good hand. He saw Aislin without looking at her.

She hit the preacher's jaw with the bottom of her palm. The blow was perfectly timed and knocked him to the ground. Aislin checked that he was unconscious before examining Ethan's shoulder. "Terrific," she said.

They stayed at the scene until more guards arrived. Lights flickered on within a few minutes, showing Ethan that his senses had exaggerated the destruction. As soon as the tarpaulins were removed and the scraps of paper swept away, only the acrid smell and a few abandoned pieces of luggage betrayed that an incident had occurred. Some of the guards took the preacher away while others took them to a back room. When Ethan and Aislin showed them their identity cards, they were ushered through to the airport's Security Commander, who shook their hands and said, "I'm sorry about this but I'll need to take a quick statement from you both, and your branch details, please. Don't worry, your flight won't leave until you're on it."

"Of course," Ethan said.

After taking their accounts, the Security Commander insisted that Ethan see a doctor. His wound was superficial and required only antiseptic and a dressing.

Aislin was sitting swinging her legs when Ethan came out of the medical office. "Come on then, I think we've earned this," she said.

"But what about… it can't just have been that one, there must have been loads of them to have set up something like this."

"Ethan, you're not taking on this job now. Am I going by myself?"

"But isn't—?"

"No. You're not going to make me have your suitcase."

Ethan smiled. "I bet you could carry both."

"Come on, we're keeping everyone waiting. This is what happens when you spend too much time at your desk. You're getting soft."

"What can I say? I agree with you."

"Finally, you're making sense. Now let's go on holiday before the next thing happens."

The plane departed shortly after they boarded it. News of the incident was not reported until two days later, when no mention was made of Ethan Thomas or Aislin Doherty.

One

ETHAN SHOOK HIS WORK MOBILE as he walked from the train station to his office, feeling the cold from melting snow for the first time that morning. It had been playing up all weekend, meaning that he had not been able to find out how many new cases had been reported since he had been away. Messages often took a long time to reach it, as the mobiles issued to agents used the archaic cellular network. That was supposed to prevent them from being hacked, as only the very poor still used cellular mobiles, meaning that they were rarely targeted by criminals anymore. However, security was not ideal, it never was. Aislin had not allowed him to take it on holiday, meaning that he was two weeks out of date.

After giving up on the mobile, Ethan observed the general stupor around him. Everyone he passed had the same glazed look of the half-awake commuter, their Monday morning sleep having been interrupted so violently that they had left parts of themselves behind in roughly made beds. The city itself seemed weary after the short lull from the underworld of its night-time economy. It too, perhaps, wanted to sleep. Ethan hurried around a huge circular fountain, always bubbling, the heights of which were covered with posters that gave colourful depictions of the developments taking place: skyscrapers that would make ants out of all existing structures. The same words were on the top of each one, visible from every angle: 'The Eternal City'.

Ethan flitted through the drowsy commuter procession. Men he passed fiddled with their ties without making any discernable difference to their appearance; women shuffled their handbags into a more comfortable position, only for them to drop back two steps later. Ethan's groggy sense of early morning meant that he struggled to distinguish any details of the people he passed; they were like dream figures in the way he could discern only their outlines.

He made his way past a line of shops, the signs of which were so dirty that they were only useful in so far as one could infer the nature of the businesses from the pictures. Their dilapidated state was typical of premises in Central Zone. Ethan had walked past them most days since he had started his job, eight years earlier. He had recommended several times that they be closed due to their suspected links to subversion, and the fact that he had been ignored made the sight of them a recurring irritation. Tattered posters fluttered against their windows, displaying cars with speed lines behind them, and future developments of statues gleaming in crowded squares.

After the shops, Ethan cut through a field. There never seemed to be anyone else going through it at that time in the morning, and he floated across its vast distance. Then he navigated through Central Zone, the amount of roadworks enabling him to move faster than those travelling by car. A coppery butterfly followed him from the field, its colour camouflaging it in the urban decay. It spiralled around him awhile before being unable to keep up with his steps. He felt driven by his surroundings, as if a figment of the butterfly's dreams.

Finally, after those long ten minutes, Ethan arrived at the headquarters of the Sleep and Dreams Monitoring Agency

(SDMA), 'the trading standards of the mind'. If the shopping centres were often called the heart of the city, then the SDMA was the blood, supplying the oxygen of well-regulated sleep. The building was so tall that one could only see it fully from several roads away. It was surrounded by a concrete pavilion twenty metres square that was filled with prongs and spikes designed to stop terrorist attacks. Ethan paused to adjust his bag; from his distance he could see only as far as the clouds that were painted on the tenth floor, beneath which were the letters SDMA, sky blue over blacked out windows.

After getting inside, Ethan felt a heavy, onerous sense of reality. When he had first received his security clearance, one of the senior agents, Daniel Lee, had led him into the building and said that the agents who worked there were on the front line of protecting society, regardless of what the ignorant or naïve decided to believe, and he had never forgotten his words. In fact, he had paraphrased them several times, both in reports and in arguments.

Ethan was peppered by a series of multi-coloured dots as he walked through the lobby. He had never asked what they were, nor had anyone ever spoken about them to him, which had made him assume that they were a restricted technology. No unauthorised tablets, Internet-based devices, cameras, or anything that could record, would work inside the building, and he had always been content to assume that the dots were something to do with controlling those types of security risk.

He went through a second set of translucent double doors, which strained his muscles to push open, muttering 'morning' to the security guards; he had never learnt their names. He pressed his identity card against a barrier, and when a light flashed green, a section of it parted, sounding like a giant sucking lip and leaving only the SDMA clouds logo visible at the top. His card was so heavy that it had long since ripped the inside of his coat pocket. They were always described as 'state of the art' in SDMA literature, although their bulk made them seem obsolete.

When he entered a lift, he pressed the button for the tenth floor and stretched his arms. In the few seconds it took to get there, the soreness of his feet, unused as he was to the walk after two weeks away, and a flash of pain across his forehead, proved that he was awake; he could still hear the cruel ringing of his alarm clock, beating its legally obligatory drum.

At his floor, Ethan walked the two metres of corridor allowed him before reaching another security barrier, with a scanner before it. For that one, he had to place his finger into a slot after sliding his identity card through, and felt a momentary sense of dread when it did not immediately register; the last time the machine had broken, he had spent an entire day walking back and forth between SDMA technical stations around Central Zone to re-register himself. However, perhaps the machine was still waking up; the barrier parted a few seconds later.

Ethan's office was at the far end of the tenth floor. Each section had a security barrier with a noticeboard beside it that gave a list of the people who worked there, their rank, information about social events, instructions about the proper usage of the gym, and summaries of workplace regulations. There were long stretches of bare corridor between the sections, punctuated only by service lifts. Ethan had to walk past countless such entrances and the distance seemed as long as that from the station to the SDMA building.

The door to his section was covered with the same posters as elsewhere, although prominent amongst them was a sign in thick black lettering that read:

'This is a paperless office. All printed materials must be destroyed at the end of the working day.'

The moment he opened the door, he frowned when seeing stacks of paper in irregular piles, from floor to ceiling in one corner, overflowing from desks elsewhere. The problem was that despite the security advantages of electronic files, the SDMA had to deal with numerous organisations large and small, only some of which could interface with their computer systems, with a few that could only reliably handle printed records. There were secure cabinets at various places around the room, taking up large amounts of space, most of which were empty. Despite the excuses different agents gave, Ethan knew that this was because most of them cared more about leaving early than protecting the organisation. He angled himself through the morass, nodding when making out colleagues. His desk was tidier than the others as he had finished and filed all his assigned cases before going on leave. There were a series of framed awards at the back of his desk, discretely hidden by his in-tray but visible from his seat. They were as familiar and comforting to him as old family photographs were to others.

"All right, mate?" Mohammed, who sat opposite him, said, his thick hair sticking up as though electrified, his grin as wide as that of a cartoon character.

"Hi. How are we getting on for cases? The work mobile's playing up again."

And with that, Ethan was released from early morning sleep deprivation. When he spoke, the weariness that had seemed as if it would last forever moved to the back of his mind, in the same way that one is entranced awhile by sunbeams bouncing off one's bed on a warm Saturday morning, until one gets up, at which point, one's consciousness of the sun fades until it barely exists. Sleep deprivation was always present when he was at work but not as a nagging presence like it was at home, and that was only one measure of its injustice.

"Yeah, good, mate. It's gone to hell since you've been off. You won't believed the bags of shit we've had to deal with."

"*The bags of shit?*" Ethan raised his eyebrows, making Mohammed hunch his shoulders to laugh.

"That's just what it's been though. I'll go through that crap in a bit. First, more importantly, did you enjoy going away with your mother-in-law?" Mo parted his lips, and Ethan knew that he was going to laugh whatever he said.

"They're not your in-laws until you're married. Before then, they're just interested parties."

Mohammed could not contain himself any longer, his head rocking back so far that Ethan saw his permanently stubbly neck.

"'Interested parties', that's good man. Whatever the fuck they are, did you manage to get through in one piece?"

"They were fine. Well, nothing beyond the norm anyway. Ash did her usual thing of getting up early with her dad to run God knows how many miles around the hotel. And Ash's mother talked about nothing but weddings and marriage the whole time."

Mohammed laughed again, and although Ethan had crouched down to switch on his computer, he could see his glowing face as clearly as if he were looking at him. Ethan suppressed a sigh. *Looks like I'll have to read the new files myself,* he thought.

"Fuck me, you're caught in the web now. Once you talk to her mum about it, that's it. I tell ya, when Hasna's mum mentioned marriage for the first time, she didn't stay an interested party for long. This is getting serious."

"We'll see. Who can know what'll happen in five years' time?"

"That's good stuff, man. I like it. That's what I should have said. When I was—"

"Has anyone found out what's wrong with Si since I've been away?"

"No, mate, no one's heard anything."

"Have there been any cases with press interest?"

"A few. There was an Ick who'd gone mad and smashed a school up. We were all running round for a few days but it's under control now. I've sent you the file to look over, I knew you wouldn't want to miss out."

"Good."

Ethan went to the end of the office to check whether anyone had bothered to print off the performance data that compared their team to those based in other city zones. No one had, and he added it to his mental list of tasks before returning to his desk. Mohammed had already wandered off.

The office had a central walkway with workspaces coming off it either side, each of which contained two circular desks facing each other. It was set up to contain security breaches, the theory being that anyone wanting to look at information left on someone else's desk or computer would have to make a deliberate effort to go there, which would be obvious to others in the office. From his position nearest the window, Ethan could see part of the walkway behind Mohammed's chair, whereas the dividers to his left and right insulated him from adjoining workspaces. The layout also meant that the two people who sat opposite each other tended to work as a pair and shared their workloads.

Ethan scanned his identity card over the screen then entered his password. A picture of a DNA spiral appeared and he pressed his index finger against the top right of his keyboard. He felt a sharp pain and the screen froze. Ethan licked the cut while the machine confirmed his sample. Agents were barred from being blood donors because of how much blood they lost at work. His SDMA computer was twenty years out of date compared with his personal one at home, except in its security measures – the screen could not even project images. The archaic nature of much SDMA equipment was something to do with contracts, something to do with budgets, and something to do with security. Apparently.

The start page of the secure work intranet loaded, depicting the SDMA logo and slogan above the words 'Always Vigilant', set against a sky blue background. The remainder of the screen was filled with exhortations to report suspicious activity, the number of the Public Safety Hotline (PSH), where people could report concerns, and advertisements for the various sponsors of the organisation. Ethan pressed the continue button at the bottom of the screen, taking him to the security warning:

'It is incumbent upon everyone to be aware of policy. It is incumbent upon everyone to follow policy. The Sleep Code supersedes all other law.'

Those were the words he saw whenever he opened his computer, and that had become a homily by repetition, albeit one he agreed with.

SDMA computers were all set out in the same way and Ethan was comforted by the familiar sight. On the left-hand side of the screen was a folder called 'Thomas_workspace', in which he kept his personal files. In the centre were a series of shortcuts to the various software used by someone of his rank. On the right-hand side was a folder called 'library', which contained a full copy of the Sleep Code, with sub-folders that grouped information that agents referred to most often, such as the conditions of commonly issued sleep licences that permitted expectant mothers or shift workers to temporarily change the hours in which they were lawfully permitted to sleep. The folder also contained summaries of relevant branches of criminal and civil law, and other useful information, such as documents describing best investigative practice.

He opened his e-mails to see that while he had been away, his supervisor Peter had assigned Ethan ten cases of suspected breaches of the Sleep Code to investigate. He added them to his spreadsheet of work; they all sounded like small jobs that he could probably conclude in a few weeks. There was also a message from the airport Security Commander, in which he said that he had made a recommendation for Ethan and Aislin to receive citations for bravery for their actions before going on holiday.

After he had finished reading, Ethan saw Peter hanging around by a pile of papers behind Mohammed's chair. He looked away but he had already seen him.

"Hi Eth. Did you err… enjoy your time off and everything?"

"Yeah, just sorted out some bits and pieces. Nothing to tell."

Peter picked a liver spot on his cheek.

"Good… good. Well, I hope you've come back refreshed. Are you free at nine? There's a meeting to discuss… various things."

"Erm… okay."

"Thanks. Are you all right with them other things I've sent through? I know there's a lot but… oh, have you had chance to look through them yet, you've probably only just got here?"

"It'll be fine."

"Good, I'll see you in the conference room then. There's also… hang on, I've just got to…"

He stepped into the main walkway, raised his hands, then said, "Hi everyone… can I have your attention a minute… yeah… thanks. We've got Dan and a few of the other senior managers coming round at nine, so can you file as much paper as you can by then?"

"How can we get rid of this lot in an hour?" one of the Sleep Investigators, Alfie, shouted.

"You don't have to sort all of it, just enough that it looks like we're trying to comply with policy. If they can see the other side of the office from the door it'd be a start. Thanks."

No one had stopped talking while Peter spoke. Ethan was irritated by the announcement, as he would not be able to do anything in half an hour, and as the brass would no doubt be at the meeting, he would be unlikely to leave the conference room before lunchtime. *It's like they go out of their way to stop you doing your work.*

Mohammed came back a few minutes later, "What's going on?"

"Waste of space said that we've got to get the desks paperless before nine 'cos the bosses are coming over."

"Yeah right. I can get rid of the top layer, I don't know about paperless."

He laughed, making his papers rustle.

"I'd put away as much as you can if I was you. This could be the occasion when they decide to enforce the policies rather than keep making new ones."

"I suppose so."

"And put your picture of Has away as well, they might check up on that at the same time."

"Fuck, man, how am I supposed to get through the day without something good to look at?"

"A reminder e-mail went round about it while I was off so they're not likely to accept any excuses."

The policy against personally identifiable items was widely ignored, although Ethan did not have a picture of Aislin on his desk.

After checking his papers in his assigned cabinet, Ethan skim-read the new cases he had been assigned.

When Peter reappeared at quarter to nine, Ethan's desk was the only one in the office to be policy compliant.

Daniel Lee, the Senior Agent, did not arrive until half nine, when he stood in the walkway with a group Ethan had never seen before. The Sleep Investigators worked desultorily for a few minutes before the pressure of a senior manager's presence proved too much, and they stood outside their workspaces like soldiers waiting for their bunks to be inspected.

Mohammed made an obscene gesture when Daniel walked past. Ethan pretended not to notice.

"Good to see you, Eth. Enjoyed your time off?" Daniel asked, shaking his hand firmly.

"I always try to."

"Thanks for your work on the Smith case, it was appreciated."

"No worries, I'm just glad it's over. I was sick of him by the end. I thought it was never going to finish."

"Well, it did get done…" He leant over his shoulder, which

was easy for him given that he towered over everyone in the room. "Remind me to talk to you about security the next time I'm here. Can you go and check that the projector's working?"

"Yep."

Peter came out of his office and paced the walkway as if uncertain whether to approach the newcomers. Ethan strolled to the conference room, knowing that they would not start for a long time yet, as Daniel always found something to say to everyone; exuding the confidence of the born to lead; his height, impeccable suit, and easy manner, made him an aristocrat among them.

Ethan stretched as he waited. The computer and projector were working fine, and he wondered why Daniel had come over. Perhaps he wanted to show Pete up for not dealing with security. Ethan hoped they would not take too long, as Aislin had said that she wanted to come round to his house that night, and he had promised that he would not finish late.

Daniel, Peter, and two men and a woman Ethan did not know entered the room twenty minutes later.

"It's all set up."

"Thanks," Daniel said. The strangers seemed to be pointedly unsmiling, as if on principle. Daniel sat at the head of the desk and said, "Right, I think everyone knows everyone, except Ethan…" He turned to the others. "Ethan is one of our best SIs and he's going to organise a lot of the work around this project. Ethan, this is Tom, who's a Senior Dream Specialist for the DIA. He's going to give the presentation today. Becky is a security consultant at the DIA and George is her assistant."

Ethan nodded and slowly cast his eyes over them, immediately on his guard. Officials from the DIA, or Dreams Investigation Agency, were notoriously arrogant when dealing with other organisations and, in his previous encounters with them, they had always made clear that the objectives of the SDMA should be suborned to their own.

"Before we start, Eth, I need you to sign a confidentiality agreement. This doesn't mean we don't trust you; it's standard procedure for the DIA whenever they give any kind of information to another agency. Pete and I have done the same."

Tom gave him a thick document from a folder. He had been expecting a single piece of paper and felt under pressure to sign immediately, as they were all watching him.

"You'll understand when Tom gives his presentation. The agreement is basically similar to the one you signed when you started working here, although it's more… detailed, legally. It's a formality."

Ethan skim read the pages before signing the bottom of each one.

"You'll have to tell your colleagues something of what's going on, but before you give any information, even to the extent of the identity of who you've met today, I want you to ring and get my agreement, and I'll make a note. Compile a spreadsheet as well to make sure I don't forget anything."

Ethan nodded, thinking that he never forgot anything, unless deliberately. He was relieved when Tom took the papers back and attention shifted away from him. *This is the thanks you get for being competent,* he thought, *being treated like shit. The others would never be asked to be involved in whatever this is. Things like this always mean spending time away from actual cases to produce documents that no one will ever read. The bosses don't know the damage they cause.*

Tom spent the next few minutes fiddling around with a memory stick, until his air of mystique shattered. Daniel shuffled his immaculately placed tie a few millimetres further up his neck before skimming through a notebook.

No one knows what they're doing, Ethan thought. *This lot must be about the Icks. The DIA aren't bothered about anything else, they'd blame them for the rain if they thought anyone would believe them.*

"Okay, it seems to be working now."

Tom pressed a button and there was a crackle of violin music, then the screen filled with children playing in a park, smiling mothers pushing their pigtailed daughters on swings. Suddenly, there was a crack of lightning then a close-up of one of the mothers looking at something unseen in horror. Lumps of flesh fell from the children before they collapsed into piles of bones. Ethan leant back, looking surreptitiously at the others. The special effects were as good as those of a film and were repulsively realistic. However, if anyone else thought anything about them, they gave nothing away, so he returned his attention to the presentation.

After piles of ash scattered, the screen exploded into white. Then, an image of a wind farm appeared overlooking a field of wheat. It turned into a nuclear power plant, then a series of other power stations, interspersed with explosions. Finally, the screen filled with the words 'OUR SECURITY, OUR FUTURE' in black on white letters, before the screen faded to white one final time.

Tom closed the presentation, leaving open a folder that contained rows of files, each of which was labelled with strings of numbers.

"Okay, I know that opening clip may seem a bit dramatic, but we like to show the seriousness of the threats we face…" He paused. "Yes, people have commented that it seems dramatic although we've stopped many similar plots in recent months. I don't know if anyone has seen in the news the rise of attacks on power plants?"

He looked around the room expectantly, but everyone was silent until Daniel said, "There was a report on the BBC a few weeks ago about animal rights protestors who were arrested trying to break into one."

"Yes, well, this subject has been in the news a lot recently. In the last two years, there has been a large rise in the disruption of power supply across the UK."

He pressed a button then stood to one side as a line chart filled the screen. It showed a similar level for the years 2030–2038, then a large rise in the following two years.

"Okay, bear in mind that these are stoppages, not necessarily attacks. Stoppages. So some of them might be caused by accidents, for example. Or illegal industrial action. However, we have information that much of this increase…" he waved at the point where the line rose as if about to perform a sleight of hand, "has been caused by the Iklonian cult. There has been an increase in their activity over the same timeframe that makes us think that the rise in stoppages is not a coincidence. That it can't be a coincidence.

"Your organisation has supplied statistics to us that shows a correspondence between the level of stoppages and the incidence of sleep related disorder. We think that the Iklonian cult may be sabotaging power stations with the aim of disrupting sleep patterns across the country. A cold country is a tired country."

Peter sat up in his chair. "Wouldn't that work the other way though? Whenever I'm too warm, I always feel drowsy."

"No. Just before the body goes to sleep, its temperature decreases. Being hot will make you drowsy but it won't make you sleep better. Being too hot at night will disrupt your sleep. Anyway, if you're cold, what do you do? You go to bed. Especially if you can't afford to turn the heating up. The increases in retail prices of electricity and gas have resulted in an increase in fuel poverty of forty per cent over the period of interest. All of which means that the Iklonians have a large potential target audience.

"Projections by our private sector partners show that sleep related disorder has reduced productivity across the economy by eighteen per cent last year, seriously harming Britain's service sector and making many businesses uncompetitive compared to their counterparts in India and China. This additional threat has the potential to cause critical damage to the national economy.

"The Sleep Code, the SDMA, and the DIA, have been in place for almost twenty years, and during that time, the national economy grew 1.2 per cent faster than in the preceding fifteen years, allowing Great Britain to claw back the competitive advantage that had developed with mass labour, unregulated economies. The current security crisis has the potential not only to undermine fundamental law, with far-reaching consequences for public safety, but to seriously damage economic security. There are many side issues, such as the rise in accidents now that subversives have started to encourage night driving, but the point does not need to be laboured."

Daniel looked at Ethan.

"So that's the basis of the project. It will be codenamed Hypnos. We'll need to break it down into manageable sections and go through exactly what's required…"

Tom must have used his most interesting material at the start of his presentation, as the rest was very boring, comprising much repetition and paraphrasing of what he had already said, numerous graphs that all looked the same, and hand movements.

What it came down to was what Ethan had suspected after the first five minutes. They wanted the SDMA, or, more specifically, him, to go through every breach of the Sleep Code in the last three years (the year before the increase was required to give a context), to determine whether any of them could be linked to 'stoppages' at power plants. Other information held by the SDMA would also need to be researched, to determine whether any further incidents could be linked to the pattern.

It was such a huge job that he could not even estimate how long it would take. From other research, he knew that the organisation had recorded 138,765 suspected SC breaches nationally the previous year and, in his experience, there would be around five suspicious incidents recorded for every identified SC case. Furthermore, the SDMA held a vast amount of information shared by other organisations that would be relevant to the task. To do a proper job, he would have to research overall patterns in the data then read a large enough sample of cases to allow him to generalise about them. It was the kind of project that might never finish. *Surely they know that my cases must be the priority.*

Ethan had never had much confidence in the DIA, and his preconceptions had been confirmed by factual errors in Tom's presentation. For example, the SDMA and the DIA had not been formed at the same time as the Sleep Code came into effect, as he had suggested. The SDMA had been created two years later, after police forces had argued that they did not have the resources and training to deal with SC cases. The DIA was created thereafter as a conduit between the security services and the SDMA. Such a basic lack of knowledge was redolent of someone seriously lacking experience. Apart from their competence, DIA agents' main problem was that they seemed to believe that the Iklonians were behind everything. In fact, they were only the most prominent of a range of subversive organisations who opposed the Sleep Code, and in Ethan's experience, most SC breaches were caused by laziness and lack of personal discipline rather than anything organised.

"Any questions?"

Ethan looked at Daniel, knowing that there was no point making an interjection at this stage. The decision to proceed had obviously been taken long ago and the best Ethan could do was to scope out the project and suggest ways to make it more practical. Daniel stood and shook Tom's hand.

"Thanks for coming today, it's been very informative. What I think needs to happen now is that we'll come up with a plan of attack then meet again to go over the finer points and set some deadlines. Eth, I'm going to send you a few files that go into more detail about what we've been talking about today. Have a look through them and draw up terms of reference about the areas you think we need to look at. We'll have a chat on Friday about how to proceed after that. Pete, I'm sure we can release another member of staff to help with this?"

"Erm…"

"We'll talk about that before I go. Okay?"

"Yeah…"

"Thanks for coming today, Eth." Daniel nodded at him then gestured for him to leave. Ethan felt awkward walking back to the office with Peter.

"So… this is exciting then. DIA, Icks, and all that."

"Yeah, yeah, it's great. What do you want me to do about my other cases, 'cos it sounds like Dan wants me to work on this full-time?"

Peter scratched his few remaining strands of hair. "Erm… what have you got on again?"

"Just the stuff you sent me while I was away. I finished everything else before going off."

"Okay… erm… leave it with me for now. I need to work some other stuff out before I decide on that."

"Right."

"So… did you enjoy your time off? Did I ask you about it?"

"I mentioned it briefly, about going away with Ash's parents."

"Oh yeah, yeah, sorry. Did you enjoy it then?"

"It was fine…" Ethan was relieved when they reached the office. "I'll have a look at what Dan sends over and start on the terms of reference. One of the cases I've been assigned is marked as mid-priority so that'll have to be done first. I'll let you know about the timeframes so you can have a look at the staff situation Dan mentioned."

"Yeah, good idea, thanks." Peter carried on looking at him as if not knowing what to do next until Ethan turned away.

When Ethan got back to his desk, Mohammed was leaning back on his seat, sucking a pen.

"Come on then, big shot, what was all that about?"

"Just something that's come from up high. I'll tell you about it later."

Mohammed sat forward, frowning and smiling at the same

time. "No, tell me now. What's this, you think you can keep secrets from me?"

"I couldn't keep anything secret from you. You'd be the first to know if I was getting a filling. I'm making an exception with this though. You're not missing out on much, you can sleep easy on that score."

"Fuck me, this is nice. You're going to be making the tea for the rest of the week."

"Fine."

Mohammed grinned.

Ethan thought about whether he could ask for someone on another team to be seconded to the project, before deciding that that would cause too much trouble.

When he looked at his e-mails, he saw that Daniel had already sent him the material he had spoken about in the meeting. There were twenty attachments and he opened one of them to see a two-hundred-page report explaining efficiency statistics in different types of power plant. Another document had the DIA logo at the top and bottom of each page, which comprised a red dagger stuck through a pillow. It was titled: 'The Hammer Project: a guide for SDMA practitioners', and contained a description of the known structure of the Iklonian cult, and case studies that demonstrated how it was linked to famous Sleep Code breaches. That was five hundred pages long. The Friday deadline was going to be a nightmare. Ethan sighed when thinking that he would not be able to even start most of his assigned cases until the following week.

The most frustrating thing about doing anything with the DIA was that he had to learn their take on whatever was being researched, which often ran counter to his practical experience. For example, one of the documents gave a 'potted history' of the Iklonians, which detailed how they had grown out of protests by the judiciary after the Subversion Act was passed. Ethan had heard that story before and had always thought that it seemed highly unlikely. He had been involved in many investigations where subversive literature had been seized, and like many such organisations, the Iklonians often made vaguely left-wing claims about 'fighting the commercialisation of bedtime', to use the phrase that had recurred in the Smith case that Ethan had finished before going on leave.

The DIA was of course right that the Iklonians had emerged at the same time as the SDMA. However, Ethan had always thought it far more likely that they were driven by a mixture of criminal elements on the one hand, who needed the freedom to sleep whenever they felt like it to maximise opportunities to commit other offences, and the natural tendency of the undisciplined to resent any limitation on their ability to do whatever they wanted, whenever they wanted. Add into that the vacuous thrills of sneaking around in a 'secret society', threatening people and property, and it was hardly a mystery why some people might get sucked in.

At the end of the Hammer Project report were pages of symbols and code words used by the Iklonians, recovered from their safe houses and through interrogation. Skim reading them gave Ethan the impression that he was looking through designs for children's stickers. The one that recurred most often was lightning encompassing an 'I'. There were dozens of variations in design, the meaning of the differences in colour and shape being described as 'unknown'. There were some secrets that no Iklonian would ever compromise, no matter their situation and what punishment they were subjected to.

Aislin had said that she was going to come over after work that night, so he decided it would be best to let her know now. Seeing her was out of the question because of the security checks he would need to complete to move floor. He accessed his landline by entering his agent number and a password, then holding his index finger against it at such an angle that the blood sample was taken in a different place from that morning. All the work landlines and computers were security locked to their owner, who had a duty to record whenever anyone else used their equipment, and was responsible for what was done with it. The security protocols were the only reason why the SDMA continued to use landlines. Needless to say, the policies were widely flouted.

"Hello, Personnel department."

"Hello Personnel department, I want to talk about some personal stuff."

"Hi Eth. I only spoke to you four hours ago, can't get enough of me?"

"You know that's true. You okay to talk?"

"Go on."

"Have you checked your e-mails yet?"

"You mean about the airport? Yeah, it's good."

"This is why you should start doing the training again. Standards have gone down since you resigned from it."

"Yeah. Maybe. It's something to think about."

"You're the one who got the situation under control, I hope he makes that clear. Look… sorry to do this but the boss has come down today and he's given me a massive project to do. I'm going to have to stay late this week."

"I thought we'd agreed about this. Why do I bother arranging anything?"

"Ash, I've got no choice. You know the score."

"Do I?"

"You know that I'd much rather be with you. All this work stuff is very inconvenient."

"Is that everything then?"

"Look, what have you got on at the moment?"

"Just audits."

"Is that that stuff you were telling me about where you'd made all the changes to the system?"

"That's it."

"You never know, this might be the thing that gets you your promotion. I'd promote you if it were up to me."

"I'd better be off then…"

"Hang on, I was just going to say that if you didn't mind staying late tonight then we could go for a meal instead. On me."

"I've only got twenty hours on my card, a few extra never hurt…" Her voice was such that Ethan could not tell whether she was joking. He laughed with the confidence as if he were certain, "… I'll wait for you tonight, I'm not doing it again though. There's no point going on holiday if you kill yourself the moment you get back."

"Yeah, that's fine, I know what you mean. I'll try to get away for eight. See you later."

"Bye then."

"Bye."

Mohammed looked up when Ethan put the phone down. "I tell you what, you're slick. 'I'd promote you if it were up to me'. That on top of her mum saying about marriage. It's a one way track…"

"That was a private call."

"It's like what they say, 'no communication made using office equipment can be considered private'. Remember that?"

"I know what the policy says."

"Is she pissed off?"

"She's all right, she just forgets that things come up in this job sometimes."

"You know what would make her feel better? A ring."

"Are you sure you wouldn't prefer to work in a different building?"

"You love it, don't pretend you don't." Mohammed unwrapped a sweet and threw it into his mouth. "Want one?" His voice was muffled by a slurp of his tongue.

"Go on."

Mohammed threw a bag of them over his side of the desk. "They were giving 'em out last week. There must have been hundreds of 'em. I do like a good suck in the morning." He grinned, showing Ethan the sweet balanced on his tongue.

"Nice."

Ethan unwrapped one of the sweets and played with the wrapper. There had been several goody bags distributed since the IT department had been subcontracted. The SDMA's 'official sponsors' were listed on the bag alongside their various logos, above the PSH. When he laid the wrapper flat, he saw what appeared to be the same information printed there – pointlessly, given that it was far too small to read.

Ethan stretched, sleepiness coming on so suddenly that it overwhelmed him for a moment. He knew that despite what he had just said, Hypnos was likely to last months, and he did not know how he was going to mollify Aislin for that long. She had always been very firm about wanting to get her promotion before starting a family, and had worked for the SDMA long enough to know what that meant. *She doesn't understand the consequences of committing to things, that's why she gets angry.* He considered the problem for a moment before re-opening the documents Daniel had sent him.

Working at that level of exhaustion was like swimming in a dream. He had moments of heightened lucidity followed by a feeling of drifting as he made notes of the points likely to be relevant to Hypnos. Sometimes, he remembered where he was with surprise; at other times, he found himself at the end of a notebook without remembering when he had started writing. He had missed this life. While he had been away, he had often found himself at a loose end, lacking a sense of responsibility and urgency. He flicked between the various reports to check how they complemented or contradicted each other. Time passed quickly and everything fell away except his awareness of his work. The enormity of his task had consumed the reality of all else.

Two

AT FIVE O'CLOCK, ETHAN REALISED that he was alone in the office. He had had enough of DIA reports and thought that he may as well look at the SC cases he had been assigned. He opened the secure intranet and gained access to his jobs by re-entering his agent number, password, and blood. The ten cases Peter had given him were listed against Ethan's name, together with their priority, a space for their section code, which represented the part of the Sleep Code that had allegedly been breached, a space for their level, which represented the seriousness of the breach, and the case status, which for the ten were all listed as being 'in transit', meaning that they had been assigned to him but he had not yet viewed them. The top case was shaded orange, as it was graded medium priority, whereas the remainder were green, for low. When he clicked on the top case, its status turned to 'open'.

The file progression pages had numerous folders where different types of documents could be stored, although only a few were generally used, as Peter did not understand the system so did not make full use of it. In this particular case, I839186D18, there were two reports attached, both in the wrong section, one from a doctor, the other from someone calling themselves 'the office manager'.

Ethan read the medical report first, knowing from experience that it would contain the crucial information. There was a lot of padding at the start, as there always was, which he skim-read until coming to a section that detailed a series of appointments that the subject, 'Kerry Holloway', had had with her doctor. Ethan committed the dates to memory: the first concerned her high blood pressure, the second was when she was worried about a mole on her breast that had turned out to be just a mole, the third was when she had wrongly thought she was pregnant. Nothing relevant, but possibly interesting context. She had to be reasonably well off to be able to afford to visit the doctor so often.

During the fourth visit that year, Holloway had told her doctor that she had left work early after feeling ill on two separate occasions, visiting a facsimile fish and chip shop near her home address both times to purchase cod substitute. On the later date, she took the food home and put it on a plate, as she thought keeping it wrapped in paper was unhygienic, but immediately fell sick after eating. Being ill had made her tired, so she had gone to bed early, falling asleep around five o'clock in the evening on the first occasion, and six o'clock on the second. In both instances, she had gone back to bed after her alarm clock had gone off, meaning that she was late for work the following day. There followed more padding, and Ethan skipped to the end to confirm that the conversations had been recorded by the practice listening devices, and 'are available if required'.

There was no indication of why the case was listed as medium priority, and Ethan started to feel annoyed as he thought that Peter had got it wrong again, until he read the office manager's report, which told him that Holloway worked in the Civil Service, carrying out administration for the Ministry of Defence. A case relating to anyone working for a critical government department was marked as a higher priority as a matter of course.

Holloway's manager was even wordier than the doctor, going into inappropriate detail about the high quality of her work and how widely liked she was by her colleagues. Eventually, he confirmed her absence on the four days in question, stating that the mornings she had arrived late, Holloway had claimed that her car had had 'engine trouble'.

Despite that the case was medium priority, given how straightforward it was, no additional reports were required unless the subject disputed the evidence. Ethan checked Holloway on the SDMA 'Mirror' system, which showed that she had never previously been accused of an SC breach, was of no interest to any police force or the DIA, and had never changed her name. She had some financial flags, including three occasions of more than four months' unemployment, but nothing out of the ordinary. She had thirty medical notifications. None of them suggested sleep related disorder, and given the reports he had just read, she seemed to be something of a hypochondriac. There was nothing else of note.

Ethan had started his career just as Freedom of Information legislation had been modified in a way that made Mirror possible, and he had felt lucky to join the organisation when he did. It incorporated data about SC cases, referrals from the DIA, the police, and members of the public via the PSH (the majority of all information came from the latter source). Further sections contained information from other state organisations, and from a selected number of the SDMA's 'private sector partners'. It was one of the most useful tools at an agent's disposal, possibly too useful, as Ethan had seen colleagues carry out an investigation purely by researching the system, without even interviewing the subject.

He also checked her manager, and was disappointed that there was nothing incriminating in his file, as that meant that there were no grounds to pursue anything in relation to him. He did, however, add a note linking his name to I839186D18, stating 'possible sympathy with person investigated for 4x SC breaches. See report attached to file, pp13–14 and p17'.

Ethan could have completed the investigation summary form in his sleep, and had in fact dreamed of them many times. He wrote his investigation notes and gave recommendations as to the section and level that the case should be considered at. Given its simplicity, the only evidence he would need was to interview Holloway. Ethan strongly believed that interviews should be carried out as soon as possible after a case had been assigned, to improve the efficiency of the organisation but also for the sake of the subject, who would not be helped by being under investigation for long periods of time, with the restrictions on their employment and movements that that entailed. He had often argued with other agents when he had found out that subjects had not been interviewed for months after an incident, which had led him to write a report that had resulted in draft guidelines on the length of investigations being issued to agents nationally. Not that they were followed, of course.

Ethan checked whether the interview room was free, which naturally it was at that time of night, and booked himself a half-hour slot. The other thing that annoyed him about interviews was when agents compelled subjects to come to an SDMA building – not only did that delay the process, but it also unnecessarily compromised their identity; it only happened because some agents could not be bothered to learn how to use the intranet. His efforts to improve that part of the process had also been unsuccessful.

The interview room adjoined his office, and he shut the door, switched off the lights, and switched the computer to its covert setting, meaning that his face and voice would be distorted, all background noise suppressed, and the area around his face would appear black. Furthermore, the IP address of the computer would be encrypted and therefore untraceable. Ethan re-read his notes before ringing Holloway's number. Her face appeared on the screen a few seconds later. She stood by an oven in a kitchen, red faced.

"Kerry Holloway?"

"Yeah."

"This is the SDMA, are you available?"

"Yeah."

She held a work surface with both hands. Without thinking, Ethan had adopted the monotonous tone he always used when speaking to the public.

"I'm Sleep Investigator number 202154T. I need to speak to you about the case you've recently been involved with. We'll probably need about fifteen minutes."

"Erm… okay."

"The first thing I need to tell you is that you're not under arrest and you can terminate this call at any time. However, you will not be given any other opportunity to dispute your guilt in relation to this matter. You're not legally compelled to answer any questions I ask you. That means that not answering any question does not constitute any further breach of the Sleep Code, a criminal offence, or any offences under the Subversion Act. However, refusing to answer, or silence, demonstrates a lack of a substantive defence and so is equivalent to terminating the call. Is that clear or do you want me to explain it again?"

"No, I… it's clear."

Interviewing more educated people was always easier, as with some street level infractions, even explaining the opening principle took a long time.

"Good. Kerry Holloway, there is unanswerable evidence that you are guilty of four breaches of the Sleep Code, section one, subsection one: 'any act of unlawful sleep that results, either by the act itself or as a consequence of the act, to hinder the effective or efficient management of a workplace, as defined in the code.'

The details are that firstly, on the first of April 2040, you wilfully left a workplace in order to sleep outside your designated shift, which is therefore unlawful sleep. Secondly, on the second of April 2040, you wilfully slept beyond the time allowed by your designated shift, which is therefore unlawful sleep. Thirdly, on the eighth of April 2040, you wilfully left a workplace in order to sleep outside your designated shift, which is therefore unlawful sleep. Fourthly, on the ninth of April 2040, you wilfully slept beyond the time allowed by your designated shift, which is therefore unlawful sleep. You do not possess any type of sleep licence, meaning that you have no lawful excuse to be asleep outside the permitted hours of twenty-three hundred hours and oh seven hundred hours.

"I'm going to further inform you that case law has identified the Civil Service, where you were working on the days specified, as a workplace. On the four dates I've just specified to you, do you remember your actions, or do you need me to summarise them?"

"I didn't leave because I was tired, I—"

"Ms Holloway. Do you remember your actions on those days?"

Her shoulders slumped and the question seemed to deflate her. She looked at the floor. "I remember."

"Good. There is unanswerable evidence of breaches of the Sleep Code on those four days. Do you have other evidence that would countermand that case?"

"I didn't feel well them days before I'd left, I didn't leave because—"

"Ms Holloway, any matters relating to your health are points of mitigation and not defences. It is incumbent upon everyone to be aware of policy. It is incumbent upon everyone to follow policy. The Sleep Code supersedes all other law. Do you have any evidence that would indicate that you did not breach the Sleep Code on the days I've indicated?"

"No."

Her word was more like the yowling of a cat than human speech.

"Thank you for your cooperation today, the results of this investigation will be sent to you in short order. Goodbye."

Ethan disconnected the call and saved the recording of the

interview before e-mailing it to himself. His interviews had become more concise as he had gained experience. The main problem was that people did not understand the difference between being not guilty, and having mitigation. Everyone had mitigation, but no one was not guilty, and he had come to realise that an agent had to explain the difference between the two as brusquely as possible, otherwise the interview would never end. Holloway was a case in point. *If we took illness and the rest of it into account, there'd be no point having the Sleep Code. Everyone knows that before it came in, we were sleeping more in a day than the average Chinese works, and that situation couldn't go on forever. But now, everyone thinks that an exception should be made for them.* Ethan chewed his cheeks as he went back to his desk.

He unlocked his computer and attached the recording to the file before updating the status to 'concluded'. That would generate an e-mail to Peter, who would (or should), read the file and decide whether anything more needed to be done. Ethan had scored the case as being level ten seriousness, meaning that it would be sent to the Sanctions department after it was agreed by supervision. The likely punishment would be a fine (and dismissal with permanent removal of vetting status, obviously). Levels one to three, as defined by the code, had to be referred to the DIA for consideration for subversion charges that would be pursued by DIA security courts. Levels four to six were dealt with as criminal matters through what was known as 'special service', meaning that they would be tried by specially vetted judges, where the agent's conclusions would be made available to a court, presented by an SDMA representative, to maintain the agent's security. Appropriate defence counsel could produce evidence of alibi, but not challenge 'fundamental facts', as defined in the Subversion Act. Levels seven to ten were usually dealt with through the civil courts.

When Sanctions received a file, they would assess the conclusions before either completing the necessary administration and sending it to a civil court, return the file to the investigator for it to be re-graded, or reverse the finding of guilt. In reality, Sanctions rarely challenged an investigator's decision because of the bureaucracy that caused, and Ethan had the strong impression that most of the time, they rubber-stamped the investigation summary form. He had never had a file returned.

When Aislin called, Ethan was looking out of his blacked-out window, thinking that he would have to tell Peter to process the file the next day. Ethan should not have to, of course, but the system tended to fall down whenever he had to rely on anyone else. What was the point of keeping Holloway hanging on at this stage? Her job needed to be advertised apart from anything.

"Finished?"

"Yeah, almost. Where are you?"

"Look out the window."

"I am, I can't see anything."

"You really can't see me?" She spoke in an ironic, high-pitched tone, and he did not know whether or not she was being serious.

"I'll be down in a minute, let me just switch my computer off."

"I'm in the car park. Hurry up."

The office had automatic lights and was in darkness except for his space. The different sections lit before him as he walked as if someone were highlighting his movements. Working in the office alone always felt strange, as if the rest of the city had been abandoned.

He stumbled over a folder when he neared the door, there still being an abundance of paper everywhere despite the tidy-up that morning. The moment he had stopped working, tiredness encompassed him in its familiar embrace. He could not imagine what it would feel like not to be walking on the verge of dreams; exhaustion was like a drug, he could not have said whether he would take the opportunity for extra sleep even if it were possible.

There was a constant pressure on his head and feet, as if they were being held in a strong grip, and he seemed to be always running up steep steps. Twenty per cent of Sleep Code breaches were committed by either shift workers or students, who worked at times contrary to their internal body clocks, and from personal experience, Ethan knew that lack of discipline in putting up with the necessary discomforts of the working day had to be the underlying reason for most of them.

Exhaustion induced in him a sensory mania in which periods of lethargy were followed by excessive sensitivity. As he walked along the corridor, he knew only the sensation of his feet hitting the floor and had only the vaguest awareness of what was around him. He would not have noticed if he had stepped over a corpse.

It was only when he saw Aislin's car that colour returned to his vision. She beeped her horn and he stooped to get inside before kissing her. She shook her head to remove strands of her long red hair from the gaps in the steering wheel. He wished that he'd brought his car that morning. Driving always made her bad tempered. The biggest car she could afford was still so small that the steering wheel stuck into her ribs – given how expensive petrol had become in the last decade, most cars, apart from those used by the extremely rich, had been designed to carry as little unnecessary weight as possible. The corollary was that they were crammed with safety devices that relayed data to insurance companies and the police.

"That's the second time you didn't see me in half an hour."

"My mind must have been elsewhere… You know that I could never ignore you…"

There was a momentary silence and Ethan held his breath.

"I suppose that'll have to do. Where are you taking me then? Or let me rephrase myself, where am I driving us so that you can take me out?"

"How about a curry? I want something that I won't have to wait long for."

"Okay."

"Your engine has been switched on for three minutes without—" the safety monitor said.

"Fuck off," Aislin replied. However, the car continued to tell her about how much petrol she had wasted until they had reached their destination. Ethan could not help but notice the graphs on the dashboard that showed that she had terrible fuel efficiency. She must waste a lot of money, although he decided not to mention the fact at that moment.

They had been to their favourite facsimile Indian restaurant so many times that they recognised some of the staff who worked there, although Ethan and Aislin had never said anything to them other than giving their order. The high price of meat and long working hours had led to the closure of many restaurants. However, in recent years, the development of meat substitutes had allowed the creation of the various facsimile restaurants, known as 'facs'.

Ethan had found this one when taking a diversion after driving home late one night. The walls were filled with holograms of India that served as lights, and pictures of smiling men with turbans and beards. The images had a blue tinge that flickered periodically, making them seem like balloons being inflated then deflated. In contrast, the staff were all white, sullen, and wore green uniforms. Nevertheless, they used the best lamb facsimile that Ethan had ever tasted.

The room had an insubstantial smell that prompted them to unconsciously take deep breaths to try to work out what it was. As they waited for their order to arrive, Aislin said, "I've not told you about the latest chapter in the scarf saga."

"Not this again. Did your dad talk about anything else while we were there?"

"You've not heard anything yet. Apparently, he was on the bus this morning going into town, and he sat next to some bloke and told him about it as well. Dad must have talked the entire way there, 'cos you know how he likes to repeat everything. He got to the part when he started saying about how it was made in the traditional Irish way, going on about all that stuff, when the bloke told him to get lost.

"Dad's never gonna let that go, obviously. So he starts up again, saying about how he was only telling him about his scarf, and what bad manners it is to swear in public. That's what he said happened anyway, so he probably had a go at him for ages. In the end, the bloke must have lost the plot and tried to grab him, or push past him or something. Whatever he was doing, somehow, his hand got caught up in the scarf, and when dad stood up, the other guy fell over and dad stood on his shoulder and gave him more advice before getting off! How mad is that?"

"Is he all right? What do you mean, he grabbed him?"

"I don't know really. I tried to ask but he kept going on about how it's a lucky scarf now. I spoke to mum and she doesn't think he was hurt. He hasn't been to Ireland since he was ten but you'd think he was the biggest patriot out listening to him. Do they even make scarves in Ireland? What the hell's a traditional Irish scarf?"

"No idea. A green one?"

"Probably. If he weren't my dad, I wouldn't know what to think."

Ethan smiled and looked across the fac to see an old man resting his head against a wall. There were so many wrinkles on his bald head that they looked like a tattoo. He was still in the way that Ethan recognised all too well as the manner of someone who was about to fall asleep. Failure to report an instance of sleep disorder was a disciplinary offence for any SDMA worker, and in some instances could be a Sleep Code breach in itself. He took out his work mobile and set the video to record, before the man shook himself and sat up.

"You're not still working are you?"

"What do you mean?"

"Come on. That's your work phone."

"No no, I was just… checking something."

Aislin licked her top lip then picked up the menu. "I sometimes think that I'd like to live closer to him. I've got the feeling that he's not going to improve. Do you know what I'm saying?"

"Yeah, yeah."

"I've never said that to mum, but I'm more sure every day."

Ethan nodded and shuffled in his seat. The old man had reverted back to leaning against the wall, as if toying with Ethan.

"You're not even listening to me, are you?"

"I was listening."

"What did I just say then?"

"You were talking about your dad… Ash, I was listening. I know how important the situation is to you. Why don't you stay at mine for a few days? Then it's only twenty minutes if you need to pop over."

"Erm… okay then, thanks."

She put her hand on his and Ethan felt relieved that he had done something right for once. When they had met at university, she had often said how much she admired his ambition and 'intensity'. He could not understand what had changed.

They held hands on their way to her car. As they went, Ethan saw the figure of a smiling man holding naan bread that was etched into a window. Despite the fluorescent colours, there was subtle shading beneath his eyes, as if he were tired. It was so faint that Ethan was not sure it was real.

He was still thinking about it when Aislin had driven off and was telling him about how her manager had caused mayhem in the office that day by not understanding the processes around the audit.

She had stayed at Ethan's house many times before and kept various essentials in his spare room.

They went to bed as soon as they got in that night.

The following morning, his alarm clock made him jump as abruptly as if his bed sheets had been torn away. Ethan had different feelings of tiredness depending on what point in his sleep cycle he was woken. Sometimes, he felt sluggish lethargy that weighed heavily on his feet, making every movement a struggle and meaning that he had to force himself to get up; on other instances, such as that moment, he had a strong sense that a dream had been interrupted, although he could not remember it. He tried to summon up the images while brushing his teeth, but it was futile.

The sound of his alarm always remained with him for several minutes, as the SDMA-approved model was designed to do. It was a very efficient alarm clock, the regularity of the tone having been calculated to destroy serenity, such that it was impossible for anyone to remain asleep or even in bed after it had gone off.

The part of the Sleep Code that dealt with alarm clocks was one of the most complex sections of the Subversion Act. All alarm clocks were required by statute to be manufactured to only go off between eleven in the evening and seven in the morning, that was, during a period of lawful sleep. They could only be modified by the use of a code possessed by the owner of a shift or other sleep licence. Tampering with an alarm clock, such as by changing the set time to get around the security (the most common method), would invariably be dealt with as at least a level six breach. An alarm clock could only be lawfully altered by SDMA technicians, who would require proof of the relevant shift licence, and upfront payment of an administration fee. When the Subversion Act had been passed, much had been made about how many of its sections were 'unenforceable'. However, they had all been enforced. The legions of disaffected neighbours and ex-partners of SC offenders had guaranteed that.

Ethan's personal mobile received an automated message from the SDMA. Members of the public could register their mobiles to receive free alerts and information. The service had proven very popular, and thousands of people had signed up on the first day, crashing the SDMA website. The message gave an updated list of the characteristics typical of sleep offenders, all of which were extremely vague; his favourite was 'often appears confused and distracted'. *Perhaps I should put in a report about Pete.* Despite being useless for any practical purpose, Ethan found it interesting to compare what he knew against what was released to the public. He spent a few minutes reading through old SDMA messages; he had saved every one since the service began.

Ethan lay on a sofa while Aislin had a shower, and switched on the Multi-View (MV). The MV provided a combined package of television channels, games, the Internet, and a variety of other amenities, depending on the level of access the user paid for. It was the only way to use many government provisions, such as registering a birth, although most mobiles could connect to an MV remotely.

He put the news on using the controller, unsure of the extent to which he was seeing his repressed dreams. A bomb had exploded inside a rubbish bin in Central Zone, and there were swarms of police and black uniformed figures behind barriers. The screen cut to a computer generated image of metal shards striking passers-by, causing them to collapse in pools of blood.

Ethan pressed a button and his lounge was filled with holograms of the scene, making the walls glow. The picture shimmered, throwing off pieces of light, before the fragments were pulled back together. After more shots of police with technical-looking equipment, a reporter interviewed an old man who a bar identified as 'Bob Culvert'.

"I was just getting my milk like I always do when there was a flash and I couldn't see anything for ages. I thought I'd gone blind.

When I could see again it was horrible, like a war zone. There was a woman with her leg… all cut open. It was horrible."

The screen returned to the reporter. "Detective Superintendent Coley, who is leading the investigation, has refused to speculate on the motives of the attack, and has said that all avenues of enquiry will be explored, including whether it is linked to the Iklonian cult."

There was an SDMA technical station near the explosion, which could have been the target of the attack. A series of them had been damaged six months earlier, which had stopped agents updating their security cards. Guards had had to check them manually for weeks.

"Did you hear that, Ash?" Ethan shouted.

"What?"

"Bombing that they're saying the Icks might have done."

"Right."

"It might be a busy day again today."

"Just finish up as soon as you can."

"Yeah."

Ethan wished that she worked opposite him. She could have been a good agent if there had been a vacancy when she'd joined. If only she could see what the world was really like, rather than the HR fantasy land, then she'd understand.

"I'll drive!" she shouted.

He did not know why Aislin had not changed departments before now, as few people joined the organisation to go into personnel. He had encouraged her to sign up by showing her publicised cases. Ethan's career had been unusual in that he had become a Sleep Investigator straight away. More typically, a new recruit would be placed into a low-grade position out of the way somewhere, where they would have to demonstrate their trustworthiness and aptitude. He had managed to get the job on the strength of his interview presentation where, using only material in the public domain, he had been able to describe the amount of SC breaches in the scenario he had been given, and how he would investigate them. After that, twelve hour days did the rest.

Being a car passenger while exhausted was a subtly different sensation from driving while exhausted, or travelling on the train while exhausted. In his hazy state, the outside world seemed to be a series of colours created by his own agency. There were as many varieties and effects of sleep deprivation as there were dreams.

As soon as they passed the boundary from Midlands Central (where Ethan lived) to Central Zone, there were roadworks every few minutes, as there had been for years. Ethan could not remember the last time he had seen any workmen. The closer they moved to the city centre, the more unfinished it became.

Ethan thought that they should have got up early to go running together, as although it would have made him sick, it would have put Aislin in a good mood by making her laugh as he trailed behind her. As he shifted on his seat, he noticed a white van in the side mirror that he had first seen as they had turned into a main road near his home. The VRM plate started 'AA', with the remainder being obscured by mud.

"Bastard!"

Ethan looked up as Aislin honked the car's horn. "What's going on?"

"He indicates then sits there. I wave him through and he doesn't do anything. Then I start to go and he goes. Idiot. I'll be stuck behind him all day now."

"People like that shouldn't be on the road."

"Excessive use of the horn can result in a fine or an increased premium." the safety monitor said.

When he looked in the mirror again, the van was gone. Ethan's personal mobile went off and he saw a message from his friend Terry. Ethan tried to understand the first sentence before skim-reading the rest. It referred to the bombing, and rambled about the links between the monarchy, the media, politicians, and the mafia, before asking him what he thought about it. Ethan sent a non-committal reply before deleting the message, thinking that it was incriminating in some unspecific way, which was the worst way to be incriminating.

"Who's that?"

"No one."

"That's it, you obviously can't be trusted."

Aislin frowned at him before sticking her tongue out.

"I can't have a moment's peace, can I? It was Terry, just saying hi."

"What's he up to these days? Is he wearing tin foil now so the aliens can't get him?"

"Not just yet. Still the same really, working at the shop and everything."

Aislin shook her head in a way that Ethan found irritating.

She parked as near as she could to the SDMA building, which was a fifteen minute walk away. Listening and replying to her as they walked forced him to concentrate to overcome the heavy feeling behind his eyes.

When they were passing the shops, a man neared them, looking determinedly at the floor. Suddenly, he grabbed a handful of posters from a wall before running off. Ethan spun round, but to his frustration, the man had ducked into an alleyway before Ethan could start moving. He ran after him for a few steps and asked a nearby woman if she had seen where he had gone, but she only shook her head, her face as full of fear as if he were holding a knife against her throat. Ethan examined the wall to see chipped brick in the space where the man had vandalised the display. The posters were all of the same design, showing an old fashioned couple looking at a sunset over a farmhouse, above the words 'Our Vision for a Beautiful City'.

"What are you doing?" Aislin asked.

"Didn't you just see that?"

"I'm not blind."

She put her hands on her hips. Ethan felt annoyed with himself that he had not been paying attention to what was before him. Not only was defacing public information a criminal offence, but there had been a case five months earlier where Iklonians had been suspected of defacing building sites. As always, they had never got to the full truth. With utmost reluctance, Ethan started walking.

There had been much internal debate about posters within the SDMA, which had focused on their perceived old-fashioned nature and expense. Ethan had always strongly favoured their use and had said so numerous times on the forums that had been set up for staff to give their views on the subject. To his mind, their advantages over electronic mediums was their visual impact, the fact that they could not be instantly deleted, and that they could be deployed in places where people had no choice but to look. And in any case, the organisation was given a budget to spend on increasing security, not to sit in bank accounts. In the end, the management had decided to continue using posters as part of its communications strategy of 'total media dominance'.

When Ethan and Aislin reached the lobby, he said, "I'll see you later then. Don't wait 'cos I don't know how long I'll be. I'll grab something to eat after work then get the train back."

"All right. Do you still want me to stay over? There doesn't seem much point in driving back to an empty house."

"Yeah, I do want you to stay. I'll tell you what, when this lot's out the way, I'll think about applying for a transfer to somewhere nearer home that's less busy. Anyway, we'll talk about it later."

"You'd do that? Is that in your contract? How would you even go about it?"

Ethan froze, as he had spoken in the spur of the moment

without thinking. "Well… it'd be Dan, I suppose. He might let me, I don't know. He'd have to look at all the legal stuff."

"Let me know how it goes."

"Yeah, will do, have a good day."

"And you. Love you."

She kissed him and went ahead, the dots dancing over her back. Ethan sighed and rubbed his eyes. There were always problems. Sometimes, his life seemed like a gigantic puzzle, always one wrong move away from disaster. He pressed his security card against the giant lip barrier, and when it opened, thoughts of what he needed to do that day seeped into his mind until he had forgotten everything else.

In the endless walk along the tenth floor corridor, Ethan contrasted the issues he had had to deal with when staying with Aislin's parents to what he would have to do about the bombing. He was happy with his own arrangement; he had moved far enough from his parents that it was only convenient to visit them during special occasions. Although he had got on fine with them since moving out, he found that a weekly call was enough.

When he reached his office, Ethan moved around a pile of papers but when he tried to take another step, he tripped over a phone cord that had been stretched taut, only just managing to force his hands out to avoid banging his head against the desk.

Mohammed roared and Ethan struggled to his feet, rubbing his leg. "Back of the net, buddy, back of the net." His laughter went through every possible modulation.

Ethan logged into his computer, blood dripping from his finger.

"Oh man. I'm glad I work with you. You had a good night then, dude?"

"Yeah fine, Ash is staying over for a few days."

Mohammed's head darted up. "That's it, it's all over. You're in the marriage club. You want me to help you pick out a ring?

Come on, you may as well go along with it. It's inevitable. Inevitable."

"I don't know about getting married but I've already got a kid."

A few minutes later, Peter walked into their section and stood by his desk. Ethan knew that he was waiting for him to say something, but the way that he hung around was so annoying that he ignored him.

Eventually, Peter said, "Hello… hi…"

"Sorry, didn't see you there."

"So… are you okay then?"

"Fine."

"Good, good. I just wanted to talk to you for a minute about… you know…"

"What?"

"You know… the thing we were talking about yesterday."

"Give me a few minutes and I'll come into your office."

"Okay."

Peter stood there a moment as if not understanding what had been said before stumbling over the phone cord and leaving without another word. Ethan picked his fingernails then looked at Mohammed. "Who the hell put him in charge?"

"God knows."

"I mean… actually, I'm not going to go on about it, I'll just irritate myself."

"You should apply next time there's a vacancy."

"Can you really imagine me doing his job?"

"Yeah, I can."

"Maybe in a parallel universe."

"We'll see."

"By the way, have you got a lot on at the moment?"

"Plenty, but I'm getting by. Why, what's up?"

"Nothing major, it's just that I might need help with something. I'll tell you about it later."

"Is it about that meeting you went to with all the bigwigs?"

"How long have you been waiting to ask about that?"

"Since you came out of it yesterday." Mohammed grinned.

"Let me see what dweeb wants and I'll tell you about it later."

Before doing anything else, Ethan logged into Mirror and wrote an entry in the 'miscellaneous non recordable incidents' section describing what had happened outside the shops that morning, giving as full a description of the suspect as he was able. Material entered into that section was sent to Investigative Support, which decided whether new intelligence needed to be investigated by the SDMA, forwarded to the DIA or the police, or filed. Ethan had always had a strong suspicion that they filed everything for the sake of an easy life.

Ethan walked into Peter's office to see him wiping the leaves of a pot plant behind his desk. The top half of the back wall was blacked out window, filling the room with shade. There were cabinets in each corner with nothing in the centre, which gave the impression that the room was enormous, although it could not have been much bigger than Ethan and Mohammed's workspace. Peter's desk was covered by pictures of his wife and daughters, who hugged each other and smiled in every one.

"What did you want to ask me about then?"

"Oh, hi, Ethan. Take a seat." Peter seemed flustered and finished with the leaves before sitting opposite Ethan.

"Right, I think we need to talk about that job Dan gave us yesterday. My thoughts are that we'll need to get some of the others to help you with parts of it, otherwise you'll never get it done with how many cases there are."

"What about security though? They seemed very hot on that yesterday, which makes me think that the fewer people who know about it the better."

"Dan rang me last night. He said that we can give tasks to others so long as we don't tell them the whole picture, and we agree it with him first."

"Right."

"So, do you want me to—"

"Why don't I make a list of all the things we've got to do, then we can see how much there is and what other people can help with?"

"Yeah… yeah, good idea." Peter tapped the arms of his chair.

"I've done the necessary on the mid-priority you gave me. It just needs signing up before it can be processed."

"Oh… okay… that was quick. Yeah, I'll try to have a look at it later."

"Can you get it done today? She's in a sensitive job so we can't be seen to muck about."

"Right… okay… Where was it again…?"

"The MOD."

"Oh right. Well, I'll definitely try to have a look then. Yeah."

Ethan caught Peter's eyes before looking away, and he knew that he would have to check the system later to make sure it had gone through.

"And the other thing is, what about the bombing? That's not going to be a quick job."

"Well… Dan spoke to me about that as well… It's been assigned to someone else…"

"Someone else? What do you mean? Who?"

"Dan said that Hypnos has got to be the priority, so I've given it to Alfie to have a look at…"

"He's gonna 'have a look at it'? Hypnos is only just getting off the ground, I could have easily started another case."

"I'm sure you could, but Dan *was* specific on that…"

"Right, fine. I obviously need to speak to him."

Ethan went back to his desk, licking his lips as soon as he was out of Peter's office. He rang Daniel's landline. When no one answered, Ethan tried his work mobile. That number was not on the contacts for the senior managers on the intranet; Daniel had given it to Ethan when they had worked together on the Smith investigation.

"Hello?"

"Hi Dan, it's Ethan. Are you all right to talk for a minute?"

"Yep, if it's a quick one."

"It is. I've spoken to Pete this morning and he wanted to arrange for other people to help with the stuff we were going over yesterday. I know you said that you wanted to be told before anyone else was brought in, so…"

"Pete rang yesterday, and I said that as long as he told me exactly who was doing what, and that you only told them what they need to know and not the bigger picture, then that's fine."

"Okay, great. I thought he would have but I wanted to check before I started anything. It'll probably be Mo who helps me out but I'll let you know the full details later."

"Fine, thanks for keeping me in the loop. I'm just about to go into a meeting, so I'll be in contact to see how you're getting on…"

"Sorry, I did need to ask something else. Did you know I've been cut out of the bombing enquiry?"

"Yeah. That's what I told him to do."

"Right… is there any reason because it looks like it might be an important job…?"

"Ethan, you know what political projects are like. If we've got to put a deadline back and they find out you've been doing something else, they'll say we're not committing to Hypnos. I've sold it to them that we're giving it full priority and that's how I've got to keep presenting it. That's the decision. I've got to go. I'll speak to you later."

"Okay. I'll see you then."

When he put the phone down, Mohammed leant over the desk. "Pete sent an e-mail round about that, didn't you get it?"

"No."

"Too important now you see. You don't have to know about the minor stuff."

"Forward it to me would ya?"

He did so, and Ethan read it to discoverer that everyone in

49

the office would be expected to help Alfie with the research that the organisation needed to carry out around 'this potentially significant enquiry'.

"He's given it to Alfie. Christ."

"Keep it down, will ya. Have you forgotten that he works here?"

"Well, he'll liven things up I suppose. He'll be good if he's got to do a presentation. He'd probably put a few pictures of bombs in for a laugh."

"How loud are you talking? If you read the e-mail to the end, it's crap anyway, just a bit of background research. The DIA are doing most of it."

Ethan nodded. There was more he wanted to say on the subject but Mohammed did not seem to want to listen.

Three

ETHAN SPENT THE REST OF the day planning the methodology for Hypnos – what aspects needed to be considered, and how long each of them would take. By the time he had finished, his draft terms of reference was ten pages long. His schedule estimated that it would take around three months.

When he printed the document, he realised that the office was empty. He had distractedly said goodbye to people as they had left but had not noticed that he was sitting alone. After skim-reading the report, he was surprised to see that Peter's door was open. Ethan went in to find Peter talking on his personal mobile. He gestured for Ethan to sit, which made him suppress a smile at the assumed authority.

"I know sweetheart but it won't be for much longer now... yeah... yeah... that's right... yeah... I will... you see, you're right, but... it won't be much longer now, when I've... exactly, then we can do what we want all the time... Okay, put it in the oven then 'cos I'll be setting off soon. Okay then, love you, bye, bye, bye."

Ethan looked at his feet until Peter had finished, when he said,

"Right, I've done the planning document we were talking about this morning."

"Planning?"

"Yeah, you know when I was saying about setting out the limits of Hypnos?"

"Right, sorry. Okay, do you want to talk me through it? Actually, let's do it tomorrow now 'cos it's getting late."

Ethan suppressed a sigh, as he had hoped to give Peter the document then leave. *It's obviously too much to expect him to fucking read something. Never mind the fact that he should have written it himself. Not that I could have trusted him to do it properly.*

Peter held it close to his face then adjusted his glasses and rested it on his lap before saying, "I think I'm going to take this home tonight, I need to work out how we're going to organise all of this."

"Well… we can talk about it tomorrow but you can't take that home, can you? It's got the codename at the top and there's sensitive material in there."

"Yeah… good point… yeah. Right, leave it with me and we'll sort it out tomorrow. In fact… come and see me about ten and we'll go through it together, that'll be the best way."

"Okay. Did you have a chance to look at the Holloway case?"

"The MOD woman?" Yeah, I have. Yep, up to your usual standards. That's for Sanctions to deal with now. Out of our hands."

"Right. I'll see you tomorrow."

"Yeah, yeah. I'd best be off. Carol wants to know where I am."

Ethan smiled. "See ya."

Peter looked into the air distractedly a moment and Ethan took the opportunity to leave.

It was only seven when Ethan got on the train. He sent Aislin a message and thought that with any luck, she would not have eaten yet and they could have dinner together. She did not seem to notice the night and would think nothing of eating at dawn if the mood took her. The one good thing about the bombing situation was that at least she would be in a better mood with him.

By the time the train left the station, the sky was so dark that it seemed to have no windows. He touched the glass and shivered as his fingertips tingled. His carriage was almost empty, as it always was after rush hour.

The train was shimmering blue and seemed to cut a path through the night, casting its hue on the landscape. The trains serving Central Zone were amongst the most technologically advanced in the country and in ideal conditions, could have taken him home in less than ten minutes. When it set off, his stomach seemed to have been left behind, as if he were on a rollercoaster. However, because of the differing standards of infrastructure in the different zones of the city, it could never get to full speed. His route took him through Midlands North West, where the track was so pitted that the train could have been overtaken by a fit cyclist. The gentle pace allowed him to nonchalantly pass his eyes over slum housing, where bedroom lights highlighted overgrown gardens filled with rusting children's toys.

It took him most of the journey to stop thinking about work, his mind racing from one point to the next as he reviewed his day. The planning document had been useful in collecting his thoughts, although given how many cases the SDMA recorded and how much paperwork there was to research, it had demonstrated just how difficult Hypnos was going to be. He decided that he would have to go through the methodological problems in more detail. Explaining the technicalities to Peter was going to be a nightmare. *I probably won't even start writing the document until next week. Maybe I should go for promotion when Pete retires. Management is easy, you just press a button to pass the problems to someone else. Could I ever give up doing cases though? Not that I'd ever get his job. Some are destined to stay in the same position forever, whereas others always come out smiling no matter that they can't tie their own shoelaces.*

When Ethan got home, he found Aislin lying on a sofa, rapidly flicking between channels on the MV. Her hair was splayed in all directions, as evenly as if she had placed every strand.

"You all right?" he asked, leaning over to kiss her.

"Yeah, fine. Busy day again?"

"You know how it is. Never stops."

"Did you ask Dan about the transfer?"

"I did but he was rushing from one place to the next when I spoke to him. I'll remind him tomorrow."

"Right… anyway, I've left you some dinner out."

"That's great, cheers. It's just unlucky that you've stayed over when this thing's come up. Sorry."

"I know what it's like, I work there remember? Have your dinner or else you won't sleep."

I'll hardly sleep anyway, Ethan thought, surprised at how annoyed he was. *The work situation isn't my fault.*

When he went into his room to get fresh clothes, he sent a message to Terry on his personal mobile, asking him if he wanted to meet up sometime soon, feeling that he had taken revenge against Aislin by doing so.

As Aislin had a wash, he logged into the MV to check his bank balance before going into the 'social' section. She had set it up for him the previous year, insisting that automating the various social networks would make his life effortless. He deleted the multitude of updates and sent a short greeting to his parents. Ethan had disabled the option of showing his face when sending messages or making calls, the idea making him uncomfortable in a way he could not have explained. Instead, as he typed on the controller, a series of multi-coloured squiggles surrounded his words, supposedly representing the sounds and movements he made as he wrote.

Although Ethan was exhausted, he lay awake for hours thinking about sleep. Aislin breathed softly beside him, her hand so light on his chest that he could only feel it when she shifted.

Shadows flashed across the walls, climbing ponderously up his spiral bookcase like spiders. He shuffled and Aislin rolled away, dragging her hand with her, making him hold perfectly still. He was relieved that she did not stir.

He woke early the following morning and sat up abruptly. The shadows had gone and the darkness was absolute now. When he lay down again, Ethan immediately lost consciousness. It was as if he had caught up with the sleep he had missed from previous nights and needed a short break before his sleep for that night could begin.

His alarm clock woke him a few hours later and he wondered whether he was dreaming. He was so groggy that he thought he could defy the insistent sound by putting his head under a blanket. Aislin started and kicked him with her heel, making a sound like a small animal in pain. The stinging sensation in his knee forced him out of bed.

Ethan rubbed his hands over his face, trying to understand why the earlier he went to bed, the more tired he felt the following morning. It was as if he could withstand a sleep famine by running on reserve energy, but as soon as he stood still, he shut down.

Aislin drove them again that morning, although she seemed distracted, resting her head against the window whenever they stopped at a traffic light.

They said little as they walked to the SDMA building, until they reached it to see a line of guards standing outside.

"What the hell's this about?" Ethan asked.

"Pass."

As soon as they were within twenty metres of the building, one of the guards shouted "stop" and four of them walked forwards with outstretched arms. Ethan thought he had seen them in reception before, although their body armour and helmets meant that he could not be sure.

"We work here."

The guards stopped just outside reaching distance, as if expecting them to attack any moment. "What floor?"

"I'm an SI, tenth floor."

"Personnel, fifth floor."

"Security cards please, slowly."

Ethan put a hand in his pocket with what seemed to be ridiculously ostentatious movements, and was worried that they would think he was making fun of them. However, he did not know how else to behave, never having been stopped by security before. One of the guards took their passes and held them under a device that flashed a blue light over them. The other guards watched them coolly, still holding their hands out. "Okay, you can go. You'll need to sign in before going to your floors."

There were crowds of people milling around the lobby, although as soon as they went inside, other guards bustled them towards the security desk, where they signed their names and departments on a piece of ripped paper attached to a clipboard, in addition to what time they had arrived. Ethan wanted to wait for Aislin, but the moment he had finished, the guard sitting behind the desk stared at him, and Ethan thought that he could not hang around.

"I'll see you later then sweetheart, don't worry about it."

She only looked at him when he touched her shoulder, red dots scanning her forehead.

There were more guards around the lip-shaped security barriers, who Ethan had definitely not seen before. They stood with their arms either folded or akimbo and watched him with nonchalant interest as he scanned his identity pass. It took a moment to work, and he was relieved when the panel went green and the lips opened.

There were guards at the entrance to his floor, and along the corridor to his office, making him nervous, as the SDMA discouraged anyone from leaving their desk unnecessarily, and there were strict security procedures for visiting another floor, which made seeing someone in a corridor a notable event. Whenever he happened to catch their eyes, they looked at him with renewed attention.

The office was silent. He sat at his desk and Mohammed leaned over and said, "They've found out that someone working here was an Ick. It's gonna be like this for weeks now."

"How do you know that?"

"I heard someone at the door when I got here this morning. They were taking computers and files away. They'd all got our markings on, that's how I know. They must be working out what they'd been getting up to. Someone was saying that even the porters were on the move, that's how big it is."

"Shit. What were they doing?"

"Tell you later. Everyone's kept their mouths shut from the moment they got here. Even Hugo, for Christ sake. That's how you can tell it's an emergency."

Ethan nodded. *The Icks are cheeky little bastards*, he thought. *They've managed to survive over the years because none of the bosses has got the balls to take the fight to them. We do a so-called 'crackdown' every so often then allow them to lay low before pulling off something like this and starting the whole thing off again.*

"What's the great leader had to say about it?"

"Well, he told us what happened then gave an inspirational speech and explained what we need to do…" Mohammed looked over his shoulder then back again, "No, not really. He was wandering about earlier then he went in his hidey hole and shut the door."

"Just like every day then really."

"Yeah."

"I wonder if it could be Si. I mean, how could he be off for this long with a broken finger?"

"I thought we'd got to the bottom of that. Didn't someone overhear that wrong? It wasn't a broken finger, it was something wrong with his muscles. Anyway, his computer's still here."

"Maybe he was having an affair with dweeb. That'd be enough to make something go wrong with your muscles."

Mohammed laughed then put his hand over his mouth. Ethan was worried that he did not know what the infiltrator looked like. They could have been watching anyone, gathering information. He heard muttering elsewhere in the office and thought about Aislin. *She won't have a clue what's going on.* He rang her landline, thinking that he would hang up if anyone else answered.

"Hello, Personnel."

"Hi Ash, it's me. You okay?"

"Yeah, fine, it was just a surprise that's all. Do you know what's happening?"

"Not exactly but one of the…" Ethan held the receiver at arm's length when seeing Mohammed running a finger across his throat. When he had got his attention, he made a lowering gesture, "…sorry, I've got to go, I'll ring you later. Love you."

He whispered the last two words. Ethan leant over the desk and asked, "What's the matter?"

"They've put out a message on the intranet, you're not supposed to use the phones at the moment unless it's an emergency."

"Why?"

"'Cos it'll clog up the network, it said."

"What the hell's that supposed to mean?"

"Fucked if I know. I'd do what they say though when everyone's like this."

Ethan nodded before looking at his screen, so agitated that he did not start work for several minutes.

Ethan worked on the planning for Hypnos before reaching a point where he could not continue without speaking to Peter for various decisions to be made. He tapped his desk before peering over the dividers. His office was shut so he sent him an e-mail to remind him of their meeting then logged on to the BBC website. After scanning it a moment to see no mention of anything that could be linked to the situation, he thought that Mohammed's warning probably applied equally to the Internet.

Ethan went into the secure intranet, thinking that he may as well look at one of his other assigned cases. He felt depressed to see the same nine from Monday. In any normal week, at least one would be added every day. He read the referral report for the top listed file. In an office block, an administrative assistant had been found asleep in a canteen after a colleague had gone looking for him when he had not come back from lunch. *I don't get the bombing, but I do get this*, Ethan thought. *Dweeb obviously took the opportunity to give me all the dross while I was away.*

The colleague had acted in an exemplary fashion by fetching his supervisor, who returned to the canteen to take pictures, as per the advice given to employers in SDMA literature. However, when Ethan reviewed their accounts, he read that bizarrely, the supervisor had taken it upon herself to speak to the offender on tape, who had said that it had never happened before and that he had become tired over the previous month because of cars driving past his bedroom at night.

Ethan researched case law and found an investigation that had taken place a year after the Subversion Act had been passed, in 2025, which stated that when an offender had been formally interviewed in relation to an SC breach by an 'Appropriate Authority', which included a workplace supervisor, they could not be questioned again 'without prejudice to the original allegation', except when the breach fell into DIA jurisdiction. Given that this breach was clearly a level ten, he had to use her interview.

Ethan sighed when writing up the paperwork with phrases he had used many times before. This was probably the result of someone putting out incorrect advice to make their life easier. Many agents would like nothing better than for personnel officers in insurance firms to do their jobs for them. The problem with that, of course, was how much would be missed by people who did not understand the bigger picture. Ethan had conducted countless interviews in which offenders had inadvertently admitted further SC breaches or implicated others. Ethan opened Mirror and researched the supervisor, only to find nothing significant. He added a note, linking her name to the file with the message: 'inappropriately interviewed suspect in 1x SC breach'. There was always the possibility that she had acted as she had deliberately, to prevent further SDMA involvement. However, given that she was technically within her rights to do so, there was nothing he could do. Ethan sat back in his chair. Still, his discovery at least meant that he had something useful to do while waiting for the terms of reference for Hypnos to be agreed. He logged into the secure intranet to search for other cases where appropriate authorities other than SDMA agents had carried out interviews, then wrote a short report about the issue and e-mailed it to Dan.

At five o'clock, Peter had still not arrived and Ethan thought that there was no point staying any longer. He rang Aislin on his personal mobile and said, "Hi. Are you ready to go?"

"Yeah yeah."

"I'll see you downstairs in a bit then."

Whenever they finished at the same time, they met outside to comply with the inter-floor fraternisation regulations. They were strictly enforced on all staff, including senior management (who were confined to the fifteenth floor, other than on pre-arranged appointments), with the exception of the porters, whose freedom and knowledge, combined with the fact that they were very rarely seen, gave them a mythical quality. They were the only members of staff given unrestricted access to the archives in the basement, where the SDMA's most confidential secrets were stored, as were original files of all cases ever recorded, including information too sensitive to be inputted into Mirror. Only porters could authorise another member of staff to move floors.

"Have you checked your e-mails?" Mohammed asked when Ethan put on his coat.

"Go on."

"I've asked everyone if they were interested in a day in another office to discuss the IT issues, then maybe have something to eat."

Peter had given Mohammed the role of 'social coordinator', which mostly involved trying to get the agents to spend time with each other outside the office. Apparently, there should be one in every team, to demonstrate how the SDMA was a flexible employer. The one policy Peter had shown an interest in.

"I'll think about it."

"Try to do it if you can. There's no point otherwise – you know no one will volunteer for anything if you're not there."

"I'll read it tomorrow. I might be washing my hair though. This is what we get for drafting in riff-raff from North East zone. I can't believe you passed the vetting."

"It's a good job I did, otherwise I'd have been shovelling shit on the street instead of in here. That's why I'm so grateful to have got the job." He smiled.

"I suppose I'm happy enough about it."

"That's what I try for – spreading the joy. Enjoy your early night."

Early night? Ethan thought. *I got here before eight.*

The corridors were still crammed with guards, and as the lips to the ground floor opened, Ethan wondered whether Aislin had been asked to do any work on the infiltrator. *There must be something we could learn from their background, what they said when they were interviewed for the job and how they had behaved during their time here.* He wanted to ask her, but although there was no specific regulation against talking about work outside the building, it would clearly be inappropriate. He felt cheerful when seeing her leaning against a wall outside. He held her hand and smiled as if he were fifteen years old. She stood on tiptoe to kiss him.

"Let's get out of here."

Finishing only an hour late was a luxury, and the evening stretched before them like a dream of eternal summer.

They went out to a fac and chatted and laughed like young lovers. Aislin ate a chunk of prawn-shaped fish substitute from the back of her fork with the utmost daintiness before saying, "Daisy rang this morning asking how I was. Did you have anything planned for the weekend?"

"Erm… not really. Why?"

"She's coming over and she wanted to know whether I was free."

"Great."

"Stop it, you."

"What? What did I say?"

"You don't have to say anything. I'm going to go back to mine tonight 'cos she wants to stay over. I need to sort out some bits for dad anyway. He said his roof's got a leak and I don't want him climbing up to try to fix it, balancing like a madman."

"She could stay over at mine you know, you don't have to—"

"Thanks for saying that, it's an improvement."

"Christ, I tell you what, that woman makes an argument even when her name is mentioned. It's a special gift, you know – most people have to be in the room."

"I'd swear to God you two were brother and sister if I didn't know otherwise."

That deliberately provocative comment made Ethan want to argue back, a dozen retorts wrapped around his tongue. Aislin took a sip of water, and by the time she put her glass down, not having taken her eyes off him since she had last spoken, he had thought better of continuing the conversation.

Aislin had known Daisy since university, when they had been in the swimming team together. Although neither of them competed anymore, they had remained close friends, despite meeting less frequently since Daisy had moved back to her parents' farm. Aislin had introduced them soon after they had started their relationship and they had each taken a vague dislike to the other, which manifested in arguments over their interpretation of the news, disagreements about what words they used in conversation meant, and barely hidden barbs about each other's appearance. Ethan had commented about the fact that she never wore make-up, which he had never done with any other woman. Daisy had taken particular offence to Ethan's job, talking slightingly about the SDMA when mentioning news articles she had read about high-profile SC cases and the size of the SDMA budget.

The last time they had met, their sniping had escalated to the point where Ethan had made a series of jokes about farmers, alluding to their sexual relations with animals. At first, Daisy had smiled thinly and replied with her standard sarcasm. However, at a certain point, his comments must have pressed some mental switch, making her screech and throw her arms into the air, causing him momentary alarm before he had burst out laughing at her desperate insults; at one point, she had accused him of personal responsibility for the 'alarm clock culture'. After that point, the two of them had made an unspoken agreement to make polite, resolutely neutral conversation that avoided any topic that might invite more than one point of view whenever they were forced into contact. Their relationship was finely balanced, with one stray comment being enough to ignite the cold war into a hot one.

"Well…" Aislin said.

"What?"

"What do you want to say?"

"Nothing."

"Your mouth twitched, I know you're dying to say something."

"I don't want to say anything."

"Okay then. You are like brother and sister though."

She watched him carefully for a few seconds and Ethan nodded slightly in such a way that communicated nothing. *She turns into her when she's talking about her.* Ethan felt annoyed that she was affecting their lives even in her absence.

"Ash, I've been meaning to ask. Are you going to do the self-defence training again?"

She had previously been one of the lead instructors for the Central Zone SDMA, after having being picked out during her introductory training for demonstrating a proficiency in the subject. Ethan had enjoyed spending time sparing together, but she had given up instructing a few months before they had gone on holiday.

"Maybe."

"It's a useful thing to have in our job with everything that goes on. And when I look round the office in the morning, some of them need to get fit."

"Like I've already said, I'll think about it, but I don't want to go back to doing something for nothing."

"But with the—"

"Do you want another drink?"

Ethan nodded and stared at the hologram of a pork pie on the nearest wall, which flashed on and off in fluorescent colours as if they were in a casino.

When they returned to his house that night, he kissed her goodbye very effusively to show her that he was not in a bad mood.

"Ash, I just wanted to say that… I really enjoyed staying with you last week. It feels so long ago now… but it was good to have some time together properly for once…"

"I'm glad. I enjoyed it too. It needs to happen more often."

Ethan held her a moment, feeling foolish. He was relieved by the plain happiness of her smile.

Walking around the house on his own gave him a strange impression, as if he had just arrived at a hotel at the start of a holiday. Aislin had joked with him in the past about moving in properly, telling him to throw away his MV because she had a better one, and to get a bigger wardrobe. He had laughed at the time, but had often since thought about the conversation.

Four

ETHAN DREAMT VERY VIVIDLY THAT night that he was
at the bottom of the stairs when he heard piteous yelps from his
bedroom, sounding as if they came from a child. When he tried
to go up, his feet stuck to the floor. He struggled desperately,
frightened of every surface in the suddenly treacherous
environment. The cries continued, battering against him like sheer
wind. He saw himself in the third person, his body flashing as if he
had been x-rayed, then the scene repeated over and over, his sense
of foreboding serving no purpose as he never learnt from what had
happened.

For a few seconds, his alarm clock only added to his nightmare.
As he regained awareness, he wished he could have controlled his
dream, as the cries were plaintive enough to be taken seriously
whether or not they were real.

However, the insistent shrieking eroded his memories like fire
to a treasured photograph. When one looks at an image of a loved
one, it is so clear that it seems it will never be forgotten, the very
idea an insult. And yet, within a moment of being consumed, the
details become hazy, and soon, only a conception of the picture

remains, as indistinct as a summer cloud. Dream memories are the same.

Ethan retained a sense of lethargic sadness that morning without knowing why. It was a feeling that continued as he drove to the SDMA building; every traffic light that turned red made him sigh, every car that pulled in front of him seemed the result of a vicious, willed evil.

He was waiting at the last traffic light before work when he looked up from changing the radio station to see a white van alongside him. It pulled away with a screech of breaks. Ethan felt alarmed. He remembered the van from the other day and his mind immediately lit up, assessing the possibilities and dangers. Unfortunately, it had left too quickly for him to get the registration plate.

He could report the incident, but that would involve completing numerous forms and being interviewed by internal security officers to assess any danger, which would take days. His position meant that his house alarm was linked to both SDMA Internal Security, and the local police, both of whom would be on the scene in minutes should anyone try to break in. It was generally unwise for an agent to identify themselves as a security risk. *Why would anyone be following me?*

It was only when he was walking his usual route that his sense of oppression was replaced by workaday tiredness, and he had an outbreak of bad-temper. *If only people didn't keep bothering me and let me get on with what I need to do, there'd be more than enough time to sleep. How can we be expected to clear this place up when we can't even get our own organisation right?* Ethan looked around as he moved into an alleyway, wondering whether his subversive thoughts would be visible to anyone watching him. Security cameras were woven so discretely into buildings that no one knew from how many angles they were being recorded at any one time.

The feeling chastened him and he relapsed into a dream-like wandering of mind. His eyes felt full of sleep no matter how many times he rubbed them, making the tops of buildings above look like the spires of gothic fantasy. Paths before him seemed to knit up like a magical maze that constantly changed shape. The one solid thing was the SDMA building, the sharp edges of which were fixed in the sky.

When Ethan neared the guards, they carried out the same procedure as the previous day. They checked his identity card despite that he would not have been able to access the area beyond the lobby without it. Strictly speaking, they could have represented a security breach themselves, their legitimacy having been nowhere established. They had never been mentioned on the intranet or by any manager, but the nature of their power was so obvious that no one questioned it.

The mood in the office was calmer than the previous day, with more talking and joking, although no one mentioned what had happened. *Perhaps the Ick was one of the senior managers*, Ethan thought. *That would explain some of their decisions.*

He knew that he could not delay Hypnos any longer, and as soon as Peter arrived, Ethan followed him into his office and dropped the planning document on his desk. Peter soon seemed overwhelmed by the complexity and agreed with everything Ethan said.

"Can I use your phone so I don't have to call Dan in front of everyone?"

"Go on then."

"Thanks… can you log me in then?"

"Oh yeah, sorry."

Peter winced when the phone took his blood and wrapped a plaster around his finger several times. Ethan looked at him pityingly before dialling Daniel's mobile.

"Hello?"

"Hi Dan, it's Ethan. You okay to talk?"

"Sure. Make it quick though."

"Right. I've put a plan together for how we can do Hypnos. I'll send you a document where I've gone into what areas we need to look at. It shows what systems the information is stored on so there's no confusion. As I said before, I'm going to give a few bits to other people in the office who've worked on various relevant jobs. It's nothing beyond the norm so I don't think there's a need to make special security arrangements. I've highlighted the stuff everyone else is going to do in the report."

"That's great. Thanks for your work on this, Eth."

Ethan glanced up at Peter. "When you've got the stuff, do you want to send a reply agreeing to it, so I can…?"

"Yeah yeah, send it through and I'll get back to you today. I'm sure it'll be fine. Okay then…"

His voice trailed off and Ethan knew that he had already taken up too much of his time. Whenever he contacted him, Dan always made it clear that his every second was precious and strictly rationed. Needless to say, the reverse was not true when Dan rang him.

"Sorry, there was one more thing. Is nothing else going to be assigned to me until I finish this? I know what you said before but it's a long time to be out the game."

"How many jobs have you got already?"

"Eight. That's stuff I had before though, I haven't had anything new since I got back."

"In that case, what I said before stands. You can keep those jobs but don't take on anything new. Make that clear to Pete. If he's got anything to say about it other than okay, get back to me."

"Right…" *But they're all the crap that can be done in five minutes*, Ethan thought.

"Thanks, Eth."

"Okay, bye then."

But he had already hung up.

"What did he say about the other jobs?"

Peter looked at Ethan over his glasses.

"Hypnos has got to be the priority, he said. I'm not to be given anything new until it's finished."

"Okay, erm… leave it with me and I'll think about it."

"He was pretty clear. He said to keep what I've already got but don't take on anything new."

"Just carry on for now then and I'll let you know what I decide."

"Fine."

When he got back to his desk, Ethan found a gold-coloured parcel. He unwrapped it to find a framed commendation for bravery from the airport commander 'for selfless and quick thinking action in the apprehension of a terrorist suspect'. When Ethan had scanned his eyes over it, he placed it at the back of his desk with the others.

Mohammed leant across the workspace. "What was that, mate? I thought they didn't accept anything that wasn't wrapped the way they like it."

"Just some paperwork. You know, Pete's nothing but a tosser."

"What's he done now?"

"It was just a general observation."

Mohammed's great shoulders shook and his mouth opened a slither, giving him a glimpse of his perfect teeth. "Come on, out with it."

"I can't be bothered to go through it now, just trust me on this one."

"Well, I can't argue with you there. You didn't apply for his job though, did you?"

"Well… no."

"You can't criticise then can you?"

"My face wouldn't fit doing that."

"But you didn't apply though did you?"

Ethan shook his head.

"There'll be another job coming up later in the year, that's what my sources tell me. You need to go for it, you don't want to be stuck here with me your whole life."

Ethan smiled, and although there was nothing in Mohammed's words that he could criticise, he was still thinking about the conversation an hour later. Because of his dealings with the majority of the management, he had turned having as little as possible to do with them into a principle. Having his logic challenged made him uncomfortable.

When he tried to print one of the documents Daniel had sent him, there was a red light on the all-in-one device. Ethan returned to his desk and asked, "Who mends the printers now?"

"You can call the same number as before… oh, hang on, is it a printer or a photocopier?"

"The all-in-one."

"You've got to ring the manufacturer then."

"What? Why can't IT do it?"

"They sent round a long e-mail the other week; it's not their responsibility anymore."

"I must have pressed delete when I saw it was from them. Christ. So if I need something printed off, I've got to either spend hours on the phone speaking to the company, or fill in a form so that the porters can take me to a printer on another floor? This place is ridiculous sometimes."

Mohammed laughed. "You chose to work here, mate."

Ethan shook his head. "I'll read it on the bastard screen. When I go blind, I'll sue the place. Who knows, this might be my way to the top."

"That's the spirit."

When Ethan got into work the following morning, he read an e-mail that had been sent at eleven-thirty the previous night:

Ethan,

Approved.

Thanks,

Dan

Ethan sent an e-mail to all the people who needed to do tasks for Hypnos, asking them to attend the conference room at eleven that morning.

"What's this about then?" Mohammed asked.

"Just that thing I went to the meeting about before. There are a few actions I need people to help me with."

"I tell you what, you love it, don't ya? You're like a sergeant major you are."

"It's a good job for some people that I'm not."

"It's a good job you're not then, isn't it?"

"Wait."

Mohammed smiled. "By the way, you never replied to me about that open day. You coming or not?"

"Sorry, I don't think I'm going to be able to with everything that's going on at the moment."

"You know best, mate."

Ethan went into the conference room ten minutes early to go through his notes. Although he had managed many large projects and often felt that he was in charge of the department, it felt presumptuous to tell agents of the same rank what to do, and he wanted to be sure that he knew exactly what he was saying.

Jo came in first and sat at the other end of the table without a word, staring above Ethan. He looked away and someone shouted in his ear, making him jump, scattering his papers.

"Jesus."

"Made you look!"

Alfie's booming laughter was as loud as his voice had been. Ethan rubbed his ear.

"Come on! It is what it is. Come on!"

He was so incessantly cheerful that Ethan was eventually forced into a token laugh, shaking his head, after which Alfie crossed his arms and whistled, poking Jo every few seconds then pretending not to notice her expression.

Mohammed nodded at him when he arrived and sat in a corner. The only other person he had invited was Hugo, and at ten past, Ethan said, "Hugh's in today, isn't he? I'm sure I saw him this morning."

"Yeah." Jo said, the effort of speaking making her face screw up.

"Right, let's see where he is."

It's like herding sheep in this place whenever you try to sort something out. Ethan went back to the office to find Hugo sitting at his computer, playing cards on the machine.

"All right?"

"Hi," Hugo said, before turning back to the game.

"Did you get my e-mail about the meeting this morning?"

"Erm… can't remember…" Ethan released his breath, which made Hugo look around ponderously, and with exaggerated movements, he minimised the game and looked through his e-mails, "… yeah, here it is. 'Meet to discuss', yeah I've got it." He started playing the game again.

"Right, well, the meeting's started, and we're waiting for you…" Given the fury he felt, Ethan had no choice but to be exaggeratedly polite.

"Give me five then."

Ethan stood there a moment in disbelief before going back to the conference room.

He did not turn up for another ten minutes, just as Ethan was about to go back and lose his temper.

"Right, thanks for coming. I've been given a project to do that involves going through some historical cases to look for various patterns, and to do that, I need help with a few bits. If I can give you this…"

He handed each of them two lists, the first comprising reference numbers of significant cases they had investigated, and the second containing various questions that needed answering, and paperwork that needed to be supplied for each one.

"… Right, it's basically about cases you've done in the past. I wanted to go through it in a bit more detail 'cos it's hard to explain in an e-mail…"

He spent twenty minutes going through what he needed in precise detail, feeling annoyed when seeing that Hugo was not taking any notes. *It'll be a fucking miracle if he gets it right*, Ethan thought.

"… I know that's a lot of work, but I've told you now so there's plenty of time. Can I ask if you can get the stuff back to me a month from today please?"

"Has Pete agreed this?" Jo asked.

"Yeah, he knows about it."

She looked away dolefully.

When he sat back at his desk, Mohammed folded his arms and stared at him, shaking his head.

"What?" Ethan asked.

"You Midlands Central types are all the same."

"What are you on about now?"

"Another meeting you've been put in charge of. You must be loving it."

"It would be better to have some piece and quiet once in a while. Anyone would think I *am* married, with all the nagging I've got to put up with."

Mohammed rocked back to laugh.

"Seriously though, it's good that Dan's put you in charge of whatever this is. He obviously wants you to get experience of the management stuff as well as doing cases."

"I suppose so. Changing the subject, I know it's painful spending as much time together as we do, but do you fancy going to the cinema on the weekend? I'm not doing anything and there's a few good films coming out."

"I'll check but I don't think I can for the next few weekends. Hasna's got a job interview and she wanted me to help her with some stuff. She gets nervous and has to memorise her answers. She'll be able to do it no problem, it's just a mental thing, you know what I'm saying? Maybe we could go the week after next?"

"Okay."

Ethan was surprised by how irritated he was. It was usually Mo who asked him to go out; the one time *he* felt like doing something, he was busy.

"By the way, what's the matter with Jo? She seems really depressed. More than usual, I mean," Mohammed said.

"Dunno. She was supposed to have stormed out the office crying again the other day after you left. I wasn't paying attention. Usual blah probably."

"All heart you are."

"We live in a world ruled by sentiment. A bit more cruelty would do everyone some good."

Later that afternoon, Ethan received a message from a university friend asking him if he wanted to go out that night. He replied that he would, then wondered whether he should invite Aislin. She had met his old friends a few times, and they'd got on quite well. He spent a long time debating with himself before deciding not to.

Ethan paced himself for the rest of the day, knowing that he did not have enough to do, not starting his remaining jobs in case his workload was even lighter the following week. *The bosses are so frustrating sometimes with how much time they waste.* He left soon after his colleagues and went straight to the hotel conference room that his friends had hired for the night.

An MV projected holographic shapes and lights over the room. Alcohol was one of the few commodities that had become cheaper in the Eternal City in recent years while largely maintaining its taste. Licensing regulation had been progressively reduced although high rent prices had forced most pubs out of business. However, there had been a boom in small off-licences, universally known as 'crammers'. They comprised mobile stalls that could be set up either in places of high demand or wherever was convenient for private clients.

Although they had of course all changed since university, some of them were working and one was married, their respective roles in the group had remained much the same since they had met as teenagers. His time with them was one of the few occasions when he was not defined by his status, which he simultaneously liked and disliked, as his childhood was foreign to him now.

When Ethan got home that night, he knew that he would still be drunk the next day, but was fed up enough to pretend to himself that he did not care. Alcohol exacerbated his sleep deprivation, and when he heard his alarm the following morning, he looked around suspiciously, as if someone was making the sound to annoy him. Ethan ambled around the house several times before ringing Aislin. It went to answerphone and she returned his call a few minutes later.

"Hi stranger, how are you?" she asked.

"Good thanks. What you up to?"

"Well, we thought we'd relive the past. I've booked an hour in the swimming baths to see if I can get out the shallow end."

"You'll be an Olympic contender again after ten minutes."

"Those days are long gone. It was Daisy's idea. I'm glad she said it actually 'cos I haven't had time to do any exercise since I got back."

"Well, that's why I said before about the self-defence stuff."

"Mmm."

"You fancy coming over later?"

"I'm sure we can squeeze you into the schedule."

"What time?"

"Give us an hour."

"Okay, see you later. Oh, by the way, did you get a parcel at work?"

"The certificate, you mean? Yeah."

"Well done, it should have been just you."

"Thanks. Right, I'll be over soon."

Ethan cleaned the house, doing jobs that he only usually did when he was on leave for more than a week, such as wiping the skirting boards and hoovering behind the sofas. He even put a fresh shirt on.

When they arrived, he kissed Aislin twice before she came into the house and nodded at Daisy. She wore a green top and combat trousers, the same as when he had last seen her. They sat on the sofa opposite him and were silent awhile.

He had wondered whether Daisy would have got rid of her braid, which, together with her red cheeks, had been his main targets for farmer jokes the last time they had met. However, she looked much the same as before, as if taking pride in the wholesomeness of her appearance.

"What've you been doing this morning?" Aislin asked.

"Nothing much. Watching the news, doing a bit of reading. I've needed to relax after how busy it's been this week."

"Have you put in the paperwork for a transfer yet?"

Aislin smiled ironically and Ethan frowned.

Daisy turned to her before he could reply. "Are you looking for something different?"

"Thinking about it. There are loads of jobs out there that pay more for shorter hours."

"That's a really good idea. There's the *social* aspect of it as well, I've always been surprised that you chose this."

Ethan sat up.

"What do you mean, 'the social aspect'?"

Daisy turned her head with haughty effort. "I mean that there's plenty of jobs out there that can benefit the whole society."

"I don't understand, more than what?"

"More than what you do."

"Really? You come into my house and tell me that my job isn't 'socially acceptable'. It's lucky for you that someone is willing to do it. I'd like to see what a mess we'd be in if no one bothered."

"Okay. Whatever. Twenty years of being told when to sleep and blah blah blah."

Her nonchalant tone infuriated him, and Ethan felt as if nothing but the two of them existed.

"No, what do you mean? You can't insult me then just say 'whatever'. First thing, we don't tell people 'when to sleep'. If you've not got a licence, then you're allowed to sleep between eleven and seven. No one says you've got to. You can party through the night if you'd prefer. You just can't sleep the rest of the time when you're supposed to be working. Twenty years of trying to put things back together, more like it. Do you want the country to fall apart?"

"Yeah right. Like everything would stop if people could join whatever political parties they want."

"Political parties? What are you talking about now? We've got nothing to do with political parties."

"Yeah, like the Iklonians aren't a political movement."

Ethan laughed. "Political parties are the people talking bullshit on the MV. They don't tend to blow up buildings or take out industry."

"I don't understand: 'taking out industry'? How can they take out industry?"

"Daisy, there are people in India and China working twenty hours a day. Productivity in this country decreased every year for the sixty years before the Sleep Code was brought in. What were we supposed to do about it? Cross our fingers? Hope that something turns up? Why should people be allowed to laze around all day anyway? We've got to introduce discipline somehow and everyone knows that excess sleep is one of the main problems. I'm asking you now. What else can we do?"

"You go on as if… How am I supposed to answer that?"

"Exactly, you haven't got another solution. You're just someone who reaps the rewards of what we do but tuts about the methods. Do you think we can afford to subsidise everything as much as your farm?"

"How dare you…"

Daisy went red and for a moment, Ethan thought that she was going to cry. Aislin stood and walked to the door.

"I'm getting really sick of this. I can't bring my best friend over to my boyfriend's house without it turning into a debate on the future of civilisation. How many times have I got to listen to this? Why can't you just both keep your opinions to yourselves? I'm going swimming, I hope neither of you have any objections to that?"

Ethan wanted to argue further but her angry tone made him think better of it. Daisy went outside and Aislin turned back to him.

"Why can't we ever have fun? We can't even talk about having kids because that might interfere with your plans to save the world. Are you going to say anything? For God's sake."

She took a step forward and Ethan breathed inwards at the thought that she might hit him. Aislin sighed then left the room.

He paced around the lounge, repeating his arguments to himself. *Why has she left with her after the way she insulted me? It's a fucking joke.* Not for the first time, Ethan thought about whether he should put an entry about Daisy into Mirror, detailing her obvious sympathy towards the Iklonians. He only persuaded himself not to do so after several hours of going over the permutations of what might happen, when he thought that he might compromise Aislin. He felt like crying when realising that self-interest prevented him from doing his duty. He went over the situation again and again as if scratching a rash until it bled.

Aislin was very attractive when she was angry, when her eyes flashed and her hair whipped around her face. Ethan knew that if only she could be placed in situations where she would have to confront subversion, like at the airport, then she would soon regain her old enthusiasm for the job.

He was determined to wait for Aislin to apologise, or at least break the ice, but by the evening, he could not stand the tension any longer and sent her a message. She replied within a few minutes, and to his amazement, he also got a message from Daisy, saying sorry for her initial comments about the SDMA. Aislin must have forced her to send it. He replied telling her not to worry then deleted her details from his mobile.

Ethan felt stodgy for the remainder of the weekend, and everything he did seemed somehow unsatisfactory. His mind wandered even as he played on his computer and listened to music, which he rarely had time to do nowadays. It was as if he were waiting for something to happen.

Five

HE TOOK THE TRAIN ON Monday morning as driving seemed too strenuous. Even looking out the window was a chore, like chewing food that would not break down in his mouth. When he got off, waiting for a space to move into as people shuffled around him seemed part of an arcane game. He thought that there were no consequences to his actions, that it would not matter if he pushed someone on the tracks or jumped himself. He rubbed the corners of his eyes, which sharpened him momentarily before he drifted back into weariness.

He received an automated message from the SDMA, which started with a headline as if it were a newspaper article: 'Home Secretary Clears SDMA of Unlawful Targeting of Protestors', before summarising a redacted report that had recently been published. Ethan could not remember all the details but it was something about a demonstration that had turned into a riot a few years earlier, when they had been tearing down posters, breaking windows, and the rest. There had been accusations at the time that the SDMA had later targeted those responsible, on the basis that many of them had committed SC breaches after the event.

Why do we bother replying to this stuff? The only people our press releases convince are our supporters. All they end up doing is giving the conspiracy nuts something else to shout about. He thought about whether to speak to someone from Communications when he got in before thinking better of it. Criticising a decision without knowing who has made it is unwise.

When he walked from the station to the SDMA building, his steps seemed to make no impression on the pavement, such that his destination became further away the more effort he put in.

He managed to concentrate on his screen for two hours that morning before exhaustion blurred his vision and he had to hold his head. He yawned so often that Mohammed asked him what was wrong, to which Ethan replied "nothing", feeling bored of the incipient conversation. He thought about booking more leave, but Hypnos hung on his shoulders like a backpack full of rocks. *Bastards. This is what you get in this place for doing your job properly. Bastards.*

The less efficient he became, the worse he felt and the longer he had to stay at his desk. That Thursday, he set himself the goal of finishing the first draft of a chapter of his report by the end of the week. However, his colleagues conspired against him; no one seemed to be able to access any system or solve any problem themselves; he walked miles around the office as people came to him with ill-defined queries, each of which was an adventure to resolve.

By the afternoon, he still had hours of work to do, and the thought of coming in the following day to the same problems made him close his eyes. He had a silent argument with himself about whether the overtime money was worth it. However, Ethan remained firmly in his seat, knowing that it was pointless to have even thought about it, because he had no choice but to do his duty.

Working alone at night was always surreal, but even more so in that state, when it seemed as if he were typing because of some monstrous punishment that mandated that he should always do so, the screen filling with more and more words in an unending sequence. He felt as if he were the only person in the city, that he had been ordered to maintain it after everyone else had been evacuated, and after a while, he thought he could discern mocking faces in the shapes of the letters.

He was surprised when meeting his self-imposed deadline, and allowed himself to leave.

As he hurried to the train station, he desired rest more deeply than he had ever wanted anything.

The train lurched to a halt on the edge of Central Zone, and a message went out over the public address system that there would be a delay, as a section of track had corroded. The very city seemed to be set against him. Ethan looked out the window with dull eyes. What used to be the limits of the old city was now a sprawling suburb, with streets cutting into each other at all angles as far as he could see. Houses glowed red then blue then green in waves as the MVs within projected characters from whatever programmes or games were playing. Although he had little time or interest in such things, at that moment, Ethan felt a maudlin sadness at being excluded.

Naturally, it was an anti-climax when he finally got home, flung himself on the sofa, and switched on his own MV. In that state, even the fact that it was still light enough that he did not need to shut the blinds was a blessing, as the moment saved felt like an eternity.

He gained then lost concentration from one moment to the next as images flashed before his eyes. Soon, he felt that he was drifting, drifting, and his thoughts dispersed…

He did not realise that he had woken for several seconds. However, the moment he did, he was immediately more alert than he had ever been. Ethan jumped to his feet. It was pitch black outside and he could only see anything by pressing his nose against the window, which shocked him with its cold insistence.

"Oh my god."

Not only had he committed a section one subsection one that, given his position, would certainly be level three, but the blinds were open – he had done it in front of all the houses opposite. It would only have taken someone to look out of a window and…

Ethan looked at a wall clock and was amazed to see that he had slept for over four hours. It had been as soft and insubstantial as candyfloss, without any dreams that he could remember. His immediate neighbours knew that he worked for the SDMA, not his exact role, of course, but he wished, desperately, that he had not told them anything. *The organisation will string me up.* He tried to think of a pretext for knocking on their doors, but after a moment's reflection, he knew that that would look even more suspicious. He stumbled to find his mobile to confirm the time. Not only was it correct but he had a missed call from Aislin that it was now too late to return.

What's the matter with me? I've worked late loads of times before without this happening. I was only off a couple of weeks ago and I caught up with my sleep then. I'm going downhill at the age of thirty-one? The organisation had special vetting that included regular checks of medical records, meaning that he could not go to a doctor without the SDMA finding out, whereupon he would be suspended pending investigation by the DIA. *Are the Icks up to something?* An intelligence report had been distributed to the organisation a few months earlier that indicated that the Iklonians were developing a device that could induce sleepiness across the city, spread by contact with an unknown agent. It was a possibility.

He thought about what he could say to defend himself. For a moment, Ethan wondered whether he could accuse anyone reporting him of lying, before realising that there was no need: it would be perfectly plausible to agree that he had been lying on the sofa but to deny that he had been asleep. *Perhaps I had a headache, so I happened to be closing my eyes when they saw me? Or the shadows in the room made them look as if they were closed?* Eventually, he decided that the dark room explanation was the best, which only left why he had not closed the blinds. *Perhaps they were broken?* He stood and snapped several of them before realising what he was doing and shaking his head. *Surely the DIA would have kicked the door down by now if someone had reported me?*

It was with a strange thrill that he realised he was now a criminal. His feet were pounding, and the moment he stopped moving, he was exhausted again. He brushed his teeth – lifting the brush taking a tremendous effort – then staggered to bed, dropping his clothes in a pile.

Early the following morning, Ethan woke, or at least dreamed that he did, feeling very refreshed, and thought that if he felt that way now, then it would be even better when he had to get up.

That morning was as different from his usual early morning state as being awake was from being asleep. He experienced a new form of consciousness. Everything he touched had a different feel to usual, and he gazed upon the shiny side of the toaster as if seeing the colour for the first time. When he touched it with his fingertips, the notches made his arm tingle; everything seemed extraordinary now that he was alert enough to experience the world.

Ethan took the train to work to give him time to think, and when he got on it, he could not sit still, constantly folding and unfolding his legs then straining his neck to look around. Buildings and trees looked more solid than usual, and he could see details in them that he had never known before. In fact, for a few minutes, he thought that he must have got on the wrong train, as he barely recognised the landscape. He was only sure of where he was when the train crossed a zone boundary then started juddering as it went over uneven track, with a motion that he knew well but had never got used to. The strips of field he passed were the only pieces of undeveloped land for miles around, and he had never appreciated them before.

A young girl sat next to him and opened a textbook, making Ethan think that he should have brought a magazine with him. Or perhaps his headphones. Although he liked listening to music, he rarely did so, as it only irritated him when he was tired. *Perhaps I could get the train everyday if I'm going to feel like this. It'd be an extra hour to do anything.* The girl looked at him and raised her eyebrows petulantly, and Ethan realised that he was compulsively tapping the window. He smiled at her then looked away.

Ethan found himself digging a finger into the top of his leg. *Calm down*, he thought. *Jesus. Act natural, you're not going to survive five minutes if you carry on like this.* There was a flap in the seat before him, where a piece of plastic could be lowered to lean on, and he found a newspaper inside. It was one of the sensationalist free sheets that glum faced men handed out in stations. His eyes jumped from one article to the next like those of a frightened cat. It was full of the usual rubbish, and Ethan found it amusing to read the cartoon version of the news. The only article that held his attention was headlined: 'Icks in baby snatch shock', in which it was alleged that 'senior officials' had uncovered an Iklonian plot to infiltrate hospitals and play music that disrupted the sleep patterns of new born babies. This would supposedly make them more likely to become Iklonians when they grew up.

Ethan liked the feeling that he had insider knowledge of what was going on, and knew which stories were true and which were planted. That article was obviously the latter, as senior officials never uncovered anything. However, the prominence of the story added to his agitation. It was of course absurd that the newspaper had been placed there to test his reaction, but Ethan knew that he had to be sensible. *I need to investigate what happened, there could have been any number of causes, or perpetrators. If anyone else found out, they'd jump to the wrong conclusions, especially people who don't know me. I've got to make sure that I don't give anyone a reason to think I've done anything wrong.*

He jumped when his mobile went off. Ethan opened it to see that it bore the SDMA clouds logo, but no message. The automated system had gone wrong before, but the timing seemed very suspicious. He looked around, wary of the other passengers. He had always known theoretically that no one could be absolutely trusted, but that was the first time he had ever really experienced it.

The walk from the train station to the SDMA building was equally strange. His steps were quick, nothing hurt, and the sound of cars driving past was amazingly sharp, as if his hearing had been turned up. He heard an engine stutter and the click of a loose exhaust, then a slap in the distance followed by a child's whine.

He noticed the dilapidation of buildings and roads, the potholes deep enough to have their own ecosystem of weeds. Light became trapped under his eyelids whenever he looked up.

"Morning!" he said when reaching his desk.

"What's the matter with you?"

Ethan burst out laughing. "I've only said one word. What can I 'ave done wrong in one word?"

"You're too cheerful. Come on, out with it. Are you going to kill me? Are you going to pull a gun out and massacre everyone in the room?"

Ethan put a finger against his lips. "Shut up."

"Have you proposed to Aislin?"

Ethan rolled his eyes.

"You have haven't you? Have you set a date?"

"Are you a woman? I've never known a man go on about marriage so much. There's nothing up, I'm just happy, that's all."

Mohammed frowned and Ethan had never seen such a look of concentration on his face before.

"I may be just a thick North East lad, but this is all very odd. You can't hide anything from me you know."

"Tell me about it. I haven't even sat down and you're on at me. You'll probably know I'm getting married before I do."

"Seriously though, make sure you get your maximum hours tonight, you look knackered."

Ethan's heart jumped. "Yeah, will do."

His voice was as timorous as that of a frightened child. Mohammed must have realised something was wrong as he did not ask any follow-up questions. Ethan did not dare to glance at him for several seconds, when he saw that he was leaning back in his chair and sucking a pen. It was then that Ethan realised what a dangerous situation he was in, sitting in an office with people who were trained to spot SC breaches. *I've got to start using my brain. Ever since the accident, I've been acting like an idiot. I've got to investigate what happened and not let it affect anything. End of story.*

His harsh words to himself worked, and within a few minutes, Ethan saw his tasks with a clarity that he had not experienced since coming back. He only stopped concentrating when his stomach rumbled and he looked at the clock at the bottom of the screen to see that it was lunchtime. He stretched his arms.

"You've been quiet today."

"I've had to crack on with this lot. How you getting on with your stuff?"

"Okay, it's just really repetitive putting everything in the right format. We shoot ourselves in the foot with the way we do things, I don't know why people can't just do their files properly."

"Tell me about it. Will you have written it up by next Friday though, 'cos that's when Dan wanted to see what progress we've made?"

"Yeah, I should have something by then."

"Make sure you do."

Ethan walked to the window behind his desk before he could reply. He realised that he had forgotten to ring Aislin back and thought that she would be in a bad mood. He called her on his mobile.

"Hello?"

"Hi Ash, it's me." It was always a bad sign when she pretended to not know who he was.

"Oh, hello. You okay?"

"Yeah, fine thanks. You?"

"Fine."

"Good, good. I was just ringing to say sorry for not calling back. I had to put my phone on silent, then I didn't get back till really late and I didn't think you'd be up then."

"Right."

"So… did you want to… Was it just to talk that you rang, or…"

"It was to see how you were, that's all."

When they had that type of conversation, Ethan usually felt annoyed after the first few stilted silences, but at that moment, he was so full of energy that he did not care.

"Right, as I said then, I'm sorry I didn't get back to you right away, you know what it's like. Everything okay with you?"

"Yeah, fine really. It's the same here as in your department, busy all the time."

"Yeah, yeah."

It's not really the same though, is it? Ethan thought. He had only ever been to Personnel once. No one had accompanied him, contrary to policy, and as he had wandered around, asking people where the files he needed to access were stored, everyone shrugged then turned back to their conversations, all carried out in low voices that filled the office with a constant hum. They glanced up whenever he passed, and moved their heads closer together when not recognising him. He had planned to speak to Aislin for a few minutes before thinking that asking anyone where she sat would be far too complex. It took him three hours to get the information he needed, their software being even worse than the Sleep Investigators used, and when he got back to his own floor, Ethan had described the situation to Mohammed in slighting terms, his brief experience having confirmed his prejudices about the admin lot.

"So… you want me to come to yours tomorrow?" Ethan asked Aislin, trying to think of something that would get him back into her good books.

"I can't. Dad rang this morning, he wants me to go over tomorrow and look at some old pictures with him."

"Look at old pictures? Why?"

"I don't know, he just called out the blue and started talking about when I was a little girl. He was getting really sentimental and I thought he was going to cry. He went on for ages about family and Ireland then he said he wanted to go through the pictures with me while he still could."

"Right. Do you want me to go with you?"

"No, it's fine. I think I should go by myself. Sorry."

"Well… hope it goes okay then. Send me a message."

"Okay, love you."

"Bye."

"Bye."

As soon as she hung up, Ethan thought over all the permutations of her words and tone of voice, trying to decide whether she was telling the truth. Although her father acted strangely before, they had got on well from the first time they had met, thanks to his toleration of his eccentricities. On the other hand, this all seemed too convenient when she was clearly in a bad mood about the lack of time they had spent together recently. However, Ethan was more worried about the fact that he was not particularly upset. He thought about the advice campaigns that detailed the nightmarish consequences of breaking the Sleep Code, about how excess sleep can change a person, about how sleep can become a drug. *I'm a living example of it. I can't be sure whether anything I'm feeling is me or the sleep.* He wondered whether he should work overtime that weekend, as he had so much energy that he had to do something.

Later that afternoon, Mohammed asked, "Do you still want to go to the cinema?"

"What?"

"Pay attention. I said, do you still want to go out this weekend?"

"Erm… yeah, sure. Weren't you going through that stuff with Hasna though?"

"We've practised enough. We've actually got to the point where she's fed up of it. A few hours on Saturday and she'll be fine. You okay for Sunday?"

Ethan paused, wondering whether he should access the Internet for his personal use after what had happened, before deciding that after everything he had done for the organisation, he deserved some leeway. "Is four okay?"

"That's fine, I often get worried that I don't see enough of you. Changing the subject to something less interesting, what powers have we got when someone's encouraging someone else to commit an SC breach?"

"What do you mean? Tell me the exact scenario."

"I've got someone here who says she saw her mate fall asleep at work and challenged her about it. Her mate said to keep her mouth shut then sent her an e-mail… she gets a bit vague at this point… basically, the offender implied that she would turn a blind eye to her friend falling asleep if she ever wanted to try it. The witness says that she deleted the e-mail 'cos she was scared. Can we question the other people in the office?"

"The best thing to do would be to have the computer away. That's section five sub-section one, 'encouraging another or others to commit acts of unlawful sleep'. You can seize communication devices if there's a suggestion of subversion; there's every chance we'll be able to recover the e-mail. Take the office MV as well, if there is one. You never know what you'll find."

"But how is it subversion if it's only her? There's no suggestion that the Icks or anyone else was involved."

"That doesn't matter. A subversive is someone who encourages others to undermine fundamental law; the fact that she's not acting in concert with other subversives is mitigation, it doesn't mean she's not guilty."

"Right, cool. You're a genius. Are you going to impart some of this knowledge in an awayday if I organise another date?"

"Maybe. I don't know, I'll think about it."

"I'll make sure that there's no laughing, nothing there to distract anyone from listening to you, if that'll help."

"I think you'll struggle to get this lot to listen to anyone."

"I wonder if you'd be the same if we were selling paper for a living. Would you go around folding it in half to make sure that all the sides were even?"

"Are you seriously saying we're the same as salesmen?"

"Everyone's the same when they're earning a living."

Ethan turned to his computer.

Before he left that evening, he received an e-mail from Daniel, saying that he wanted to meet on Monday to 'get back in the loop' about Hypnos. He had got as far as he could on the section of the document he was working on and was waiting for the other agents to get back to him, meaning that there was no point coming in over the weekend.

When he got home, Ethan felt the difference in his feelings even more acutely. At work, the rank structure, the expectations, and the deadlines meant that he could hide his mental state behind a public façade. At home, out of sight of the world, the significance of the change was plain. He took a long time to wash, cook dinner, and put his work things away, fearful of what would happen now he was finally alone with himself.

The house was silent. He stood in the lounge, wanting to put on the MV to fill the vacuum but at the same time resisting. The thought occurred to him that anyone walking past could see him, and although strictly speaking he was not doing anything wrong, that prospect worried him. *You can never know who's an Ick or where they could be hiding. There could be one across the road and I wouldn't know. They could have targeted the town for infiltration.* He hurried around the house, closing all the blinds.

Soon, he was in the lounge again, staring blankly at the now covered patio door. *It's not surprising that I've gone mad in the last few days. I could have handled it better, but I could explain everything if I needed to. It's what happens next that's important.* Ethan yawned.

He had worried that his criminal act would mean that he would not be able to sleep that night and that he would wake exhausted the following morning, his knowledge of sleep disorders filling him with dread. However, when he got up, he felt as energetic as the previous day.

As soon as he had put his shirts into wash, he realised that he had nothing to do. Feeling like a man who drinks alone, the day stretched to absurd lengths. He wished Aislin was there and sent her a message:

Hi sweetie, hope your ok.let me know if you need anything.xx

She liked him using pet names and kisses, which meant that he reserved them for occasions when he needed to say sorry or ask for a favour. *I should tell her that I love her more often. You never know what's going to happen.* He kept his mobile in his hand until he thought that she would probably be driving.

Ethan put on the MV but felt discontented after a few minutes and sent a message to one of his university friends, asking if she was free for a drink that night.

After a few minutes, she replied that she was.

Aislin sent a message half an hour later:

Just got here.going to be a fuss about nothing prob.will call later.xx

The kisses made him relax for the first time since the incident.

He did not leave anything in the crammer they hired that night, making his friend comment about it. Ethan did not get home until one in the morning.

Aislin rang the following day.

"Hi sweetheart."

"Hi ya, sorry I didn't get chance to call yesterday. You'll never guess what's happened."

"Go on."

"Well, we went through the photos for hours, I'd forgot that he'd taken so many. There must be a dozen albums full to chocka. Anyway, when we'd gone through a load of them, mum said that she wanted some stuff from the shop and I said I'd go with him. We were standing in a queue when this bloke next to us asks dad about his hat and where it had come from.

"I don't know how it happened but they ended up arguing about it. Dad took offence to something he'd said and kept going on and on about how it'd come from Ireland and that you can't buy them anywhere else, and the other guy was taking the piss, saying that you can get them from the pound shop. It ended up with dad saying that 'the likes of him' could never understand, then the man swung a punch at him."

"Jesus, is your dad all right?"

"Yeah yeah, he never got hit. The idiot swung so hard that he'd have smacked him into next week if he'd connected, but he fell into a stand instead and knocked the stuff over the floor."

"Was he drunk?"

"I think so. I've never seen anyone run so fast in a circle before. He must have gone round the shop five times before he got out."

"I'm surprised you didn't deal with him."

"He was more likely to hurt himself than anyone else. It was the most embarrassing thing that has *ever* happened."

Ethan chuckled.

"You can laugh but it's only a matter of time before this happens to you. He likes you, remember. Anyway, I haven't told you the worst of it yet. I just wanted to go, but the woman at the till started to put our stuff through before I could say anything. Then, she said that we had to wait 'cos it was policy that they always call the police when a crime's been committed! It was bad. I had to stand there for an hour 'cos there was a manager watching us the whole time. Dad must have thought I needed some entertainment because he explained at great length why he likes queues. Apparently, they're one of the few places left where people are equal and spontaneous. They are when he's standing in one. I don't know what people thought was going on. They probably thought we were shoplifters. Then we had to give statements to the world's most bored policeman. Ethan, what can I say? What can you do about someone like that? For most people it's a once in a lifetime thing, but for dad, every day's a sitcom."

"What did your mum say?"

"Nothing. Just shook her head. Took one of the onions off us then carried on cooking. She's used to it, you see. I was too, it's only now that I don't live with him that I notice."

"Is this what I've got to look forward to then? Are you going to end up as mad as he is?"

"Worse. So you're planning to stay with me forever then are you?"

"Of course."

"That's a relief. I'm going to need someone to change my nappy when I go wrong."

"You can count on me."

"By the way, have you spoken to Dan yet?"

"About what? What do you mean?"

"About what you said you were going to talk about. Your workload, and all that stuff."

"No, I haven't yet. To be honest, I've had a massive pile of jobs to do and I just forgot. Sorry."

"Are you going to?"

"Yeah, I will. Leave it with me."

"Okay, I've got to get off. You up to anything today?"

"Not much, just going to the cinema with Mo."

"What you going to see?"

"That aliens thing."

"*Aliens*. You're proper boys, you two are."

"I hope so."

"Right, I'll ring you at work tomorrow."

"Okay. Do you want to stay over next week?"

"Erm, yeah, why not."

"It's just that I haven't seen you properly for ages, with work and everything."

"Okay, shall I come over tonight then?"

"Yeah. I'll be back around seven, eight?"

"That's fine, I won't leave here until late."

"Okay, see you in a bit."

"Bye then."

"Bye."

He missed her very much at that moment. *I don't have problems when Aislin's around. She'd never have let me act like an idiot.*

Ethan met Mohammed in a fac around the corner from the cinema, which was bedecked with advertisements for an ultimate combat match that was going to be shown in a hour. Fighting sports had become more popular in recent years after the regulations surrounding them had been relaxed, which had increased the chances of spectators seeing someone get killed. Holographic projections gave a three hundred and sixty degree view of injured bodies.

The tables were close together and the smell of alcohol was heavy in the air. Elderly men occupied the spaces nearest the bar, sipping pints and gazing around.

Mohammed turned up a few minutes after Ethan.

"You all right?"

"Yeah, good thanks."

"I've got the drinks in."

"Mate, all the things I ever said about you… I only meant about half of them."

Ethan laughed. "I must be a right shit then. Sit down before I make you pay."

Whenever he saw Mohammed outside of work, it took him a moment to recognise him, as his beard looked odd over a jumper. His work shirts hid his stocky physique, the width of his shoulders being evident in his casual clothes.

"What you getting then?" Ethan asked.

"I'm hungry, I'm gonna have a burger."

"Sounds good. In fact, to hell with the menu, I'll have the same as you."

"Be careful. People'll think this is a date if we have the same thing. They'll bring a candle over."

Mohammed smiled, sticking his tongue out like a lizard.

"Bring it on, I'm game."

"That's enough of that, I'll get the order."

Ethan gave him the money then watched him queue at the counter. Despite that it was only mid-afternoon, the fac was already busy. Ethan checked his mobile to see whether Aislin had sent him a message.

Drinking that early made him drowsy, and the sounds of the fac seemed to retreat, as if he were floating away from it.

"Thirty minutes, they said."

"That's not bad. I'd forgotten the fight was on."

"Cheers, mate," Mohammed said before drinking the beer Ethan had bought him.

An old man at the bar mechanically lifted a pint to his mouth, his movements seeming as artificial as if he were made out of wax. Someone came out of the toilet and joined him, and when Ethan saw her, he hid his face behind his hand. It was Holloway. *What the hell's she doing here? Everything in her Mirror record had suggested that she lived on the other side of the city. She should have been removed from her position by now.* The old man looked in his direction.

"Let's go into the other room."

"What's wrong with you? I won't be able to see the fight from in there."

"Mo, I'm going in the other room whether you come with me or not."

"Right…"

Ethan zipped his coat up to the top and pressed his nose into it. He held his breath then made for the other room without looking over there again. *It's the Icks. They're up to something.* Things started to make sense. The incident, how tired he had felt. They'd poisoned him somehow, followed him, entrapped him. He had finally got an explanation. He sat at the table nearest the fire exit.

"What's the matter, Eth?"

"Nothing, it was just really hot in there. I was about to faint."

"You're getting fucking eccentric, you are. You'll be turning up to work in your slippers next."

They sat in silence for a few moments, Mohammed stretching his limbs.

"By the way, I've got some news for ya."

"Yeah… yeah…"

Those bastards will stoop to anything. It won't work with me, I'm stronger than that…

"I wanted to tell you before everyone else at the office. Not that it's a secret, but… anyway, I wanted you to know. Well… it's that Hasna's pregnant."

"That's brilliant, nice one. Congratulations."

"Thank you."

What about Aislin? If they can get to me then they can get to her. Why didn't I think of this before? His eyes suddenly focused and he saw Mohammed looking at him.

"So… how many months is it then? Are you going to know if it's a boy or a girl?"

"Four months and it's a girl. It just seemed the right time, you know what I mean? We've talked about it on and off for ages, about the money and everything. We got hung up on stuff about her job at first, but as soon as you decide, that lot doesn't matter anymore."

"Yeah… yeah… 'Scuse me, I'll be back in a minute."

Ethan went out the fire exit and was immediately hit by wind that swirled up his nostrils. He rang Aislin. She did not reply. He looked at his mobile and thought about sending a message before deciding that that was not immediate enough. He rang again, pacing the grass and kicking the fac wall.

A few seconds later, the call connected.

"Hello?"

"Hi Ash, it's me. Are you okay?"

"Yeah fine, what's up? You sound like you've just run a marathon."

"Nothing… I was just checking you were okay."

"Right… I haven't fallen down a well since yesterday if that's what you were asking."

99

"You know I… love you, don't you?"

"Ethan, what's up? You're acting very strange."

"Nothing… it was just… I'm out with Mo and he was telling me that one of his uncles has died. It makes you think when you hear something like that… that you should let people know…"

"I'm going to outlive you so you've got nothing to worry about there. Look, I've got to go, Daisy's waiting for me. I'll talk to you properly tonight."

"Yeah, bye then…"

He looked at his mobile and for a moment wondered whether she was in danger and unable to speak. *I've got to calm down.* The fire exit would not open from the outside, so he walked to the front entrance. He checked that his zip was fastened as far as it would go and set his work mobile to record, hiding it in the palm of his hand. Ethan went into the fac expecting everyone to turn round and stare at him, but his appearance caused no reaction. In fact, the fac was noticeably quieter than before, even though the fight had started. No one reacted when a hologram of one of the fighters launched across the room, flickering when it went through tables. It was all very suspicious, but at least Ethan was not in any immediate danger. He went through to the other room to find Mohammed picking his teeth.

"What was that about?"

"It's all right. I just realised that I'd forgot to tell Ash something. Panic over."

"Right. I'm finished. Let's go or we'll miss the start of the film."

Ethan remembered what he had said about the baby. "You'd better get your paternity sleep licence in, I don't want a file of your dodgy activities landing on my desk."

"Mate, I'll make sure I fill the form in first thing tomorrow. I wouldn't want you going through my affairs."

"Make sure you do."

Mohammed took his coat and brushed past him. *What's his*

problem? Ethan thought. *He doesn't have anything serious to worry about.*

The seats were arranged in rows around the edges of the screening room, with a wide open space before and above them where the images could be projected. Ethan felt as if he was going to fall asleep when the lights went out, so he pinched the backs of his hands and neck. The pain was dull and signified nothing, making him more irritable than alert. His thoughts drifted as the tinny music of the advertisements began. He wondered whether he should tell Aislin about Mo. She had always said that she did not want children until she had got her promotion. He decided not to mention it.

Ethan wondered whether he could have been followed. After all, so much can be found out about someone from their leisure activities: their lifestyle, their associates, inferences about their political views… And the cinema would be the perfect place to observe him. He consciously controlled his blinking until his eyes felt sore.

The film did not live up to the boastful descriptions that had been beaten into his consciousness by the advertising. When they came out, they walked in silence for a few seconds until Ethan asked, "What did you reckon then?"

"Crap."

"Agreed."

They walked to their cars in silence.

"Right, I'll see you tomorrow then, mate."

"Yep, see you tomorrow. Tell Has that I said congratulations."

Mohammed nodded.

Before setting off, Ethan checked his mobile to find a message from Aislin, saying that she was too tired to come over that night. While driving home, he further debated with himself about whether to tell her about Mo. If she found out, the first thing she would ask was why he had not said anything, which he would be unable to answer.

His mind drifted and he realised that he was approaching a traffic light too quickly. Ethan stepped on the brake.

"You have stopped closer to the vehicle ahead than the recommended distance. Your insurer has been informed."

A graph appeared on the dashboard, which showed a spike in his otherwise optimal use of fuel over the last month. He became angry as he thought of how ridiculous he was being. *Back to this again. Not being able to leave anything alone. Thinking the same things over and over and going round in circles. Upsetting Aislin over nothing. I'll not be happy until I've driven her away.* The thought of not seeing her again was so painful that he was as upset as if they had actually had an argument.

Ethan shuffled on his seat. The car suddenly seemed very hot. He lifted himself then sat down again, his trousers stuck to his skin. A horn beeped behind him, making him jump. He glanced at the front mirror before seeing that the traffic light had turned green. He blushed before driving away, feeling as if his whole body was burning. He had not blushed since he was a child.

It was only when he was out of sight of the irate driver, and thus when Ethan was no longer concentrating on whether he was gesturing at him or would suddenly make an aggressive move, that the exhaustion came. It felt as if he had stepped through a thick layer of spider's webs then found himself unable to move his arms, the strands constantly brushing his face. His feet were heavy and felt as if they stuck to the pedals whenever he touched them. The sky flickered around the edges of his vision; the car seemed sluggish as if it were a living thing only reluctantly following his commands.

He did not think he would be able to get home and considered pulling over several times, only not doing so because of his awareness that if his behaviour came to official attention then everything would be over. Not that there was anything in the policies about his situation; no rulebook could be so comprehensive as to cover every eventuality, but suspicion ran far and wide. If they wanted him out, if someone risk assessed his behaviour as falling into the wrong category, than an investigation would be sure to turn up something. So he carried on as if driving into a nightmare, the streets becoming narrower the further he went.

After parking, Ethan looked around in amazement when finding himself outside his house, before relief hit him like a slap on the cheek. His rational sense told him to relax, that this was only an exaggerated version of a situation he had known throughout his working life. However, the memory of his illicit sleep was too strong, the previous breach in his discipline having more weight on his behaviour than the remainder of his life, and he could not get inside fast enough, fumbling his keys as if Aislin was waiting for him.

He shut the blinds in the lounge then stared into darkness, trying to calm himself. However, waiting only heightened the anticipation. It was only when he went into his bedroom that he realised the enormity of what he was doing, and was so ashamed that his exhaustion momentarily abated. He was only able to get into bed after half-convincing himself that he was merely going to lie down, not to make a conscious effort to sleep, that at least his intentions were pure. As he rolled back the sheets, he had to justify every step to himself; why he was taking his shirt off, why he was covering himself with the duvet, why he was closing his eyes...

He found himself swimming deep underwater in a dark blue ocean. Ethan continually debated with himself as to whether or not he was asleep, sometimes thinking that he was and deciding to pinch his legs to check, but always forgetting before he could move his hands. There were shoals of darting silver fish, always just out of reach. Suddenly, he thought that he could not breathe underwater and started to gasp. Pressure from above stopped him rising to the surface. There was something in the distance and he swam frantically. Breathing in hurt and he could sense his body filling with water. Eventually, he reached a reef with a pink tendril unfolded down its side. There were pulsating bulbous orbs at various points along its length, which became darker the further up it went. He grabbed it but his hands were stung and he drifted into the inky depths, screaming wordlessly…

When he woke, he looked around as sluggishly as if he had gone to bed at his usual time, and could not understand why the blinds were prominent silver, which they only were at night. He was too groggy to think about the significance of what had happened, or the curiosity that he was as tired now as if he had been starved of sleep rather than glutted with it. The temptation to lay his head back on the pillow was tremendous, and his movements were so slow that it seemed hours before he finally managed to drag himself to the bathroom, his every movement as laboured as those of an old man. Setting his alarm clock took the effort of a final breath, and his trousers fell off him as if he were shrinking. He did not remember getting back into bed.

He sat up listlessly for a few moments before realising that the light outside was flickering and patchy. His vision shook and he felt as if he had been shunted through time. Sun danced around his bed like light caught under his eyelids after he had been spun on a merry-go-round.

The two hours before his alarm went off were filled with lighter sleep, which flickered into semi-consciousness where he thought he was reaching out to touch clouds, moving them closer then further away by squinting. He had a constant feeling of floating, and imagined that he would never get up unless ordered to, that the early stage of NREM sleep, insubstantial and wanton in its hold over him, would keep him alive for a hundred years, untouched by material needs and safe in his bed.

When his alarm finally went off, Ethan jumped as if electrocuted. Sleepiness hit him like a wave and he rubbed his cheek on his pillow, wondering how long he could remain there before being caught. A few days, at least. *There's no way dweeb knows what the missing persons policy is; he'd just let things drift on like he always does. Aislin would do something before him.* How good those stolen days would be, in which he could get rid of his sleep deficit and feel as good as now all the time. They'd put him in a DIA prison, of course, but after you're ruined, you're free. *If I got sacked and became a nobody, I could do whatever I wanted. When I got out, I could lock the door and sleep away and no one would bother to check. And if they did find out, what would happen? More prison then back here again…*

Somehow, he had become oblivious to the alarm, and when he finished daydreaming, it made him start as it reached a point in the tune that he had never heard before, after which, it went back to the beginning. It was then that Ethan got up.

When he went into the lounge, he realised that he must have been staring at the wall for ten minutes since the alarm had gone off, and he ran around the house, tripping over several times. He could not remember it being so messy the previous night, with several pairs of trousers slung over the arm of a sofa, including one that was inside out. There were crumbs everywhere and several computer game cases had fallen off a display in the lounge, leaving splinters of plastic on the floor. *What the hell happened? Do I sleepwalk now?*

Ethan had such energy as if he had drunk coffee and eaten chocolate bars all morning. He felt as if he could have run a marathon as well as Aislin, and brushed his teeth so hard that there was blood in the sink when he spat the toothpaste out.

As he drove to work, Ethan hummed tunelessly, becoming aware of the sound during pauses on the radio. When a traffic light turned green, he waited for a few seconds to annoy those behind him before driving off laughing when one of them honked their horn.

He was headily unselfconscious as he walked to the SDMA building, not seeing anything around him but having a vague impression that all the cameras and eyes of the city were turned on him, none of which would be able to identify anything wrong.

The additional security was gone and he only managed to suppress his cheerfulness with great difficulty as he got in a lift with half a dozen other workers, each of whom wore the familiar expression of weary dissatisfaction.

When he reached the office, he tapped Mohammed's shoulder before quickly moving past him, making him turn around a fraction.

"Oh my god. This day will live in infamy. I can't believe you fell for that."

Mohammed shook his head then held it in his hands. "You'll pay for that. This is no word of a lie, you'll regret that. I'm gonna bring your whole world crashing down, mate. Let the games begin."

"Doesn't matter if you do, you can never take this moment away from me."

Mohammed slowly shook his head with a wry smile. "What are you so happy about anyway? Did you propose last night?"

"Yeah right, nice try. Don't change the subject."

"We'll see who has the last laugh. Give me a week."

"Bring it on."

The pain from the blood sample was so acute that it made him sit up in his seat. While Ethan waited for his computer to load, he sent Aislin a message:

Hi sweetie, sorry you couldnt come last night.love you loads... E XXX

When he logged into his e-mails, he saw that several agents had sent him the details of the cases he had asked for. There was nothing that could have improved his mood at that moment.

His fingers glided over his keyboard as if he were playing the piano that morning, doing more work more quickly than he could ever have imagined, words multiplying as if he had cast a spell over them.

After he had done as much as he could on Hypnos, Ethan decided to treat himself by opening one of his remaining cases. Given the progress he had made and the difficulties he had identified, he could easily justify himself if necessary. He logged into the secure intranet and opened the top case in the list.

There was a referral from the police in the reports section, which described how a warrant had been carried out at an address as a prelude to arresting a postman for a robbery that had occurred at three o'clock the previous morning. When the police arrived at seven in the evening, the man was sluggish and had clearly been sleeping. He did not have a shift licence. In addition to items stolen during the robbery, police had recovered subversive pamphlets, possibly Iklonian in origin, behind a sliding panel in a cupboard. The suspect had been released on police bail.

Ethan leant back in his chair then stood and paced around his desk. Not only had the case been wrongly assessed as low risk, when it was clearly medium due to the links to serious crime, it had been wrongly classified as a single matter, when there were at least two: the illegal sleep and the pamphlets, in addition to possible wider links to subversion suggested by the fact that the suspect had a legitimate job. It was entirely possible that he was an Iklonian agent taking a 'revolutionary tax' from premises that were somehow linked to alarm clock manufacture. Worse yet, the police had requested a response by a deadline that had expired while he was on leave.

Ethan looked over a divider to see that Peter's office was closed. *This has happened one time too many, he can't be long for this world.* Ethan scanned through the report again to find the contact e-mail of the submitting officer. He then logged into the operation name generator, which was required whenever a case was likely to be assigned as level six or higher.

DS Tomalin,

I have been assigned the Inderjit case, as per your referral (henceforth: 'Operation Amber 518'). Unfortunately, your initial deadline could not be met due to other operational commitments.

Please let me know when you are available so that we can discuss our requirements in this matter.

Yours,

SDMA

Hopefully, the police would be sufficiently intimidated by the mystique of the organisation not to complain about the delay. They usually were. *Something's going to have to be done about that idiot.*

Ethan spent the following three hours researching the suspect on Mirror, wanting to make up for the initial poor impression the organisation had made. There was a lot to research.

He sent some of the documents to print, and when he went to the all-in-one, Hugo was casually putting a ream of paper into the machine. Ethan looked around the room then tapped his feet. Eventually, he said, "Is it working?"

"Think so."

Hugo yawned, looked at his nails, then pressed more buttons. Eventually, the machine started printing. Pages stacked up and it stopped, making Ethan peer over. It started again.

"You got much more?"

"Almost done." Hugo rocked backwards and forwards from his heels to the balls of his feet, before turning to Ethan. "It's my personal strategy whatsit. Took ages that. Loads of copying and pasting."

"Are you being serious? You know the consequences of doing that?"

"Kiss on the cheek?"

Hugo banged the papers on the side of the machine for some time to line the edges up straight before going back to his desk. Ethan ran a hand through his hair.

"You're quiet," Mohammed said.

"What?"

"I said you've been quiet this afternoon."

"No different from normal then, is it?"

"Hmmm. You're a funny 'un sometimes. I'm watching you, remember that."

His voice was so deep that Ethan for a moment thought Mo was being serious, until he rolled his eyes. The break in Ethan's concentration reminded him that he had to read through his notes for Hypnos before Daniel arrived. Preparing for a meeting with him was as hard as every other aspect of working with him, as he would not accept any ambiguity, despite how well they got on.

"I am going to talk to you now and you might have preferred it if I'd kept quiet."

"Go on."

"I've got to see Dan at twelve for him to check up on the work he gave me. I need to compile a list about how long everything's going to take and any problems I've been having."

"Oh right, okay. What do you want to know?"

"We'll have to go through everything, you know what he's like. Sorry about this."

"No problem, go on."

"Right, so… the stuff about the shift licences, where are you with that?"

"I've got the data. The problem is, I've found out that admin don't input half the stuff from the forms into the system. Some crap about how they prioritise things when they don't have enough people there. I've had to work with what's on the system for now 'cos it'd be a nightmare even finding the paperwork, never mind typing it up."

"Right… okay… have you spoke to admin about it, is there any chance of getting them to change their process?"

"I've not spoken to them, they'll never listen to me. Perhaps that's something Dan could sort out. They need rank to give them a kick up the arse."

"Yeah yeah, I'll mention it. Next thing, have you started filling in the document I sent over?"

"Yeah, I've started it."

"Okay, can I have a quick look? Just so I can tell him enough to keep him happy."

Mohammed opened the file then turned his screen around. He had not followed Ethan's instructions exactly, and the graphs he had created to display the data looked untidy, with different fonts for the title and axes, and too many colours, meaning that he had to squint to work out what it meant.

Ethan nodded and said 'thanks', wishing that he had the access to do everything himself. It would be a nightmare, of course; he would not have been assigned any new cases for even longer, and would have to work like a slave for months, upsetting Aislin even more than he already had. But it would have been better than this. The problem with working in a team was that no one else ever did anything right. *I can't say anything until I don't need them anymore.* Ethan had made that mistake before but it took a lot of effort to remain calm.

He went through the other tasks he had assigned to Mohammed, cracking jokes whenever he sensed him becoming annoyed by all the questions. By the time they had finished, there was only an hour until his meeting. His energy level was such that the moment he stopped talking, he compulsively tapped his feet, banging his knees against the desk.

"What's that?"

"What?"

"Well, unless there's an earthquake going on, you're doing something with the desk. It's making me write in Chinese. Pack it in will ya, you've already got me once today, you don't have to stamp me into the dirt."

It was only then that Ethan realised what he was doing, and as his attention drifted, he found himself tapping again and had to put his hands on his legs. He looked around, but of course, hemmed in by dividers on all sides, no one could have seen anything.

Ethan did so much work in the hour before Daniel arrived that he had to revise his notes about his progress. *How strange is it that in this place, where we monitor thousands of people in the minutest detail, the management don't have the first idea what their own staff are doing? It's not surprising we've got Icks working here. Are all the regulations myths? Perhaps we've got so many that they're impossible to police and you only get caught by chance. We collect so much information that we don't even know what we've got, never mind doing anything with it. The admin department doesn't do something because it doesn't feel like it, and no one cares. We're more like a junkyard of information than 'the trading standards of the mind'.*

He was thinking about the best way to confront Peter about the wrongly assigned case when Daniel strode into his section.

"Busy?"

Ethan jumped, making his head jerk out of his hands, not knowing whether he was being serious. Daniel smiled wryly and he still didn't know.

"Hi Dan, how you doin'?"

"Yeah, good. Solving the case for me?"

"What? Oh, yeah, yeah. This is no problem, you should give me something hard next time."

Daniel looked at him knowingly. "Just wait, I've got plenty of things lined up. Have a seat in the conference room while I do a bit of meet and greet."

Ethan did as he said, smiling to himself at how he did not feel the need to conceal the artificiality of what he was doing.

He waited for half an hour, as he knew he would. Inevitably, someone would have mentioned a problem to him without thinking, which would have prompted him to investigate, making whoever told him regret ever having mentioned it. Then he would have berated Pete for his latest idiocies. Despite their obviously frosty relationship, Daniel had always been too professional to criticise him in public, and Ethan wondered how he dressed people down: whether he shouted, or gave his arguments in a cool rational tone that brooked no response, or else was sarcastic, like a teacher. Whatever the case, Pete must dread the sight of him by now. It took some brass neck for him to even be here after all this time; anyone else would have left from embarrassment long ago.

When Daniel finally arrived, he spoke in the slow, laconic tone of a man whose perfect confidence means that he never expects to be challenged.

"How you doing then, Eth?"

"Yeah, good thanks. Battering through everything, you know how it is."

"Good. Your eyes look like piss holes in the snow, have you had to extend your hours again?"

His words were unexpected; Ethan could not remember him swearing before and laughed nervously before the sound was cut down by the unceasing gaze of his sky-blue eyes. In a flash of panic, he wondered whether he had worked out what had happened.

"I'm fine, I've just got a lot on at the moment, that's all. Aislin has had some issues with her dad, things like that."

"Why, what's wrong? Is he ill?"

"No no, nothing that serious. It's just that he can't do stuff round the house as easily anymore, so he needs help but won't ask for it. Silly things really. Nothing to worry about."

"Right. Be sensible with your hours then. Not too sensible, but look after yourself. I said before that I'll have a vacancy for you soon, and I want you to be in a position to take it, yes?"

"Yeah, I know what you're saying, will do."

"Good. Let's see where we are then."

They went through the material in as much detail as Ethan knew they would, and he found it hard going at first, but after a while, he realised that he had anticipated almost all of Daniel's questions, and felt confident that he was on top of the process. Eventually, Daniel smiled behind his hand.

"… Okay, good, I'm happy with that. I need a few things from you then for next week. We need to give the DIA a steer about where we are to keep them off our backs. So if you can summarise everything we've said today into a few paragraphs and send me an e-mail. You're going to wow them, you know. I've worked with the DIA more than once over the last few years and they'll never have seen anything like this."

"What do you mean?"

"How to put it. They don't think things through *systematically* like you do. Whenever you talk to them, everything is connected, but in a vague way that they can't quite explain. And how you present things is a lot better as well. In the DIA, if you give someone a chart they'll look at you as if you've just shown them a light bulb for the first time. They'll be amazed at what you've done so far, I don't know what's going to happen when they see your full report.

"Our problem is that because we're such a young organisation, the fifteenth floor doesn't have enough tradition to fall back on. Allowing people to make decisions without any reference points creates difficulties."

"Right, I'll get something to you in the next few days."

"The other thing I need you to do is to fill in the gaps around the occupations of the subjects of the level one to six SC breaches. I know I didn't mention that before, but I've been asked about it more than once now."

"Okay. Does that need to go in the summary?"

"Yeah. Is that okay?"

"That's fine."

"Good. Has Pete been supporting you and releasing the people you asked for?"

"I've not really spoken to him recently. I had a few minutes when I was first given the project then I've just got on with it."

"Is he managing your case workload?"

"I've got some of the jobs I was given while I was away still to do but it's not a problem. I've been doing them when I've got a bit of downtime or when I'm waiting for people to send me stuff."

"Right. That's not ideal because the deadlines might clash. Can they be handed over to someone else?"

"To be honest, it'd take longer to hand them over at this point than to do them myself 'cos of how long it'd take to go through everything. I'm pretty sure I'll be all right."

"If it becomes an issue, speak to Pete about it and tell him that I expect Hypnos to be the priority, and that he needs to give you the support around it. If it really becomes a issue, let me know and I'll sort it."

"Okay."

"Has he kept to the security arrangements we agreed?"

"So far as I know. As I say, I've not seen much of him lately. I will say one thing. He's still not doing the initial notifications right."

"What do you mean? Since you've come back?"

"Yeah. One of my jobs was classified and risk assessed wrong. And 'cos it was given to me while I was on leave, we missed a police deadline."

Daniel ground his teeth. "Noted. Anyway, I'm pleased with how it's going, keep it up…" Daniel sat back on his seat and put his arms around the back of his head in an expansive gesture, as if posing for a photograph. His legs reached across to the other side of the table and he seemed even taller than he was. "How's Aislin these days?"

"Yeah, fine, carryin' on, you know. She's worried about the privatisation though, she thinks that she'll be lucky to keep the money she's on now and that there won't be any chance for promotion while our 'sponsors and official partners' are doing their thing. It's not right 'cos she's the best there by miles."

Daniel snorted. "Our 'partners'. You know what partners do? They fuck each other. Tell her to just keep going. The worst of it will be over in a few years; it'll be hard, but if she sticks it through then she'll be in a good position. The strongest always come out on top somehow. Anyway, I've got to get a move on, send me the summary through and I'll be in touch in a few weeks for another meeting, yes?"

"Sure."

"See you later then, Ethan."

Daniel was on his feet immediately. He patted him on the back then was out the room before Ethan could say anything. He stared into space a moment then summarised the instructions in his notebook.

Daniel was the only person he knew who could make him feel like a child; praise from him felt like that he had received from his father when getting good marks on a spelling test at school. Since the first time he had met him, the personal side of their relationship had been one way, in that Daniel would ask him about Aislin, but he could not imagine enquiring about his partner, if he had one.

Ethan stretched his limbs as far as they would go. He walked aimlessly around the room a few times until his legs ached then sat down again and rested his head on the desk. An indeterminate time later, he jolted and realised that he had closed his eyes. Feeling foolish, as anyone walking in could easily have had the impression that he was sleeping, he jumped to his feet, his conversation with Daniel still fresh enough in his mind to make him purposeful.

When he sat at his desk, Jo walked into the workspace. She stood in front of him and tapped his chair.

"Hi. Pete's asked me to run something by you before I put a file in. I don't know why, don't blame me."

"I don't think I was going to. Go on."

"He didn't know whether we should put a finding of an illegal alarm clock through to the DIA liaison. I've said it was only one but he couldn't make up his mind."

"Right… what's happened then exactly?"

Jo breathed inwards sharply and spoke quickly as if having already told him several times.

"Basically, the police were round some druggie's house and they've found an illegal alarm clock. He was sleeping in the middle of the day so we've got that, it's just whether we've got to do the forms for the alarm clock as well."

"What do you mean, it's an illegal alarm clock?"

"You can change it to whatever time you want apparently."

"Okay Jo, I know what illegal means, but how can we prove it's illegal? Have you seized it?"

"No, but that's what the police have said."

"Right, the first thing you need to do is get it over here and have it examined. It's all very well saying it's illegal, but he might deny that. Then, who else has used it, where did he get it from…?"

"So, do I need to do the report?"

"Jo, this is what I'm trying to tell you. You can't just hand it over to the DIA without doing any of the work. I mean, they might be interested in the bigger picture around the black market, but they're not going to investigate the clock are they? The illegal sleep is probably a nine, but the clock is definitely a six. If there's a bigger network then it could be a three."

"Well, I'm not being funny, Ethan, but what do you want me

to do? Peter asked me to find out whether to make a referral, he didn't mention anything about all that other stuff."

"It's section three sub-section… thirteen. I'll tell you what, Jo, just e-mail me the file and I'll mark up what you need to do."

"Thanks…" She turned away as she spoke before pushing past Mohammed.

He waited a moment before saying, "Boyfriend trouble again then. You'd have thought he'd have made up his mind by now. Can you imagine having to listen to that every night?"

"I have to listen to it most days, I probably see her more than he does."

Mohammed laughed. "Very true, mate. Depressing, isn't it?"

Ethan nodded. Despite having laughed off the situation, he felt furious after thinking about it a moment. *Why does she think we're here? To paint our nails? We're supposed to be giving society a kick up the arse but we need one ourselves sometimes.*

After reviewing the file and writing a list of actions for Jo, Ethan worked on the summary Daniel had asked for until his landline rang.

"SDMA."

"Hi ya, it's me, Aislin."

"Oh, hi. You all right?"

"Yeah fine, you?"

"Good."

"Can I ask you a massive favour and I'll remember it forever?"

"Go on."

"You haven't promised yet."

"I've got to promise before I know what it is? You haven't sold my organs have you?"

"No." Aislin laughed perfunctorily then immediately continued. "I'm seeing Daisy tonight and it's hard to meet her near mine because she's coming over on the train. She'd have to get a taxi if she was coming to my house. Is it okay if we meet up at yours?"

"Erm… yeah…"

"And if we stay over, 'cos we'll be back late and I don't want to drive when I'm knackered? It'll only be for one day, then she can stay at mine for the rest of the time she's here."

"That's fine but I'll be late tonight; Dan's been over today and given me a load more stuff to do. Is it all right if you let yourself in and I'll see you when I can?"

"I suppose. Are you still angry at her?"

"No, I've just come out of the meeting, I was going to ring you in a bit. That's completely fine. Do you want me to give you a lift?"

"I'll be okay. What time will you be back?"

Ethan paused before deciding on being slightly later than usual rather than suspiciously absent the whole night. "About… eight?"

"That's okay, we'll probably still be there by then. See you later, love you."

"Hang on, before you go, can I ask you to look at a Strategic Personality Review? It's for—"

"I don't manage them anymore. Send an e-mail to the generic personnel account and it'll get picked up from there."

"Oh. I thought you did them, you spent ages setting that up."

"The problem is, Ethan, it was something else that I didn't get paid for and that nobody but me cared about. Anyway, I'll be over soon."

As soon as he put the phone down, Ethan started calculating whether he could contact her before she left work to say that contingency had turned against him and that he would be back later than he had thought. However, she had not sounded convinced by his explanation, and if he added more to the story then she would doubtlessly question him about it and catch him out. He had used Dan as an excuse to get out of commitments too many times to be believed unconditionally. Just like she had used Daisy too many times.

He repeatedly thought through the information he needed before deciding that he could not trust a generic e-mail account, meaning that there was nothing he could do. Although he always praised Aislin to anyone who would listen, his words of encouragement had felt like homilies recently. He could not help but feel a little disappointed in her.

Six

AFTER SIX O'CLOCK, WHEN EVERYONE else had left, he continued typing desultorily for a few minutes before wandering around the office, kicking the air, feeling annoyed that he had tied himself into his excuse; he could not even walk around town for fear of bumping into Aislin. He was trapped within his fortress. As he moved through the workspaces, gazing out the windows, all of which were covered with the same dark security sheets that turned the city into shadow, he saw that many of his colleagues had left files strewn over their desks, the error compounded by the fact that whoever had been last to leave had left the door open. After all the times everyone had been told about security, the tardiness made him depressed.

After thinking about what he could say to Daisy, Ethan went back to his computer. His mind worked very quickly late at night, as if all the excess parts of him fell away to reveal a machine underneath his flesh.

When Ethan switched off his computer, his feet hurt in the way they did when he was so tired that he would fall asleep if he lay down, and he was very tempted to do just that.

The security barrier lips near the lift made a grinding sound when he scanned his card. He sighed and it seemed a lifetime before they finally opened. *No one else is ever in the building after four. Except the porters, who probably sleep in the basement. Perhaps I could apply when one of them dies.*

The gloom of his security-sheet-impaired vision became writ large when he stepped outside, as a despondent air hung over the city. The way was dark and sinister; his steps hesitating and clumsy, like those of a drunk. Everything seemed significant; the holes in the pavement, the way his laces slowly unravelled, horns from cars skidding past, the sound of retching in the distance… He felt like he did when half-awake early in the morning, dozing and unsure of himself.

Abandoned, half-finished building works looked surreal at night, as did the yellow roadwork signs that had been there since he had started working in the city. Posters flapped on walls he passed, the pictures obscured. Only the words were visible, giving orders that were senseless without any context.

He could not remember the last time he had had a headache. He could feel the circumference of his skull. He turned down a path to find himself in a concrete square where an ugly bronze statue towered over open space. There were names written on a slab underneath it, generic in their grey layout. A group blocked an alleyway. They were bedraggled and one was covered in blood that streamed from his head. Knowing that it was unwise to associate with such events, Ethan hurried away and ducked into a shop, the window of which was translucent with grease.

He rubbed his hands and blew on them. Ethan peered inside a freezer to see that it was empty but for shiny chunks of ice. Not that there was much of anything else on the shelves. This was why he did not like to shop in Central Zone. There was no facility to pay with his mobile or even to see a hologram of the chocolate inside the wrappers. Everything was dirty. He tried to think of an excuse to not go home; despite the vast variety of entertainment in Central Zone, the better parts of it, at least, there was nowhere he could sit and pass the time; in fact, it would be prohibitively expensive to do so given the cost of entrance to the 'green spaces', or of renting a bench.

He suddenly became aware of the silence, and when he looked around, the sales assistant was staring at him. The shop seemed to be naturally deserted, his presence there an intrusion. Feeling embarrassed, he walked to the counter and picked up some chewing gum from a display.

The sales assistant looked at him for several seconds before moving. She had thick strands of multi-coloured, interwoven hair, which were squashed together in places. There were black patches around her eyes and she wore an inscrutable expression that seemed to exist beyond her grey clothes. She served him with mechanical movements and the merest hint of a mocking smile.

There was a piece of card on the counter, on which was written a series of special offers for chocolate bars in felt tip pen. An Iklonian lightning symbol was drawn at the top of the list.

Was she an Iklonian? As he hurried from the shop, Ethan realised how few he had actually seen. In various briefings he had had on the subject, he had viewed pictures of a typical subversive, where the features of different agents had been spliced together into bizarre hybrids. Only a small number of his investigations into Sleep Code breaches had identified direct Iklonian influence, and he remembered every confirmed Iklonian he had ever interviewed. However, speaking to them for a few minutes in strictly controlled conditions before they were transferred to the DIA was very different from free interaction.

Ethan wondered whether he could get into trouble for talking to such a person, whether the DIA had her under surveillance. It was impossible to know, of course, fruitless to speculate, although that did not stop him from doing so. When Ethan looked at his watch, the pressure of a practical deadline came to him with relief and he hurried his steps. He threw the chewing gum, unopened, into the road.

He had often thought it strange that he never felt tired when driving. No matter how exhausted he was when getting in or out of his car, the moment he sat, his judgement seemed impeccable, his eyes sharp. He had investigated several instances throughout his career of car crashes caused by people falling asleep at the wheel, and had given presentations to other SDMA agents on the subject, without ever connecting them to his personal circumstances. Half an hour earlier, he would have fallen asleep if he had rested his head on his desk; now he could have travelled any distance without a problem. His thoughts drifted and he wondered whether driving induced chemicals in the brain that suppressed sleepiness. Adrenaline? *Perhaps I wouldn't have any problems if I drove around every evening after work.*

He was so ensconced in the folds of his thoughts that he was surprised when finding himself home, as if he had leapt through time. It was ten past eight. The driving cocoon continued to protect him as he got out the car and he felt jaunty when walking up his path.

He opened the door and called out. "Hello?"

"Hi Eth, we're in here."

He was grateful that Aislin had warned him. *She's only going to stay for a few minutes. Just count down the time.* He paused before going into the lounge.

"Hi ya, how you doin'?" He put the question to them both ambiguously, to test whether Daisy would answer.

"Hi Eth. You get your stuff done?"

"Yeah, just about. It never ends does it? Sometimes, you feel like you could be there twenty-four hours a day and you still wouldn't do all that you need to. How are you then, Daisy, found your way here okay?"

He knew that he sounded fake but thought it best to brush over everything that had happened. Most people cannot stand much reality, but for some, even a glimpse is too much.

"Yeah, we got here."

"Cool. Good. What's the plan for today then?"

He looked at Aislin, thinking that he had done enough for her not to be upset with him. She was wearing a blue dress and her hair was tied in a ponytail, which she had not done for awhile. He wished they were alone.

"We're just getting ready actually. We should be back here for eleven, then we'll drive to mine in the morning. I've booked a few hours off so I don't have to go in until later."

"Okay. Well, make yourselves at home then. Sorry to be rude, I've got to get something to eat. I'm starving, I've not had anything all day."

He smiled at them both with a generic expression that could be applied to anything from an unwanted birthday present to a picture of a cute animal, before going to the kitchen, acutely aware of the possibility of Aislin testing him by leaving him alone with her.

He remained there for several minutes before thinking that he needed to maintain an appearance of cooking. Aislin came in as he was peeling carrots.

"I'll see you later then, Eth. I'll meet you at work tomorrow 'cos there's some stuff we need to talk about."

"Fuck!"

He had been compulsively rubbing the peeler against his forefinger, and when she had said they needed to talk, he had forced his hand up.

"What have you done, are you okay?"

"Nothing, sorry, it's fine. Sorry… what were you saying?" He held his hands behind his back.

"Just that I was going to meet you tomorrow. I'll call at lunchtime."

"Is something wrong?" Ethan's voice was high pitched. Aislin seemed serious in a way that worried him. *She couldn't have found anything out, could she? If Mo noticed, perhaps it's obvious.* His mind raced through everything they had said to each other throughout the week, analysing the conversations for clues.

"I'm fine, I just think we need to talk about some things, that's all. Sorry, I've made it sound like a big deal now. It's just about the job and that, it seems like I haven't seen you for ages. Anyway... we'll talk tomorrow."

"Okay, enjoy yourself then..."

He kissed her cheek and smiled. They held each other's eyes a moment.

"See you later, Daisy."

He heard her mumble something back, and hoped Aislin would think that he had made an effort.

He stood in the kitchen for some time, hearing a constant clack clack clack before realising that he was tapping the peeler against his leg. He examined his finger to see what looked like black blood dripping to the floor. The amount seemed disproportionate to the length of the cut. Drip, drip, drip.

Ethan felt aching soreness in his shins that always presaged exhaustion. It was as if he had been kicked with steel-toe-capped boots, and the temptation to lie down was overwhelming, as if sirens were calling him.

The terrible thing was that it did not feel as bad as the first time; he knew that having given in once, he would inevitably do so again, that his previous actions had created a grove that he was now compelled to walk along. It was as if invisible hands were holding his shoulders, such that even before he moved, he had lain on the sofa several times, telling himself that he was only resting, that he did not have to sleep, that relaxing for five minutes would give him the energy boost he needed. For a moment, he even believed himself.

Ethan felt excitement dart around his stomach and limbs.

He slowed his steps before reaching the lounge, his attempts to dissuade himself only increasing the anticipation. His mobile went off and he rushed towards it, hoping that it was Aislin. It was an automated message from the SDMA. He switched it off without reading it.

I can't lie here again. Someone's bound to see me, it's poking fate in the eye. I'll be one of those who appear on a video, who people laugh at before saying to their friends that they can't believe anyone could be that stupid. An idea popped into his mind that he at first dismissed, but the more he thought about it, and the more his legs ached, the more sense it seemed to make, until the invisible hands pushed him into the next inevitable course of action. He switched off his house alarm.

As he dragged boards from his shed, Ethan thought that he must look incredibly suspicious, that he was drawing attention to himself in exactly the way he was trying to avoid. He dropped the wood on the grass and put his hands in his back pockets, doing a bad impression of being casual. When he had convinced himself that no one was watching, he picked up a stone and threw it at the patio door.

It made a clang and Ethan blushed as he tucked the boards under his arm. Not only had the glass not shattered, but the sound had been very feeble. At least no one would have heard. He thought that he had not caused any damage, but when he approached the house, he saw thousands of thin lines that turned the glass into a multitude of hexagons. It was the best possible result, as it provided an excuse to put the boards up while not making a mess or making the house freeze at night. On an afterthought, Ethan kicked the stone back on the grass.

His hands fumbled as he fitted the boards over the glass. Pain ran through him like electricity as splinters were forced into his cut. By the time he finished, he was breathing heavily. He went into the house, threw his shoes aside, and drew the curtains.

When he lay on the sofa, he was fearful for a moment, as he

did not feel tired anymore and wondered whether the exertion had washed away his exhaustion. However, as the intensity of his thoughts faded, he started to relax, until the sensation of nestling his head on his arms felt like an incipient dream. He was safe now, the boards and curtains hiding him from prying eyes. His sleep very deep and he dreamt only of colours…

Ethan was woken by something so loud that he sat up and waved his arms as if swiping wasps, until realising that it was the front door opening.

"Hi Eth."

Replying seemed impossibly complicated, and when he put his hands on the sofa to lift himself, he immediately had a headache.

"Ethan?"

Aislin sounded annoyed and her voice cut through his grogginess, feeling like fog slowly clearing so that he could see two metres ahead instead of one.

"What's happened?" His heart froze when she dashed into the room. "Are you all right, Eth, what's the matter?" She stroked his face, looking closely into his eyes, "Are you okay?"

"Yeah, yeah, fine."

He felt very heavy.

"What's all this, what's happened?"

"It must have been those kids again. Look, it's broken…"

He pointed at the patio door with a feeble gesture, his arm barely lifting from his side.

"Show me your hand. Shit…"

She scrunched up her eyes as if something had been sprayed into them. Ethan felt awake for the first time since she had come back.

"Don't worry, it looks worse than it is. It's nothing really. I just slipped when I was putting the boards up. I'm going to wash it in a minute. Seriously, it's nothing to worry about."

He hugged her with his free hand and she pressed herself

against him. Ethan felt sick. "I'm sorry for scaring you, I was just cleaning up when you came in. I was hoping that I'd have got things back to normal by the time you got here."

"Don't be ridiculous, I wasn't scared. I'm just fed up that it's something else to deal with. Perhaps it's time to think about moving if things like this are going to happen all the time. It's getting rough round here."

"We'll talk about it in the morning; it's late now, you'll be knackered tomorrow. Have you enjoyed yourself?"

"Yeah, yeah…"

Aislin sounded as if she were talking in her sleep.

"I'll take the sofa tonight if you want to go upstairs…"

She pulled away from him. "No, it's okay, we'll stay at mine. We've got back earlier than I thought."

"Aislin…"

"It's fine."

Ethan suddenly lost the will to argue with her.

"Come on then."

He walked out the room with his arm around her, imagining that Daisy would be annoyed to see them like that. *The one sure way to cure my addiction would be to live with Aislin. I only go mad when I'm alone. Why's she so emotional at the moment? She never normally gets this flustered.* Ethan felt worried when remembering the tone she had used when saying that she wanted to talk to him the next day.

"You enjoy yourself, Daisy?" he asked as they went into the hall, not being able to prevent his voice from being breezy.

"Yeah."

"Good."

They walked past her into the kitchen, where Aislin picked up her bag.

"Are you sure you're all right?" he asked.

"Why wouldn't I be? It's just that… I don't know, you've been very distant lately."

Ethan thought that she was not making any effort to lower her voice.

"You're right, I've had things on my mind… Anyway, you need to get off now. We'll meet up at work tomorrow like you said and we can talk about… everything."

"Okay, love you."

She sounded as if she were asking him a question.

"Love you too."

He kissed her and she examined him with an artless smile, such as he remembered from when they first went out at university and he had walked her to the train station. He had been unsure how well it had gone and so whether or not to kiss her, but knew what to do when seeing her face. That moment had set a benchmark for how he measured beauty.

He thought she was going to say something else but she only shouted "See you tomorrow!" from the hall before leaving.

Ethan stared at the floor, thinking about how much trouble Aislin would be in if anyone found out what the Iklonians had done to him. *She wouldn't be able to carry on working.* Even if they didn't find something to pin on her, it wouldn't be long before a stolen pencil was found in her bag or her performance mysteriously went downhill. *There's always a way of getting rid of someone. The organisation becomes efficient very quickly when it needs to. I wonder how many SDMA people make it to retirement? It can't be many. Promotion is the only sure way to security.*

She's in an impossible situation. What would she have done if she'd come in and found me asleep? It would have hurt her so much. Ethan was surprised to find himself crying. *I've not thought of her since this started. The intrusive nature of exhaustion tends to obliterate all other considerations, but even so… they really are bastards, they don't care about any of this.* He vowed that he would force his sleep patterns to normal by a supreme effort of will. *That's all it takes, how long have I been carrying on before now? If I can just guarantee myself six hours a night, everything will be fine.*

When Ethan went back to the lounge to sort out the mess, he saw that it was eleven and realised that he must have been in the kitchen for over an hour. *I should be in bed. I can't give them a chance. What happens to missing sleep? It must swirl around in the sky just out of reach, always threatening to be absorbed into rain clouds.*

His movements gained impetus as his limbs started to ache. *I won't be able to claim on the insurance because there's no way they'd believe my story. I'd have to report it to the police, and that's just asking for trouble. So a few hundred quid down the drain.* As he tidied the lounge, he calculated how many hours he would have worked to get the money to repair the glass. *A good way to spend my overtime.*

When he went to bed, he thought through his situation until it seemed inexplicable that he had acted like he had. Ethan had a sense of regaining control over his life and felt like an adult for the first time in weeks. *How long would it have taken me to get a grip if Ash hadn't come back when she did?* He felt very animated until suddenly becoming aware that he had lain there a long time and was tempting fate again. He closed his eyes and tried to block out everything, but his mind was buzzing. After what seemed several hours, he turned and went over everything he had already decided, his fervour increasing even though he was only repeating himself.

He slept fitfully that night, as if he had a fever. Being woken by his alarm clock felt like being slapped in the face while talking, and it took several seconds for him to remember where he was.

Up until the point when he got to work that morning, Ethan was filled with the sensation of renewing an old routine. In the same way as when getting back from holiday, he had a sense of inexplicable excitement. He was overwhelmed by long-suffering irony, a futile knowingness that made him want to laugh hysterically.

Ethan tried to remember what his usual hours were; his life had lost order in the last month, with time no longer fitting his days; night no longer allocated to sleep, work having no limits, in-between moments attacked by invasive thoughts… Mohammed was in the office when he got there.

"All right, mate?"

"Hi."

Mohammed glanced at him and Ethan knew that he wanted to ask why he looked so tired. He laughed.

"What?" Mohammed asked.

"You, the look on your face. We could be sitting here in a hundred years time and you'd still have the same expression."

"We probably will be here in a hundred years. You don't think we're going to get a pension do you? The only pension we'll get is throwing ourselves in the sea so that no one has to pay for a coffin."

"What's got into you? You're a rebel now, are you?"

"I just watch the news."

Ethan smiled, trying to understand the import of his mysterious comment, before thinking it best not to say anything. The organisation was very sensitive about changes to pensions. That was one of the reasons why unions, or any other form of 'combination', were banned in the SDMA.

"Yeah right, I bet it's nothing but cartoons in your house."

"What's wrong with cartoons?"

"Nothing. I'm just saying that I don't believe you watch the news."

"It's nice to count how many ways I'm being screwed over. But forget about that for a minute. I might have figured out why Si is still off."

"Go on."

"Jo was looking depressed yesterday so I got her some cake, you know, for comfort food, and she told me that she'd overheard dweeb talking about him on the phone."

"And?"

"Well, the rumour is that he's had to have an operation. You know. Downstairs."

Mohammed looked at his knees portentously. Ethan shook his head and rolled his eyes.

After everything that had happened, Ethan's work had faded into the background of his mind, despite the hours he had put in, and when he opened the Hypnos files, he felt as if he was looking at the project for the first time.

However, as the morning passed and he became more confident, Ethan relaxed and rubbed his shoulders, realising that they felt sore because he had sat hunched forward as if ready to spring to his feet. Whenever he was working particularly well, like that day, he would watch himself thinking, counting the lines on the screen while typing and estimating the amount of words. He was energised.

He had made good progress on the project and started work on another theory, which was that in addition to disrupting the power supply, the Iklonians were trying to damage food distribution in Central Zone. By dull and painstaking research, he had compared the amount of various types of SDMA investigations against the movements of known Iklonians and unsolved attacks on infrastructure. That gave some evidence of a pattern of small-scale sabotage and SC breaches in particular suburban areas, which resulted in SDMA resources being prioritised there. After around a month, there would be an attack on a weak point in the power infrastructure, not necessarily at a place that would cause significant damage, but in locations that would be unlikely to be immediately detected, such as pylons in isolated areas. Spikes in SC breaches in poorer zones would be accompanied by shortages of basic foodstuffs with an apparently disparate set of causes, from illegal strikes to warehouse fires.

The upshot of everything he had learnt was that the Iklonian attacks were organised in some unidentified way. Needless to say, the DIA would never release any intelligence reports that gave more detail about the internal mechanisms of the Iklonians, if, indeed, they knew that much about them, which Ethan doubted. All the DIA agents he had ever met were the same: always asking for information but never releasing any in return, making veiled comments about the extent and reach of their intelligence networks but not knowing the answers to specific questions. However, if the system worked, they would be able to overlay his report with any information they had, and perhaps even do something about it.

Despite the progress he had made, Ethan thought that he was missing something, that if he fitted some other factor into the puzzle then the patterns would become obvious and his theories would be proven. *Perhaps there's something significant around SC breaches relating to companies that supply agricultural plant?* Testing that idea would require a very long and boring search through the records, as the SDMA did not record information in a format that would make such esoteric searches easy. However, now that he had had the idea, he had to see whether it was true… he opened the intranet and started the long trawl.

As he worked, he wondered whether he could get away with not telling Daniel the whole story during his next update. He had not misled him last time, but had concealed the inferences he had drawn. Now that his research was more advanced, it would be very difficult not to say more. The problem was that if he told him everything then Daniel would inevitably ask dozens of questions and want to take the matter to his superiors immediately. He would then require a draft version of Ethan's report, which would mean taking out the incomplete sections and re-checking what he had already done, stopping him from researching anything new and keeping him from his cases.

Within a few days, he would be told that given the nature of the findings, the deadline had been brought forward. Furthermore, at the back of his mind was the thought that if he could keep a little to himself then Daniel would not be able to take the whole credit for presenting his work, and Ethan would have to be invited to the meetings with the bigwigs, which never did any harm.

He had made the mistake of giving too much away before. The difficulty in this instance was that the importance of the project made manoeuvring dangerous. Knowing that he had a few days to decide, Ethan lost himself in his work.

Later that afternoon, his mobile went off, making him jump.

Hi honey. Can you finish 5 tday? xx

Seeing the message made him nervous, as he had forgotten about Aislin wanting to talk to him. *Weren't we supposed to meet at lunchtime?* He sighed and tapped his desk before deciding that he had to leave when she said that day. *Fuck.*

Sure see you in a bit. xx

I should get her a present, I haven't surprised her for ages. I've been so tied up with my sleep patterns lately that I've ignored Ash. That was almost certainly what she wanted to talk about, to ask him whether there was anything wrong and to say that she wanted to spend more time together. It would be nice, everything else being equal.

His stomach rumbled and he saw from the clock on the bottom right of his screen that it was almost three o'clock. He locked his computer with a flourish of his hands.

"Right then. Want anything from the shops?"

"No, I'm all right, thanks."

"See you in a bit."

"Yeah, see you later."

There were few people around the city at that time. Ethan walked quickly, knowing that he was breaking SDMA policy concerning lunch hour, which should start between twelve and one, and be staggered so that there was a least one person at every workspace during office hours, or at all times during national emergencies, or as required by the SDMA General Director.

It is incumbent upon everyone to be aware of policy. It is incumbent upon everyone to follow policy. The Sleep Code supersedes all other law.

Those words had never seemed more true and they stuck to his shadow.

Ethan went from shop to shop until he found one that sold greeting cards and cuddly toys. Aislin was always happy with any present, even thoughtless ones from distant relatives at Christmas. Ethan bought an elephant with 'to someone special' written on its ear.

As he made his way back, Ethan approached a jewellery shop that he had often passed. It was half three, such a long absence aggravating his policy breach. He crossed the road and went inside.

The shop was tiny, smaller than the lounge of his house, with rows of necklaces and rings on slanted displays in glass cabinets. The size of the place meant that he could not help but immediately look at the woman behind the counter, who smiled and asked, "Are you looking for anything in particular?"

She had the artless kind voice and messy hair of a grandmother.

"I wanted something for my girlfriend. I was looking at some necklaces in the window…"

For some reason, he felt nervous that she would ask him which ones he had viewed, and did not know why he had lied.

"Do you want to take a closer look at a few?"

"Okay."

The woman produced a key out of the air as if performing a magic trick before opening a cabinet and taking out a series of necklaces. He nudged one of them with a finger then looked at them one after the other. However, apart from the ones that had different coloured gems, there was no way he could tell them apart, other than by price.

"Which ones do you like?"

"They're all nice, it's hard to choose."

"Do you know what kind of jewellery she prefers?"

"I've not asked her, I wanted it to be a surprise."

Ethan was suddenly embarrassed by the thought that he had never bought Aislin any jewellery, a fact that he was sure the woman would find scandalous.

"Okay. How tall would you say she is?"

"Not very. About five six."

"And is she fair skinned?"

"Yeah."

The woman nodded as if that information was very significant.

"I've got a picture here."

He scrambled to take it out of his wallet, feeling the gentle pressure of her waiting eyes.

"She's very pretty, isn't she?"

Ethan felt proud in the same curious masculine way that he had felt when his mother had commented on how beautiful Aislin was after first meeting her, such that he could only nod.

"An emerald would match her skin tone. Either of these would suit her very well." The woman ran a hand above two of the necklaces.

Ethan did not understand her reasoning but respected her authority on the subject. "That one's really nice."

"It's my favourite as well, it's a lovely shape, isn't it?"

She picked it up with her fingertips.

After a few seconds, he realised that she was inviting him to hold it, and when he did so, he found that it was so light that he could hardly feel it, which he was not sure whether or not was a good thing. It twinkled even though he held it still. "I'll have that one then please."

Ethan was surprised to hear himself, as he had not intended

to buy anything and never spent that much money spontaneously. He could not wait to see Aislin's reaction, and thought about what he would say when they were alone.

The woman handled the necklace very carefully, placing it into an ornate purple box, which made Ethan feel even giddier.

"Do you want any insurance?"

"No thanks."

"Are you sure? We can—"

"No, I can just add it to the house insurance."

Now that they were talking about something he was confident about, Ethan felt back on sure ground. He paid for the necklace and placed it inside the bag containing the teddy bear.

"I'm sure she'll love it. Sleep well like the world."

The woman made a circular gesture with a palm. Ethan nodded, not understanding her or knowing how to respond. Her eyes were very penetrating, and he felt her watching him as he walked out the shop.

He hurried back to work, the uneasiness he felt drowning out his anticipation.

He approached a point where the pavement narrowed as it joined a car park. A man wearing a hoody stood in his way, meaning that Ethan could not get by without going into the road. He turned his shoulder to squeeze past but the man followed his movements. Ethan took half a step back but the narrowness of the passage meant that the man had only to shift his weight to obstruct him again. Ethan thought that he did not want to get into a confrontation, his recent experiences having dented his confidence in his self-defence abilities. When he remembered that he was carrying Aislin's presents, he felt close to panic.

The man stepped forward and pushed him out of his way with the blade of his hand. Ethan braced himself against a car. As the man moved past, Ethan was inclined to shout something, but was prevented from doing so by the realisation that he had pressed something into his fingers. Ethan slowly opened his hand to find a scrap of paper, creased and covered with stains, like a piece of torn treasure map. It contained two words, written in thick black ink: 'Iklonian five'. That was one of the unidentified codes he had read in a DIA document that Daniel had sent him.

Ethan scrunched it up and looked around, thinking that the whole thing was a trap, that if he was detained now, the evidence against him would be unanswerable. The street was almost empty; there did not seem to be any eyes on him. He put the paper in his mouth and rolled it around his tongue; he could only swallow with painful effort.

He imagined cameras recording his every move, shadowy figures darting from one alleyway to the next. The words of the woman from the jewellery shop now almost made sense; was everyone he had ever met either an Iklonian or a DIA agent? Every scenario he had ever faced a test to determine his loyalties? It was unreasonable, unfair, no one could be expected to pass a trial like this, when those playing the game could instantly reverse all that had previously been agreed.

Ethan realised that he had closed his eyes, expecting to be either arrested or spirited away by robed figures any moment, depending on which side had set him up. However, if it had been a test, then he had not passed or failed it sufficiently to start an endgame. He stared at everyone who passed him, preparing to grab and shake them if they so much as glanced up, which would have proven that they knew what was happening. However, it was as if he did not exist; even those who brushed his shoulder did not look at him.

He wanted to go back to the jewellery shop to confront the old woman, and decided to do so several times. However, the shop shimmered as if it were a reflection in a puddle whenever he tried to move towards it, until the strain of his efforts made him realise that unless he was going to attack her, there was nothing he could do. *There's no way she'd ever say anything. Am I going to kidnap her and force her to tell me what's going on? Given how disciplined they*

are, she'd only laugh, no matter what I did. That's if she really is...
The mystery that gnawed him to pieces was that there was no way
to know which parts of his life were real. The actions he would
have to take to find out which of his associates were Iklonians were
so extreme that they would destroy him.

After he did not know how long, Ethan reached the SDMA
building, his every step as if he expected to tred on a mine.

The guards in the lobby stared at him, and he smiled back in
a way that seemed horribly false. As he pressed his identity card
against a slot and the lip-shaped security barrier slithered open,
he felt a pain in his stomach he could not understand at first, but
that as soon as he stepped into a lift, he knew was the note, cutting
him open from the inside out. He imagined that if anyone studied
him at that moment, the words 'Iklonian five' would be blazoned
across his chest, and they would have no alternative but to point
and shout at him, identifying a security risk as they were bound
to do by duty.

When the lift door opened to reveal an empty corridor, Ethan
released his breath.

He felt as if he had walked for miles, and when he looked at
his watch to see that it was quarter to four, the fact only added
to his agitation. *Is there anything they can't do? Or was I really
away for that long?* The jewellery bag was very heavy and when
he transferred it to his other hand, he felt as if a piece of his
flesh had been ripped off where the handles had dug into him.
He closed his eyes and imagined a schematic of the building
with a red dot representing himself, visible to anyone with eyes
to see.

Ethan was exhausted by worry and whims. *They won't leave
me alone, that's obvious now. What can I do? Just carry on, I suppose.*

As he strode through the corridor, the unchanging noticeboards
displaying their widely ignored exhortations to take up sport and
go to staff social events, he became angry at the thought that he

had not done what he needed to do for Hypnos that day. He imagined building a machine that could freeze time, which would allow him to sleep all he needed then sort out the crap people gave him. *Then I could relax.*

He pushed the office door open harder than he intended, making his colleagues turn to look at him. Pete moved to head him off.

"Eth, can I—?"

"Not at the moment, I'm busy."

When he reached his desk without any comeback, Ethan had to stop himself smirking.

"All right, mate, where've you been?" Mohammed asked, resting back in his seat. Ethan thought that he must not have heard him speak to Pete, otherwise he would not have been so casual.

"Just picking something up for Ash. Here, have a look."

Ethan handed him the jewellery box, for some reason embarrassed about the cuddly toy, and analysed his every movement. He was suspicious of the old woman's motives.

"That's nice, really nice. Is there any occasion?"

"No, not really, it's just that I've not seen her much lately with all the stuff going on."

"Well, she'll be pleased with that. I thought it was going to be a ring for a minute then, I was disappointed that the box was that size."

"Fucking shut up, will ya. I'm tired of hearing about that."

"I was just joking."

"Get some new jokes then, I'm sick of that one."

Mohammed smiled in a strained way and seemed to take particular care when placing the necklace on its felt backing. He handed it to Ethan then frowned at his screen.

Ethan breathed inwards sharply when giving his blood sample to get into his computer, feeling acute pain for several seconds. A bubble of blood welled up as large as a teardrop.

He took a perverse pleasure out of the awkwardness of the

next hour of working in silence, feeling the tension when both of them happened to stop typing and they could only hear their chairs creaking.

Later that afternoon, he had a return e-mail about Operation Amber 518.

SDMA,

No problem, when are you available for an initial meet up?

Thanks,

DS Tomalin

Ethan smiled. Although the mystique of the organisation allowed certain people to get away with a lot, he could not deny that it was useful sometimes. He arranged the meeting for the following week.

When Aislin sent him a message, his mobile sounded harsh and abrasive.

Meet outside in 10? xx

He sent a return message:

Okay.

Now that the moment was nearly there, it seemed anti-climactic. He wished that he could have given her her presents as soon as he had bought them, when he was excited. Now that he had had time to think about the situation, he had an uncomfortable feeling that she would conclude that he was trying to bribe her, that she would think he had guessed that she was annoyed with him and was trying to get out of the situation. *Maybe that **is** what I've done. Hopefully, Aislin won't mind not seeing me for a few days if tonight goes well.*

Ethan switched off his computer, mentally preparing himself for the event that he had built up in his mind. Everything had become so complicated since his sleep problems had started. *This might be a medical condition.* Ethan had investigated many cases where punishment for an SC breach resulted in diagnosis of a sleep disorder, with the offender having to submit themselves to 'a rigorous programme of physical and psychological evaluation to establish the best ameliorative course of action, including further medical treatment, lifestyle adjustment, or any other course of action determined by the SDMA,' in the words of the official literature.

Of course, being diagnosed with a sleep disorder would result in immediate and permanent removal of his security clearance. No one who had ever had one was allowed into an SDMA building. Indeed, a history of sleep disorder, even after treatment, was a recognised 'risk factor' in becoming a subversive, which was why medical records had been incorporated into Mirror. That must have been why the Iklonians had done whatever it was that they had done to him.

Ethan spun on his chair to look out of the darkened window. Receiving the note would have changed his life a month earlier but was only another incident now, something else that he had to suppress to maintain the façade of his public persona. *It's amazing how quickly the extraordinary becomes the ordinary. In fact, there's not much extraordinary about the extraordinary.* He looked at his watch and jumped when realising that fifteen minutes had passed since Aislin had contacted him.

"I'll see you tomorrow then," he said to Mohammed.

"See you tomorrow."

Ethan was surprised to hear his voice sound strained, until he remembered their argument. It seemed entirely inconsequential now, to the extent that it was ridiculous that Mo cared about it. Nevertheless, Ethan was sure that he would not hold a grudge; Mo would forgive someone who had broken his nose half an hour earlier as long as they sounded sad when apologising. Ethan nodded at him before leaving.

As he waited for the lift to arrive, he thought about when he should give Aislin her presents. Doing so straight away might result in an awkward scene and spoil the moment, as she would probably open them but not want to say anything while standing outside the SDMA building. On the other hand, if he waited until she had told him what was wrong, then it might seem as if handing her the bag was a tactical move in an argument.

In the few seconds it took for the lift to reach the ground floor, he felt uncomfortable when thinking about the old woman in the jewellery shop. Had the Iklonians picked out the necklace for him?

When he saw Aislin, holding her handbag in both hands, her hair blowing around her back, Ethan thought that she was very beautiful. Somehow, she did not seem like an SDMA worker, subject to all the rigorous discipline that that entailed.

"Hi ya."

"Hello!"

She beamed and stood on tiptoe to kiss him, and Ethan thought that perhaps he had built up her words out of all proportion; if she was angry with him then she was certainly hiding it well. When she took his hand and they slowly walked to the train station, he decided not to give her her presents just yet.

By happenstance, they walked past the jewellery shop, and when Ethan saw it, he tightened his grip on her hand, preparing himself for who knew what. He could not stop staring at it, knowing that he would not be able to answer if she asked him what was wrong. He walked away as quickly as he could, pulling Aislin in his wake.

She was very affectionate on their way home, resting her head on his shoulder as soon as they sat on the train. He put his hand around her waist and watched the landscape pass. They jolted apart whenever crossing a zone boundary before reaching out for each other again. To his surprise, he saw many things that he had never seen before, and thought that he was always so busy that he must rarely see what was before him. When travelling to and from work, he stared blankly with glassy commuter eyes, seeing as if in a waking dream whilst compartmentalising the work he had done and needed to do, all images seeming only an extension of himself.

Aislin was very still, her breathing audible and regular. Ethan shifted on his seat and she cleared her throat with soft irritation before settling down again. The easiest way to deal with everything would be to talk to her. *If only I knew how she would react.* He stroked Aislin's hair, pleased to see her unambiguously happy for once.

When they reached their stop, they decided that they were too tired to cook, so they went to their Indian fac. They ordered and Ethan looked out at the gathering darkness. It was late autumn, when night descends as stealthily as an assassin, when one can talk awhile then be no longer able to see beyond the window of one's room when one looks outside. Harsh streetlights gave the suburb the air of a metropolis.

"I was going to wait till we got home, but I wanted to… Here, I've got you something…"

Ethan thrust the bag, which he had hidden in his lap, across the table. Now that they were together, he felt embarrassed and could not bring himself to explain.

"What is it?"

He smiled at her, and she rolled her eyes when taking out the elephant.

"Thank you."

"There's something else."

When she opened the box, she looked at the necklace a moment before walking around the table and hugging him so hard that his neck ached. When she returned to her seat, Ethan saw a solitary tear on her cheek.

"I'm touched."

He was about to launch into an explanation about why he had got her a present, but instead put his hand on hers and they looked out of the window together.

He did not know what to say for several minutes, and when their food arrived, Aislin told him about her day.

"What did you want to talk about then?" Ethan asked.

"Nothing major really, nothing that's a big deal. Just… various things…" Aislin scratched her nose. "It was just about work and a few other bits."

"Go on."

"I've found it hard going lately having to do all this travelling. It's over an hour to get to work and over an hour to get to mum and dad's; I'm in the middle of nowhere."

"It has been tiring you out."

"I know. And as well… I don't know, we've been drifting along… you seemed to be not very happy with how things are going."

She frowned at him.

"No, it's not that, I'm sorry if that's what you thought…" He looked away. "It's just… I don't know, it's what our jobs are like, it's a life we've chosen rather than a career. I always say that when whatever project I'm on has finished then things will get back to normal, but there is no normal. The problem is that too many people are too comfortable. They forget how important the things we're looking at are. You have to save the management from themselves but that takes so much time."

"That's why you'll be running the place soon."

"Yeah right."

"You will though. I know that you… anyway, thank you for today."

"It's okay… it's okay…"

"I've been thinking recently that the organisation might not be the place for me to get ahead. They might even outsource the whole of HR and I'll have to start at the bottom somewhere else. What I wanted to ask you… I want us to live together."

"I want to as well."

She pushed her thumb into the side of his hand and her smile turned her face into a series of dimples. Despite all the reservations he had had in the past, Ethan had answered without hesitation. He knew that she was not serious about leaving the organisation. No one ever left.

"So… what do you think would be the best thing to do? Would you want to sell your house and…?"

"Why don't we get a new place? That way it'll be ours. Anyway, I think it's starting to get bad round by you, with the window and everything. Why don't we have a quick look when we get back?"

"Okay." Ethan thought that in the best case scenario it would take several months to sell their houses, and longer if they were in a chain. Although he was happy with his decision, he felt glad that he had that time cushion. "I'm sorry about everything that's gone on, I know I get distant sometimes. It's hard not being able to talk about what I get up to during the day."

"Why, do you want to tell me something about you and Mo?"

"You'd know if there was something going on between us. I wouldn't be able to walk."

Aislin laughed then shook her head. "I know what you're like, I was just worried that you were getting bored, that's all. You're obviously younger at heart than me. When I joined up, I thought about nothing other than work and promotion. I feel old at twenty-eight now. Everyone I speak to is getting married and having kids, it's weird."

"Yeah… yeah…"

"And the job… after a while, you… lose enthusiasm, I suppose. It just ends up seeming like a load of rules, like a strange game."

"You sound run down, that's all. It's nothing to worry about."

"Anyway, let's not go over everything again. I've not finished yet."

"Oh? You've not got more revelations for me, have you? I don't know how much more of this I can take, I'm already this emotional." He held his shaking hand by his forehead.

"Stop it, you. What I was going to say was that my dad wants me to go with him to Ireland, to the town where he was born. He rang yesterday and said that he's lost touch with his homeland. He started telling me all this stuff that he's told me loads of times before, about when he was naughty at school, things like that. But now he says that he's got to see whether his hometown is still there. He's going at the end of the week."

"Right…"

"I know, it sounds mad doesn't it? He was getting really upset though. He was almost crying at one point and he's not cried his whole life. He didn't cry when his mum died."

Ethan nodded.

"He says he wants me to go with him. So he can show his little girl her roots, he said."

"So… what are you going to do then?"

"The way he was talking about it… I've got to go, Eth. I know how mad it sounds, but I have to."

"How long does he want to go for?"

"A month."

"A month?"

"Yeah…" she said apologetically, looking out the window while stroking his palm with her little finger.

147

"Erm… what does your mum say?"

"You know what she's like, she doesn't say anything these days. She just accepts whatever he does."

"And what do you think?"

She sighed. "It's so hard to say. In some ways, he's always been like this. But I suppose it is strange that he's getting worse as he gets older. Most people get boring."

"Haven't we already had three weeks off this year?"

"I can take it unpaid. They put out an e-mail about unpaid leave a while ago. They don't mind you doing it now, with the budgets and everything. If you do it at a time to suit them, anyway."

"Ash, are you sure he's all right? I know what you're saying, but this does seem… out of the blue."

"Yeah, I think so. It's just something he's got in his head. He's obviously been thinking about it for ages, the detail he went into about things. I can't remember half of what I did yesterday in as much detail as the stuff he was going on about from forty years ago."

"I want to come with you."

"He said that he wanted it to be just the two of us."

Despite what he had just said, Ethan was glad that that was the case. "Well… it looks like that's what you've got to do then. Can I ask one thing though? If he isn't better when you get back… just speak to someone about whether he needs help with things. I mean, help around the house and that. We just need to… you know… make sure he's all right."

She nodded then leant forward and kissed him.

"I will do. And you'll have time to start researching houses and everything while I'm away."

"Yeah… yeah…"

Ethan suddenly felt discomforted.

"Has Dan come to a conclusion about transferring?"

"Erm… I haven't spoken to him for ages."

"You've never spoken to him about it, have you?"

"I have. I have mentioned it, I just haven't pushed the point. It's hard to get hold of him when he doesn't want anything from you."

"Ethan, I thought you just said that you were going to think about us a bit more now? There's no point us living together and me coming back to an empty house every day."

"I think…" Ethan looked at her and wished that he had not started speaking, as the pause became unnaturally long very quickly, "… well, I don't think transferring is a solution. The organisation is the same everywhere. It's just a matter of… being stronger with them…"

"Ethan… I don't think that's ever going to happen…" Her voice cracked, which immediately made him feel that he was about to cry. "… I want you to have sorted something out by the time I get back. I'm not saying it's got to be a transfer if you're committed to being an investigator. Come to some formal agreement about your hours, whatever. But I need you to show me what's most important to you."

"Okay."

"No, it's not a one-word answer. Things will have changed when I get back or I'll know that you don't want us to be together." Aislin reflexively made her right hand into a fist and cradled it with her left.

"Look… I understand. When things go so far… I know what I need to do now. Go and sort out your dad and everything will be fine by the time you get back."

She smiled and drew a circle on his hand. Ethan looked around nearby tables, his emotion of a moment earlier having dissipated into annoyance when she had said that he was an investigator. No one gave any indication that they had heard anything.

After having finished with all the serious topics, they chatted and enjoyed themselves for the rest of the evening before driving to his house. Aislin did not leave until very late.

As soon as he closed his eyes, Ethan was in the ocean, drowning from the very first moment. He swam in circles, tendrils all around. He somehow retained a dream memory of how much touching them had hurt. He watched his limbs changing colour as they filled with water.

Seven

ETHAN WOKE THE FOLLOWING MORNING with a jump, and the familiar surroundings seemed strange, as if he had forgotten that his life would have to continue unchanged a while. He felt tired in a way that he had not known since before his sleep problems. For the past two weeks, he had often felt a preternatural sense of normality before falling asleep, like a man with a terminal disease who convinces himself that he will make a recovery on the basis of a sudden lack of pain. Ethan had grown to fear that listless calm, to distrust himself. *The Icks **must** have done something to me. Maybe injected me with something. Bastards. Bastards.* There had long been rumours about them developing secret technology to manipulate their targets' dreams. He had not given those reports any credence before. Now, anything seemed possible.

As he got up, his shoulders felt stiff, which made everything he lifted seem heavier than it should be. Then there was the constant dullness behind his eyes, which felt puffy no matter how many times he rubbed them, that seemed somehow connected to the dry itchy feeling in his hair. In one sense, he hated feeling that way.

However, it also gave him a strange relief that he was experienced enough to cope with that level of tiredness.

Ethan decided to drive to avoid the hazy sensation that the train induced, and the familiar sights gave him the sense that he was on top of his life and work, that nothing of any importance happened outside them, that the world was but a reflection of his frustrated dreams, that everything was gnawingly the same as it had always been or could ever be.

He could not rest his head in his hands, his nose bobbing against cold glass while he absorbed the landscape, like he did when on the train, and his vision rejected any excess stimuli, turning the suburbs into marshmallow: pallid colours, buildings that seemed to sway as he passed, objects straining too hard to be real.

The feeling persisted when he walked his usual route from the car park to the SDMA building. His physical discomfort lessened as he went, the mild exercise jolting him into acceptance of what was happening, his sleepiness instead projected on his surroundings, giving him a constant sense of colours being out of synch, that they were bleeding into each other, that his brain was not being updated quickly enough. Those were the familiar, crude yet vibrant, sensations roused by exhaustion.

Ethan's eyes focused when he went through the first lip-shaped security barrier. Dots of colour shone in his eyes, making his vision spin as if he were on a roundabout.

Mohammed nodded at him when he reached his desk.

"You all right?" Ethan asked.

"Cool. How you doing?"

"Yeah good. Is dweeb in yet?"

"Don't think so. He hasn't been out here this morning. Not that that proves anything. You mates with him now, are ya?"

Ethan smiled. "Don't worry, you don't have to get jealous. I just need to tell him to do a few things."

Mohammed laughed silently. Ethan switched on his computer. The police officer dealing with the robbery had replied to his e-mail to say that he could not make the meeting after all, but that he would send the relevant material to SDMA headquarters. Ethan tapped his fingers against the keyboard, then said, "I've got some news for ya."

"Okay."

"I'm telling you now so you don't get the wrong idea if you overhear anything… well, me and Aislin were talking about stuff last night, about how difficult it is to see each other with all the travelling… Anyway, we're going to get a new house and move in together… it's not going to be for a bit yet, we're going to put both our houses up for sale and God knows how long that'll take. But that's what we're going to do."

"That's brilliant, mate. Genuinely. I'm pleased for ya. Hasna won't stop talking about it tonight."

"You tell Hasna about what me and Ash get up to?"

"Course. She loves all that stuff. She says you sound cute when I tell her about you."

"Cute? Anyway, changing the subject, I've got a work-related question."

"Go on."

"Okay. I've got to find out what the term 'Iklonian five' means. You ever heard of it?"

"No. Where's it come up, in one of the case files?"

"Yeah, yeah. Are you all right to research it for me? The only reason I ask is because I've got to do another progress report for Dan by the end of the month and I've got a hundred and one other things to do before then."

"Okay, what does it relate to, can you narrow down what to look for?"

"Sorry, I know next to nothing about it except that it was mentioned in an intelligence report somewhere. I'll need you to run searches through every system; start with the case files and

Mirror, then anywhere else you can think of: miscellaneous reports, anything from the hotline, from the internal files, anywhere."

"Oh, man. You're taking advantage of me now. Just because I love you doesn't mean I'll bend over for you."

"And there's one more thing."

"Another thing? Are you kidding me?"

"I'm gonna have to go to the basement at some point about this so I need the right references. You can't tell anyone about this, not even dweeb…"

"That's not likely. I don't say morning to the bloke if I can help it."

"Well, keep it that way."

"I tell you what, you're on your way now, hobnobbing with porters and everything. Why've you got to go there?"

"Just to check a few original files for bits and pieces. Nothing major."

"Okay, mate. Going to the basement is 'nothing major' these days. You'll be having the prime minister over for tea next and she'll be curtsying you."

Ethan smiled then they both started typing. He had no choice but to get the information this way, because if the DIA had tried to set him up then he could not afford to have any evidence of the term stored on his computer. He did not think about it any further that morning.

His stabilised condition helped his concentration, and that afternoon, he made two further breakthroughs. Firstly, by overlaying electricity prices from United Power with SDMA statistics, he was able to posit a direct link between attacks on power infrastructure and the retail price of electricity, giving further credence to his theory that some of the incidents were carried out as part of a wider plan. There were some incongruities in the information that he needed to further research, but that would be much easier now that there was only one utility company to deal with. When he had first joined the SDMA, there had been three, each of which had their own mutually incompatible way of recording their data, which had been a nightmare.

Secondly, there was a clear performance pattern in the success rate of SDMA cases over the same period that to his knowledge had never previously been identified. The SDMA was required by statute to collect statistics about the amount of investigations that had resulted in proven breaches of the Sleep Code. The recognised recording practice was that one proven breach in a case was counted as success, regardless of the nature of the incident or how many people were involved. This meant that if an investigation proved an SC breach, it went down in government statistics as a positive result, even if the investigation had identified ten suspects and the SC breach was only verified against one of them.

Official statistics showed that the agency had a consistently high and improving rate of success over the last three years. However, the amount of people identified as committing SC breaches was reducing, and the amount of prosecutions brought on a per-case basis was also decreasing. The organisation relied far too heavily on official records and therefore struggled to investigate those who did not have an MV. Furthermore, the amount of Iklonian agents uncovered was lower the previous year than at any time since the agency had formed. In short, the SDMA was only identifying the obvious, investigating shift workers who had been caught asleep on the job by their supervisors, and homeless people who had been seen asleep in the street by a crowd of onlookers. Eighty per cent of successfully identified breaches were for section one, subsection one. Many of the other sections had no proven cases. Increasingly, the SDMA was blind as to what caused breaches and was unable to identify Iklonians or other subversives.

Whether as a cause or consequence of those problems, the amount of referrals through the PSH had decreased thirty per cent year to date compared with the previous year, and thirty five per cent compared to two years earlier. The organisation had long depended on the public for the majority of its information, which was why it had always spent such a large proportion of its budget on advertising. If the public had lost confidence in the system then the organisation was in serious trouble.

Ethan's first instinct was to look around the office and think about the faults of his fellow investigators; how they did not pursue cases to their logical conclusions, how they did not follow procedure, or in some cases even know it, how the work was unequally distributed to hide the blushes of the lazy, and finally, of course, the fool in change of the section, who was as unaware of what was going on around him as an anaesthetised patient.

Ethan locked his notes in his drawer, unsure whether to give the unvarnished truth. Daniel was as hard on poor performance as he was, but even so, he was a senior manager, and Ethan had never known a senior manager who had been happy to have a systemic problem pointed out to them. In addition to the implicit criticism that they had not known what was happening, detailing a problem in writing meant that it could no longer be swept under the carpet, creating a necessity to do something. And doing something invariably caused problems.

After giving the matter considerable thought, he decided to put some of the truth in the initial document and give Daniel a verbal update on the more unpalatable facts, such as the amount of SDMA agents who had never uncovered multiple suspects in any case they had ever investigated. Then at least he would not be embarrassing him in front of the DIA, and he could decide what he was willing to disclose.

He opened his e-mail to let Daniel know about his progress, but a blank window opened that crashed his other files when he tried to close it. "Is your e-mail working?"

"It's been crap all day, mate, you just have to keep restarting it until it works."

"I already have twice this afternoon. I spend hours waiting for things to load."

"You know why, don't you? I've heard that they've found that five of the new IT contractors are Icks. God knows what they've been doing with the system."

"Where did you hear that from? Anyway, wasn't there that lock-down the last time it happened?"

"They don't do that anymore, it's too high-profile. They do it in secret now."

Ethan looked at Mo to see that he had a perfectly serious expression. "I swear to God you talk a load of shit sometimes."

"Is it really that far fetched?"

Ethan shrugged.

As he was walking to the car park later that evening, Ethan's mobile rang and he saw that it was Terry. *Where did he dissapear to?*

"Hi Tez, how you doing?"

"More importantly, how are **you** doing?"

"Erm… fine… is there any reason I shouldn't be?"

"With everything that's going on, how can anyone be fine?"

"You've got me."

"I'm only messing around with ya. I was just going to say what are you doing tonight? We were supposed to meet up ages ago but it never happened."

"Erm…" Aislin had earlier told him that she had some things to sort out that night, and Ethan thought that he would not have to mention anything to her. "Sure, okay. Do you want me to come straight to yours?"

"Why not? No problemo."

"Right, I'll see you in a bit."

Ethan paused, thinking about whether he should go. He probably wouldn't still be in contact with Terry if it didn't annoy Daisy so much. She had not liked the fact that they were friends when they were going out, and the sound of his name was enough to make her grind her teeth now. That just about overcame his distaste about associating with someone so unreliable.

There was a new poster that seemed to be on every wall of every building. It depicted a man with a sinister moustache sleeping with his head resting on a desk. Workers were loading a crane with metal bars behind him. The slogan was 'Our City Our Security – don't take any risks'. The image was oddly incongruous – there had been no heavy industry in the Eternal City for at least fifty years.

When he reached Terry's house, Ethan saw that the curtains were closed and there were no lights on. After knocking twice, he was about to ring Terry's mobile when the door opened a slither. A nose appeared.

"All right?"

"Come in then, hurry up."

He bundled him inside and shut the door before he could say anything.

"What's going on?"

"What do you mean?"

"Why are all the curtains closed?"

"Well, you don't know who's looking, do ya?"

Terry stared at him as if highly offended before going into the lounge. Ethan followed him, to see that the room looked precisely the same as when he had last visited, six months earlier. There were still beanbags in place of chairs, and one of the walls was given over to a montage of musicians cut from magazines and newspapers. There were photographs of Terry and Daisy on the mantelpiece, placed in front of a picture of a magnificent fish leaping from a river. Light flickered off its scales and the cascade of droplets was as dramatic as if the water had been pierced by gunfire. Terry had been interested in photography since they had met as teenagers while working in a supermarket, and he had always said that he would look for somewhere to send them to, someday.

"Have a seat, wait there a minute."

Ethan looked around as there was nowhere obvious to sit, before clearing a pile of magazines from one of the beanbags. He was looking at the pictures when Terry returned, carrying a plate like a waiter.

"Here ya go. Food fit for kings."

It was a crisp sandwich like they used to have in their lunch break.

"Cheers."

"You ever see Daisy these days?" Terry asked.

"Occasionally. Through Ash."

"What's she up to?"

"Couldn't really tell you. I only tend to see her for a few minutes at a time."

"Does Ash ever mention about her having a new boyfriend?"

"No, but we hardly ever talk about her."

"I think about calling her sometimes. I'd like to know how she's doing."

"Yeah."

"Anyway, fancy a game?"

Terry waved a controller at him.

"Of course."

Terry had one of the earliest models of MV, which was compatible with his old games console. Once Ethan started playing, he enjoyed himself like he used to. Terry was intriguingly old-fashioned; Ethan had never met anyone else who owned a camera with lenses. Meeting him was like reminiscing over a bittersweet film.

He got so competitive that he lost track of time, and when realising that light was no longer filtering through the folds of the curtains, he looked at his watch to see that it was ten o'clock. He brushed the crumbs from his clothes before mumbling an apology, ignoring Terry's suggestion that they play on, leaving with assurances that they would meet again soon.

Terry slammed the door shut as soon as Ethan was outside. He straightened the collar of his coat and saw a flash in the window of the house opposite.

"Nice to meet you…" he shouted, waving at whoever it was. He saw a darting movement then everything was still. He held his breath while walking up the path, feeling like he was about to be shot.

As he got into his car, Ethan went into his mobile to see that he had had an automated message from the SDMA:

INFORMATION EXCHANGE. A suspicious male wearing a mask has been seen in YOUR area between 23:00-03:00. Described as tall, medium build, shaven head. Call the Public Safety Hotline today with any information. Why take a chance?

He bit his thumb. No one's ever described me as tall. I'm medium height. No one could say any different.

The rest of the week conformed to the pattern of his life as he had known it for the last eight years since joining the SDMA; long, hard hours, and eating out with Aislin late at night. However, there was a heightened quality to his experience; he took particular care with security procedures as he realised that the scope of the project was incrementally widening to involve investigating his colleagues. Mo's statistics were average, which was to say poor. (His own were of course by far the best in the section.) The amount of people he could trust was now very small.

Since their agreement to move in, Aislin had not been annoyed with him for finishing late and they had been as happy together as when they had first met. He left at eight on Friday, meaning that she had had to go home to pack before meeting him. He had thought that the hassle would have pushed her too far, even with how well things were going, but when she sent him a message saying that she had set out, it contained ten kisses.

When he reached their fac, he went to the table Aislin had reserved for them and did not recognise her for a moment. She was wearing a new red dress that made her arms look very long and elegant. When she saw him, she stood and kissed his cheek.

"You look very beautiful tonight. Not that that's any different from normal."

"Trying to make up for keeping me waiting?" She smiled, giving a very bad impression of being annoyed.

"Sorry. You know I'd end the world tomorrow if it meant I could spend more time with you."

"That's all right then."

After they had eaten, Ethan felt their time together slipping away, as if the passage of time was a punishment that they had uniquely to endure, and wished they could always live that way, enjoying each other's company without any complications. The accumulated sleep deprivation that was always worse at the end of the week made him feel a giddy headiness.

They remained at their table for a long time. However, eventually, Aislin looked at her watch with a flick of her head.

"I've got to go, they'll be wondering where I am. Dad'll be forced into doing something desperate, like asking mum to go with him instead."

"She'd love that."

"Oh yeah, you can imagine her, can't you? Traipsing around following his whims all day long. There's only one fool daft enough to do that."

Ethan put his hands over hers and said, "I'll miss you."

She smiled and looked away, and Ethan thought that if he complimented her again, she would be happy enough to stay a little longer.

"I wasn't joking before, you know. You are always beautiful. I'll joke about anything except that."

Aislin smiled while biting her bottom lip.

She squeezed his hand several times on their way to the car park. Such a commonplace thing as love did not seem possible at that moment. He was expecting an emotional scene before she left but Aislin only kissed him with probing lips, resting her head against his chest before getting into her car.

"Remember what I told you," she said. He nodded, feeling annoyed that she had alluded to her ultimatum on such a night. She paused before driving off, making the safety monitor admonish her for the fuel she had wasted.

When he returned home, Ethan wandered from room to room, feeling as if he wanted to do something, anything, rather than go to bed. It felt nonsensical to remove himself from the immediacy of the world at such a time. A thin, hazy sleep soon snatched his thoughts of Aislin away, without even the consolation of incorporating them into his dreams.

Ethan woke feeling startled the following morning, hearing his alarm clock as if for the first time. He had planned his every moment the previous week so as to see Aislin as much as possible before she left. Now that he could do anything, he felt at a loss.

After eating a banana for breakfast, he lay on the sofa and idly made different figures appear in the lounge using the MV, before sending Aislin a message. He tapped his feet for a few minutes before thinking that she was probably driving.

Ethan thought that he had not contacted his university friends for a while, and he rang one of them to arrange to meet the next day. Even with half of the weekend accounted for, time stretched before him as if he were looking at a starless night sky. They could think of nothing else to do other than hire a crammer. His friend slept at Ethan's house that night.

He felt refreshed on Monday morning. Aislin had sent him messages and a brief e-mail over the weekend, in which she had said that her father had been as excited as a child from the moment he got on the plane, and that she had had to treat him as such: "I'm going to be knackered at the end of this". Ethan had smiled when reading her words, as he could imagine what had happened as vividly as if he were there.

The next interim report for Daniel had to be finished by Friday, and now that Ethan had only himself to think about, there was no reason why he could not put in the hours to get it done for Thursday, then perhaps go out with Mo at the end of the week. Ethan wanted to ask his advice in private about living with a woman, never having done so before.

He planned to finish most of Hypnos by the end of the month. That way, when Aislin came back, they could concentrate on looking for houses and he would not have to upset her by missing showings. Of course, there would still be meetings, presentations, briefings to management, and all the other rubbish that followed the completion of any major project, but one-off events of that type were easier to justify than unconditional devotion to the SDMA.

Ethan plunged into work as soon as he sat at his desk. Diligence seemed paradoxical, as the harder he worked, the more he discovered, expanding the project still further.

After a few hours, Mohammed said Ethan's name, making him jump before looking round his computer.

"What are you daydreaming about?"

"What?"

"I had to call you ten times. You weren't thinking about me again, were you?"

"Yes, mate. I wasn't going to say but you've forced my hand. What do you want?"

"I've found out about that thing you were interested in, 'Iklonian five'."

"Oh right."

"It came up in a report that Ben filed a few years ago. You remember him, he used to—"

"Yeah, yeah…"

"He did a few jobs around infiltration of the fire brigade. Apparently, there was some suggestion that a few people in the back office of a station had been recruited by the Icks. The original report said that they were going to use their influence to allow certain buildings to burn down, but that wasn't proven. A couple of firemen were caught up in minor SC breaches and were sacked; two stats people were arrested but the criminal case was later discontinued.

"Iklonian five came up in stuff recovered when their desks were searched. There were a whole series of weird notes with patterns scribbled over the paper. There were pictures of… demons, or monsters or something… anyway, the phrase was written underneath them. They were sent to the DIA for analysis but nothing ever came of it. Nothing they told us anyway."

"So it doesn't mean anything as far as we know?"

"There was one other reference. Do you remember the big who-har a while ago about the symbols being graffitied on buildings that were supposed to be a secret language the Icks were using?"

"God, not that again. That lot was a nightmare."

"Tell me about it. Well, one of the symbols drawn in chalk in a hospital toilet might have read Iklonian five, although it had been partly worn away by the time we got there. There was a press report to say that it refers to an initiation ritual, about the number of them who've got to be there and the position they stand in. We had the journalist in who wrote about it but he wouldn't tell us where he'd got the information from, so the job was filed."

"Okay… right. That's as much as we've got then?"

"Yeah. The DIA have probably got more 'cos it was their intel in the first place. You want me to put an inter-service request to them?"

"No. It's all right. They'll never give us more than they already have, with how high profile it was."

"Okay, do you want me to send you the full files?"

"No, that'll be enough for the report."

"What about the references?"

"Yeah, I could do with putting in the sources."

"Right, the fire brigade cases are 1XT, forward slash, 1095 dash K12. There were a few of them but they were all investigated under one number. The symbols job is I409186D12."

"Cheers."

"Anything else? Warm your chair for you?"

"It would be nice."

Mohammed laughed before going back to his work, shaking his head. Ethan stared at his screen. The information floated around his mind for the rest of the day, in the same way that one chews gum without conscious awareness of the movements of one's jaw.

That afternoon, he received an e-mail to say that Security Support had received a package for an operation linked to him. Ethan immediately felt excited, as it was the first package he had received since he had been assigned to Hypnos. Usually, he would receive at least one a day.

He logged into his Security Support account and arranged for it to be delivered to his floor. All agents had access to the system and had to input which cases they were assigned to, verifiable by a unique reference number. All mail sent to the organisation had to be labelled with either the SDMA case number or operation name, which was checked before the porters delivered it to the relevant floor.

The system was designed to ensure that anyone dealing with the organisation could not identify a particular member of staff. Ethan thought that the officer had labelled the package in the specified manner without being told what to do. *He must have dealt with us before.* Nevertheless, he was annoyed with himself for the omission. Unlabelled mail or parcels were liable to be destroyed, and the organisation occasionally carried out disciplinary investigations against those who had failed to follow policy.

Items were conveyed to each floor every three hours, and by convention, agents would retrieve them ten minutes after delivery, so that they would not see the porters. Ethan constantly looked at the clock and paced around his workspace at five past.

He retrieved the department's post from a space near the lift and gave the various packages to the other agents. The amount of mail they received was a good measure of how busy they were, as they should be having material from other agencies all the time. No one had more than a single item.

He opened his box like a child who has been waiting impatiently for their birthday for months, going to bed every night thinking about the toys they had been promised. It contained photocopies of various police statements, and the seized pamphlets, each separately wrapped in a transparent exhibit bag. The policeman was obviously experienced in these matters.

Ethan read the statements so greedily that he had to go over them again to grasp their meaning. They confirmed what DS Tomalin had told him in his initial e-mail about the suspect sleeping when they had arrested him. They were very detailed and well written, also giving information about the state of his bed, describing how the sheets were dirty and that there were no pyjamas in the bedroom. Ethan noted both facts in his investigative report, as they were common occurrences in hardened sleep offenders.

Each pamphlet had the Iklonian lightning symbol printed repeatedly around its edges. They criticised aspects of the Sleep Code, and argued in demagogic terms about the supposed difficulties it caused. They were very similar, and he had to place them side by side to see the differences in phrasing. After giving the central argument, the bottom of each leaflet gave statistics about the problems caused by lack of sleep.

After looking at them for several minutes, Ethan thought that they must have been designed for people working in different occupations. *This is seriously well organised subversion.* He noted the inference in his report.

There was already almost enough to prove a case of section one, subsection six: illegal sleep connected to other criminal activity. If any of the other agents had been assigned to the case, it would certainly have ended there. However, if his inference was correct, then there was a clear possibility of a section two, subsection five: undermining fundamental law by encouraging Sleep Code breaches through use of extra-parliamentary measures.

He wrote up his reasoning in his report, then prepared a covering letter for the pamphlets to be examined by the SDMA's forensic experts, recommending that fingerprints be taken, and for tests to be carried out to establish the origin of the paper and ink.

The final action he needed to complete before sending them on was to check the suspect in Mirror. When he saw that he was connected to over fifty records, Ethan ran a 'lifestyle sweep' to produce charts showing how they were connected, and bringing back information from other agencies in a format that would allow him to request further details if necessary. He resisted the temptation to read it now – there was no point when he would have to do so again when the pamphlets were returned, and wrote the system reference on his covering letter, before labelling the box containing the pamphlets and taking it to the space near the lift.

When he got back to his desk, Ethan thought that, given how professional the policeman had been, it was surprising that he had not thought to say whether there had been an alarm clock in the house and whether there had been any evidence of tampering if there was. He sent him an e-mail about it.

It felt surreal to be able to come and go as he wished, without a call to Aislin to justify what he was doing. He had sent her a message earlier in the day asking whether they had settled in, but on the basis of her comments from the weekend, he did not expect a reply until that evening.

He felt as alone as if he were looking out from a ship into the boundless waves of a storm. He remembered his first day at the SDMA, when Aislin was still at university. She had met him before work and could not stop adjusting his suit, saying how smart he looked. Some of his mystique had dissolved when she had started working for the organisation.

Ethan scared himself on his way home, as he became so lost in reverie that he thought he had fallen asleep. The strain of everything that had happened that day: the hard work, the subterfuge with Mo, the intensity with which Ethan had thought about Aislin, was such that he felt as if he were sinking into his chair.

When he got back, he opened the door to find a thick wedge of post on the floor, as if he had just returned after a fortnight long holiday. He put it on a window ledge before yawning and putting his bag in his bedroom. Ethan was hungry but did not feel like cooking. He put insurance renewal letters into a pile for later. He thought that he had found something interesting when he saw a multi-coloured envelope, but it was only coupons from the local supermarket.

At the bottom of the pile was an A5-sized parcel. It was so light that it seemed to be empty and he had to shake it several times before a black rose fell out. He rubbed a petal between his thumb and forefinger; it felt thick and rubbery, as if it had been spray painted, but when he checked his fingers, nothing had come off. There were two pieces of notepaper inside. The same handwriting was used on both of them, so neat and perfectly spaced that he at first mistook it for typeface. On one piece of paper were the words 'Iklonian Five', underneath which was written an address and Wednesday's date, followed by 'six o'clock'. On the other was written 'Aislin Doherty', her home address, the address where she was staying in Ireland, her mobile and home numbers, date of birth, and a sort code and account number.

Reading the notes made Ethan feel what it had to be like to be driving and see another car swerve in front of him, giving him a moment to realise that he was going to crash. *This is it then. They know my address now. I'll never get away. One mistake and they have you. How the hell did they even find out that I'd fallen asleep that night? I'd been worked into the floor, how was it my fault?* For a moment, he was consumed with childish rage and wanted to tear up the note and kick something; he would have enjoyed smashing the MV and hurting himself so as to have something else to concentrate on.

I've got no choice, I'll have to report myself tomorrow morning. It was past the point of SC breaches; he knew cases less serious than the situation he was in when people had been arrested under the Subversion Act for associating with a prescribed group.

Will Ash still want to know me? It seemed unlikely. She would lose her job for sure, but it was more than that. For the first time, he realised the dishonesty that his sleep problems had induced, this whole aspect of his life that he had kept from her. When he thought about how much better they had got on lately, he had to stop himself from crying.

He stood perfectly still, looking out the window. The inclusion of Aislin's phone numbers had to be only a threat, as she would have contacted him had they rung her. Ethan did not recognise the sort code but had no doubt that it related to one of her accounts. Neither side would ever let him go. Someone with his knowledge who had been shown to associate with Icks would be considered a high priority for the rest of his life. If he was lucky, he would be put into some covert DIA operation to infiltrate an Ick safe house; if unlucky, he would be charged in a DIA court and be sentenced to indefinite detention in DIA custody under whichever provision of the Subversion Act proved most convenient. He was depressed that the Iklonians had found him first.

Eight

HE DID NOT GET TO sleep until very late, constantly going over all the injustices he had been subject to and the unfairness of everything that had happened. When he woke reluctantly into darkness, he turned over in a confusion of groggy miasma. He lay still, imagining that he would soon fall back asleep. However, he was too unsettled, his worries retuning within a few moments of consciousness. Ethan got up to see that it was three in the morning.

His stomach rumbled and he ate a packet of crisps in the dark, not wanting to put the lights on and give away to the street the fact that he was up so late. The food barely dented his hunger, and he remembered that he had not had any dinner the previous night. After searching through the cupboards with his fingertips, he found some soup. Ethan lit the room with his mobile and listlessly watched the red glow of the hob.

He ate in front of the MV, continually going back to the kitchen to get more bread until he had eaten half a loaf. Ethan lay on his back and flicked through the channels, allowing the mixture of advertisements, repeated news reports with jaded presenters, and pornography, to wash over him. He switched on the holographic projector and watched two naked women for a few seconds, their vacant eyes being no more real in three dimensions than in two.

His stomach felt distended. He knew what he was doing was stupid, and yet another risk, as the SDMA sometimes checked patterns of electricity and gas usage with United Power when investigating a suspected SC breach or Iklonian agent. A high usage early in the morning often identified sleep problems and therefore a vulnerability to subversion. Ethan could not be bothered to justify to himself what he was doing, so caught up was he in his suffering. He was sore all over, felt that he had no control over anything, and that there was no way out. It was unfair.

Although he soon started to feel tired again, he could not bring himself to stand until five in the morning, when his stomach gurgled. He had barely noticed the room starting to lighten and felt out of alignment with time, that he should be doing anything other than what he was doing. His intense exhaustion felt like having two black eyes, and his legs tingled, a feeling that would not go away no matter how many times he rubbed or shook them. Just under an hour and a half of sleep before he would have to get up. He debated with himself as to whether he would feel better by staying up all night, before deciding that at least his stomach might calm down if he had a nap before leaving for work.

He spent his time in bed turning, stretching, listening to his stomach, then catching a few moments sleep before waking with the feeling that his alarm clock had gone off, then realising that the house was silent. The nightmarish intensity made him acutely aware of the fact that he was alone in the darkness, that everyone except him and the SC criminals were enjoying their rest.

The sound of his alarm clock hit him like a punch to the nose. Just lately, he knew whether he was going to have a good day seconds after waking. His limbs would not move in the way he wanted them to; getting up seemed no longer within his power, so he remained where he was, being beaten by the sound. By the time he was able to stand, Ethan struggled to his alarm clock to see that he had been lying in bed for twenty minutes.

He felt that he should be rushing around to try to make up the time, but did not have the energy.

After being unable to fit slices of bread into the toaster, he angrily scrunched them up then rested his arms on a worktop with his head bowed, stupefied by the pettiness of his actions. He closed his eyes, and for a moment felt the comforting embrace of semi-consciousness. Ethan had an urge to lie on the floor and sleep where he was. *Perhaps I should. I'm bound to get caught sooner or later, so why not sooner?* None of it made any sense. Even assuming that he had not slept after going back to bed, he had still had five hours the previous day, which was longer than normal. Why did people have illegal sleep if it made no difference? The more you have, the more you need, like a drug.

He had to drive because he had missed his usual train. As he was leaving his street, the shapes around him seemed to move closer then further away and he stopped to rub his eyes. When he had recovered, he found that he was in the middle of a road, so close to a parked car that he had to wind his window down to see whether he had hit it. Multiple red lights flashed on the dashboard. *This is so dangerous.* It demonstrated the truth of the warnings against tired driving: every hour less than the recommended quantity of sleep was the equivalent of five units of alcohol.

He steeled himself before setting off again, and by a supreme act of concentration, he remained aware of everything around him, his eyes darting from one side of the road to the other. However, when he became caught in a traffic jam and relaxed, he blacked out for a moment and jumped when a car horn sounded behind him, finding himself resting his head on the steering wheel, his arms lolling down his sides as if he were dead. He was too frightened to look around to see whether anyone had seen what had happened. He turned around and drove to the train station.

Fear kept him alert throughout the journey; he constantly checked the makes and models of cars around him to see whether he was being followed. He did not think he was.

"There were five instances of harsh breaking during your last journey. Your insurance company has been informed."

Ethan stared at the graph on the safety display, which demonstrated that the car's fuel efficiency had reduced significantly during the last two weeks. He chewed the inside of his cheeks. *No wonder the premium went up. Something else I've ruined.*

He was already half an hour late by the time he arrived in the city. As he stumbled along the pavement, Ethan felt his exhaustion like a terrible, wearying drubbing, as if all the negative feelings he had ever experienced had combined into a moment. The events of the previous night had wiped out his recent happiness with Aislin, to the extent that he hardly remembered her.

He found walking as difficult as driving and had to promise himself that he could rest when he reached an alleyway. When he got there, he pushed against a wall to stretch his arms. From his angle, irregularly laid cobblestones seemed anachronistic under the shadows of the skyscrapers and wide glass structures that dominated the city. The alleyway was near the entrance to one of the old high streets from the time before the cities had merged, the battered shops unfamiliar despite him walking within a few metres of them every day. They were mere backdrops to reality, desperately clinging to their meagre existence without ever actually disappearing.

Ethan remained there for several minutes, knowing that there was nowhere else he could stop before reaching the SDMA building. He ignored his mobile buzzing in his pocket and took a deep breath before willing himself onwards.

None of the guards challenged or even acknowledged him. When he reached his office, people glanced up as he passed them. He stumbled over the carpet and Mohammed looked at him from over their divide before ducking down. Ethan felt instant annoyance, knowing that he was going to have to explain himself.

"All right?" he asked, as casually as he could.

"Hi."

His throat was very tight.

"Did you get my message?" Mohammed asked.

"Oh, was that you? I thought I heard my phone go off but I was rushing."

He checked his mobile. The message read:

Hi you okay? Dweeb asking about you.

"Right. What's his problem?"

"He didn't say much, he was just walking backwards and forwards, and after about the fifth time, he asked if I'd seen you today."

"What did you say?"

"Just that I hadn't. He flapped about a bit then went away."

"That's strange. What's made him come out of his cage? When's the last time he was interested in what's going on?"

"It had to happen sometime I suppose. Perhaps he felt guilty. You know, with all that money he makes for doing not a lot." Mohammed typed loudly for a few seconds while Ethan stretched and looked at his keyboard. "Anyway, were you okay this morning? I was worried for a minute."

Mohammed peered around his computer to focus on him.

"Yeah fine, just… just a bit of a family crisis. Aislin rang early and woke me up; she's been upset with some of the things going on with her dad. To be honest, it's been hard work lately. You know what he's like, I'm fed up with it all now."

"What's been going on?"

"I don't want to go through it all again now. Sorry… Thanks for asking but I've had hours of it this morning."

"Okay."

Mohammed looked into the air for a moment then leant across the desk as far as he could go. He glanced around again, making himself appear very suspicious. "Be careful. With all that stuff going on about the infiltrators, you know how paranoid they are at the moment. I've heard that they're looking for any excuse to sack people so that the organisation will be easier to sell to whoever puts a bid in for it."

"Yeah, I know, it's—"

"Just be careful, mate. Whatever you're doing, be careful."

Ethan felt a twinge of annoyance at the implied allegation and wanted to ask him what he meant, but was oppressed by the silence of the room and did not know whether their colleagues were listening. Although there were no rules about partners whispering to each other, he was aware of how suspect they would look if someone walked past. He gritted his teeth when giving his blood sample, wanting to punch the screen when the pain in his finger did not ebb.

It felt strange to start typing at almost ten o'clock, as he had usually carried out several enquiries or been immersed in research for hours by that point.

He had only written a few sentences when Peter walked past his desk. Peter paused and glanced at Ethan in a very obvious way. *Christ. It's a good job he's never done any fieldwork or actually had to talk to a member of the public.*

Peter walked past several more times until awareness of what he was doing made Ethan so irritated that he could not concentrate and rested his head in his hands.

When Peter next appeared, Ethan asked, "Looking for someone?"

Peter stepped into their space and tried to look anywhere but at Ethan, until his steady gaze eventually forced Peter to meet his eyes. Peter rested his hands on the back of Mohammed's chair, making him turn around. Peter pulled back.

"Hi, Ethan. Yeah, I need to talk to you for a minute."

"Can it wait 'cos I'm really busy at the moment?"

"Well… no, I need to go through it now."

"Right."

Ethan smiled a strained smile. He wanted Peter to go ahead but he only stood there, and Ethan felt the stares of his colleagues on his back as he went to his office.

When they reached it, Peter picked up a policy manual and put it on a windowsill. Ethan felt himself becoming more and more angry. *Just get on with it you idiot.* He tried to temper his feelings, not wanting to make trouble for himself, but as he sat waiting for him to stop messing around, he knew that he was not going to be able to force himself to be polite.

Eventually, Peter sat before him and crossed his legs. "I just wanted to say first, thanks for all the work you've done lately, it's been noticed by a lot of people and it's been appreciated."

"Yep."

How can he say that? He doesn't know what work I do. He doesn't know the first thing about what goes on in the department.

"So this isn't about you. You mustn't think that. But there is a policy about lateness and it says that I've got to fill in a report."

"I know what the policy is, I wrote the policy. I've enforced the policy more than once."

Peter winced at the reference to the fact that Daniel had chosen Ethan as the representative for their section to the SDMA disciplinary board, which meant that he had updated the guidance for supervisors around disciplinary and performance issues. He was the only person of his rank at the monthly meetings, Daniel having evidently not trusted Peter with the task. After he had presented various case studies of investigations that had shown that lateness to work was often an early sign of sleep disorder, the policy around attendance had become harsher, and required all supervisors to complete a red report (so called because of the colour of the form), whenever anyone was more than half an hour late, to be sent to the local DIA attaché. Failure to comply with the policy was a disciplinary offence.

"You know what needs to happen then. What were you doing this morning, Ethan?"

"This is the intrusive questioning then, is it?" he asked, referring to one of the requirements of the policy, "… It was personal stuff. There's nothing wrong."

"Okay, but you know I can't put that. What personal stuff?"

"I don't feel comfortable talking to you about it. Put in the report if you want and I'll speak to the DIA. I will say one thing though. You know what it says about extenuating circumstances. Well, what would happen if I mentioned about the hundred hours I've got on my card? I've never put all my hours on overtime. Perhaps I should, then we'll see what happens to the budget."

"That's a separate issue."

"Oh right, a separate issue. When we've finished here then, I'll go over my time owing card and put in overtime for all the occasions I've stayed over. Strangely enough, I don't seem to remember anyone else staying with me. But we'll see what happens when Dan finds out that I've been taken off Hypnos, shall we? Perhaps you can carry on with it. There might be a question or two raised about the lack of supervision around some of the jobs as well. Have we done here then, or did you have more to say?"

Peter looked at the ceiling, and for a moment, Ethan thought he was going to reply, but he only shook his head. As he left the office, Ethan could not help thinking that he was displaying all the classic signs of someone with a sleep disorder; even the speech Ethan had just made was partly quoted from a subject of one of the case studies he had researched when updating the disciplinary policies. He was safe on that point, of course, because there was no way that Peter would have read it, or remembered it if he had.

He squeezed past Mohammed and stared sullenly at his screen. Ethan knew that he would not be able to get away with saying nothing about what had happened but did not want to initiate a conversation.

"What did he want?" Mohammed asked in a low voice.

"Just a load of shit. Let's talk about it later, I can't be arsed to go through it now. How are you anyway, is Hasna getting on all right?"

"Yeah, fine, thanks for asking." Mohammed looked around the screen to grin at him.

I hate it when he gets like this, when he can't say what he wants because he thinks it'll upset people.

"Right. Better get going on this then I suppose, I've got a million and one things to do before Friday."

They did not speak again that morning.

Ethan could not stop yawning. The first time it happened, he felt embarrassed, but after surreptitiously holding still and flicking his eyes from left to right, he satisfied himself that no one had noticed. It struck him as ridiculous that he was sitting in the SDMA headquarters and no one had identified that anything was wrong. On the other hand, knowing his colleagues as he did, that was hardly surprising.

He thought about the whispered conversation he had had with Mo before being called into Peter's office that morning. He knew that Mo would keep his secret as long as he was able, up until the point where he fell asleep in front of him.

When he yawned particularly loudly, Ethan sunk into his seat. However, after that, he became blasé, thinking that he was working himself up over nothing. After all, there was nothing specific against yawning in policy, it was only his belief about the discipline that an SDMA agent should possess, which was a voluntary code he had imposed on himself that anyone else would have laughed at if he had told them.

He was able to work for an hour before exhaustion rose in his chest, eroding his concentration until he had to stop and turn around.

The city took on a gothic, sepulchral air through the blacked-out windows, every building seeming elongated, every roof a spire. The security glass turned the city into a patchwork of shadows, a place of ubiquitous suspicion, which was amplified by the feeling behind his eyes.

He yawned then stretched his arms until they hurt, before forcing himself to concentrate, until the feeling returned a few minutes later. Ethan worried that his last redoubt from exhaustion, his workplace, had been breached.

When he went to the other side of the office to do some photocopying later that day, he heard Alfie telling Jo that Simon was not ill after all but had been seconded to the DIA. Ethan made several copies of the same pages to have an excuse to continue listening. Alfie said that Simon was enjoying himself so much that he was using any excuse to stay there. Jo asked him how he knew and Alfie said that he just did in a serious tone that Ethan had never heard him use before. Although he could not be sure that it was true, the thought that someone who had worked with him might now be DIA added to his anxiety.

Jo delivered a box to his desk that afternoon, pouting at him when meeting his eyes. When he opened it, he was amazed to see the pamphlets from Operation Amber 518, together with the forensic analysis report. The fastest he had ever previously got a medium priority case back was a month. The report identified eleven sets of fingerprints on each pamphlet, and described the type of paper and ink used. Most significantly, there was a reference number with '90% hit' written beside it. That meant that they had matched the combined paper and ink to a Mirror record. Paper and ink would most likely be linked to a safehouse where propaganda was produced.

Ethan opened Mirror and typed in the reference number. A warning message filled the screen:

'This is a restricted record. Your attempt to access this record has been logged. A security access form is required to view this record'.

Ethan scratched the back of his head. He had never heard of restricted records before. After all, the amount of people who could access Mirror was very small, and if any agents could not be trusted to view anything stored there then they should be thrown out of the organisation.

He logged into the secure intranet and searched it for 'security access'. He found the form, filled it in, and sent it to the e-mail specified. He looked at his screen for several minutes afterwards, feeling an inexplicable sense of dread. It was as if he had thrown a stone off the roof of a tall building and was watching it fall with the sudden realisation that it could kill anyone who happened to be walking past.

When he had recovered enough to be able to move again, Ethan realised that the policeman had not replied to his request to confirm whether there had been any alarm clocks in the house. He sent him another e-mail. His mobile went off, making him jump. It was an automated message from the SDMA, giving performance figures for SC cases in his area, which his research had shown were entirely unreliable.

Strangely, Peter was one of the last to go that day, and paused at the edge of his workspace before leaving. However, he did not say anything and went a moment later.

What's he up to? He doesn't have enough work during his normal hours, never mind staying late. Ethan's curiosity was such that he had to talk himself out of breaking into Peter's office and searching his drawers.

Being on his own, typing in the darkness after all the lights had gone out except those in his space, made Ethan's exhaustion move from his eyes and settle over his skin, like a fine powder he could not brush off. He was always aware of it but could struggle on, in the same way that one can ignore a dull pain but not an acute one. His concentration was only broken when his mobile buzzed, which made him stop, as only Aislin would contact him at that time. The message read:

> Settled in now after all that lot thank God! How you?Missing me?

He smiled at the screen and was thinking about how to reply when the feeling behind his eyes returned, more severe than ever.

Ethan stood and lights in the walkway flashed. Shadows flitted between empty workspaces and darkened windows. His heart leapt and, for a moment, he imagined someone sitting at one of the desks, staring at him. There was no one there, and as he moved along the walkway to stretch his legs, lights lit up three steps ahead of him in whichever direction he turned. His feet hurt as if he had trod on spikes and he had to hold a divider to stop himself from doubling over. With a supreme effort, staggering as if he had been stabbed in the stomach, he managed to get back to his desk and lay his head on it. There was no struggle this time against the urge; it had been all he could manage to stop himself from collapsing on the floor.

When he woke into darkness, he heard a click and the light above him turned on, making him wince. He felt as sluggish as if he had slept for a lifetime, and had to press his hands against his desk to stop himself from putting his head down again, knowing that he would return to sleep if he did. He fumbled in his pockets for his mobile as if he were drunk, eventually finding it to see that it was one in the morning.

"Shit."

His arm brushed against his keyboard and the screen glowed as harshly as the light. He saw the time again in the bottom right corner.

His mind roved over his problems, unable to focus. *Will I be able to get out of the building at this time? Do the security cameras cover my desk and will they be able to pick me out in the dark? What other security measures are there? Even if I can leave, will the guards think it suspicious that I was still in the building? Will leaving activate a security alert? How am I going to get home? The last train left hours ago.*

"Shit."

His feeling of compulsion, of wanting to lay down his head, was as strong as before, although he was able to resist now, making him despair of his previous weakness. However, there was no time to think about that. Ethan picked his landline up and was about to ring for a taxi, when he thought that that would be too easy to trace. *Even easier than sleeping on my desk.*

What can I do, other than walk out of the building and hope for the best? He had momentarily considered going back to sleep and setting an alarm on his mobile for five o'clock, so as to pretend that he had got there early, but that seemed to be tempting fate, even for him.

Lights flashed on before him, and from the corner of his vision, he saw them flickering off behind him as he went. When he walked along the corridor, posters on noticeboards fluttered without evident cause, and there were red dots on every door leading to other sections. He did not know whether they were from security cameras or the edges of his imagination.

The lip-shaped security barrier made a sucking sound as he scanned his identity card and was cool to the touch. Ethan paused in the lobby, scrutinizing the poorly lit circular counter, before realising that a guard in its centre was staring at him. Feeling his fingers clench, Ethan nodded at him and muttered 'night' before hurrying to the door, expecting to be called back any moment. He was peppered with dots of light.

There was a line of guards outside, all muscular and looking outwards, their uniforms scruffy. None of them paid any attention to him and Ethan wondered whether there were always that many on duty at night.

As soon as he was out of their sight, he closed his eyes and pinched the bridge of his nose when remembering the feeble way he had spoken to their supervisor. Of course there would be someone there, of course they wouldn't leave the building undefended. *Why didn't I just act naturally?*

He had not been out so late since childhood, and felt a certain professional interest mixed with giddy excitement at the wantonness of the night, lit as it was by sensually twinkling stars. Most companies operating in Central Zone could afford only the most basic holographic projectors, making their advertisements blink rapidly. There was degeneracy evident on the faces of the drug-addled sleep offenders who rested against walls and lamp posts, their vacant stares seeming to pierce him, their eyes distended by the rings underneath them. Ethan was careful to look through everyone he saw.

The only way he knew to get home at that time was the taxis behind the train station. Most of the drivers plied their trade illegally without a night-shift licence, meaning that using them probably made him party to a crime, but doing so was hardly more dangerous than everything else he had done that night.

Although the jewellery shop was shuttered, he crossed the road to avoid it. Ethan had investigated the activities that took place in areas like this many times, but had never before seen firsthand the prostitutes dressed in red, the colour chosen to attract the attention of the sleep deprived. Many of the men walking the streets were painfully thin and limped with their heads down. Those involved in the night-time economy of drugs, weapons, and women had become implicated in SC breaches soon after the Sleep Code was introduced, with drug dealers trading in counterfeit night-shift licences to allow their clients to legitimise their lifestyles.

It was likely that nine out of ten people around him were sleep criminals of one description or another; the performance problems he had identified in Hypnos meant that in the inner cities, SC breaches and other crimes were carried out more or less openly.

The world at night was slow moving, with things always shifting in the corners of his eyes. Several times, Ethan saw, or thought he saw, people nodding at each other, handing over packages, then slinking into alleyways. Lights flashed across windows and glistened over the city. He felt very vulnerable, painfully aware of his status as an SDMA agent. Whenever anyone seemed about to talk to him, he increased his pace until all he could hear were the rhythmical thumps of his shoes against the floor.

The taxi rank was quieter than when he passed it during the day, with only a dozen or so cars in the concrete space that was once designated for an expansion of the train station. A group of Asian men watched him while smoking, the pleasure they took from their cigarettes evident in the way they relaxed and stretched their arms after every few drags.

Ethan approached one of the taxis and knocked on its window. No one answered so he knocked again, and the driver pointed to the cab at the head of the line. When he knocked on the window of the lead taxi, the doors unlocked and he got inside. He told the driver his address and he drove off wordlessly.

There was a sweet smell inside, like incense, and Ethan rested his eyes for a few seconds before feeling himself going drowsy. He pinched the top of his legs venomously, leaving a persistent dull sting. He could not tell whether the driver had seen him. In any case, it was unlikely that he would have cared. Taxi drivers were notorious for facilitating SC breaches. Ethan was more concerned with the cost of the fare, as the ticker facing him, white on oblong black like an old fashioned alarm clock, increased by ten pence every few seconds.

The view of the city from inside the taxi was sanitised; the windows were steamed up and cold to the touch, obliterating everything in a grey haze. Nevertheless, Ethan was so absorbed by what had happened that night and the feeling in his legs, which he pinched several more times when the initial pain was no longer effective in focusing his attention, that they soon reached his home. The ticker had stopped at over fifty pounds.

"Do you mind if we go to the high street? Sorry, but I need to get some money out, I didn't realise it'd be this much."

The man put on the handbrake and turned his head a fraction, so that he must have been looking at him partly out of the corner of his eye and partly through the mirror.

"Forget about it. We'll take it as down payment for tonight."

Ethan froze and his teeth clenched. It was only then that he saw the pink beads that hung over the seat before him. He immediately thought of his recurring dream and rocked back as if the stringing tendril had wrapped around his neck. He seemed to have to climb over himself to get out the car.

It sped off silently and he desperately tried to remember what the man looked like. Ethan did not know why it was important although he believed that it was with absolute conviction, meaning that he stood on the pavement for several seconds trying to build an impression of his face. However, Ethan's memory of that night was a series of fragments, and he could only recall a generic Asian complexion and accent. When he came to himself, his hands were very cold.

Chill stuck to his skin like oil on water as he moved around the house, the heating making no difference, nor did burying himself into the sofa.

When Ethan saw that it was three o'clock, he realised that if he was to have any chance of avoiding a repeat of what had happened, he had to drag his sleeping pattern back to normal; even though going to bed at that time was absurd, it was a three-hour improvement on the previous night, and would at least be movement in the right direction. However, he put on the MV and listlessly flicked through the channels. It was all tedium and pornography, the Security in Broadcasting Act having placed restrictions on the length and types of programmes that could be shown at night, futilely, of course, given the ubiquity of the Internet. Nevertheless, he watched anything that held the remotest interest, continually promising himself that he would go to bed after the next set of advertisements or when a programme had finished. Yet he remained there, unmovable.

When he could not stand glass-eyed nudity any longer, Ethan switched the MV to the Internet and browsed with equal languor. He watched time pass in small increments on the clock at the bottom of the screen.

Ethan went on the BBC website and automatically scanned for security and sleep-related stories, quickly coming across a feature on the north of England where a far right group had carried out a series of attacks on immigrants, with an anonymous leader posting messages on websites, including: 'Paki scum are all Icks and thieves'. The local SDMA had put out a press release stating that: 'There is no proven correlation between the amount of immigrants, asylum seekers, or members of BAME communities in an area and the prevalence of SC breaches or sleep based subversion'. Despite everything, Ethan allowed himself a smile. *At least I don't have to deal with that crap.*

He went to bed an hour before he had to get up, the same time as the previous night, when he thought that he would be too weary to move if he did not at least close his eyes before leaving the house. Ethan needed a symbolic divide between one day and the next, without which his life would feel like reading a book without paragraphs.

He was not sure whether he had slept or only lay still in pain when his alarm clock went off. His eyes jolted open as if someone had shouted into his ear. Being forced back into reality was harsh and unyielding. The ceiling moved closer then further away.

Ethan knew that he had to go to the address on the note that night. The decisive factor was the threat against Aislin; once he had checked that the phone numbers they had given were hers, the decision was as natural and obvious as that of whether or not to go to work. *Anyway, I can gather information while I'm there. They're making a mistake allowing me into their territory. They're not in control.*

Nine

HE DROVE TO WORK THAT morning, not trusting himself to remain awake on the train. When reaching the car park, Ethan's stomach fizzed with excitement. The more he tried to distract himself by counting blue cars, the more he knew that he was in desperate trouble, and when he gave way to his imagination, he thought that he might have less than a day to live.

He had grown used to the new type of exhaustion since his sleep patterns had become distorted. An oppressive weight fell on his shoulders at random points throughout the day, as if he were the subject of a practical joke. During those times, it seemed as if he would fall over should anyone so much as bump into him, and concentration was impossible. On the other hand, there were moments when he felt elated, even manic, when he wanted to run around shouting, using up his last store of energy.

Time fell through his fingers. Ethan tried not to concentrate too hard, knowing that doing his work would make the morning pass. He constantly interrupted Mo to chat about anything and nothing, only stopping when seeing that he was becoming annoyed. Ethan constantly calculated the time left before he had to leave in hours, minutes, and seconds, before browsing the Internet in the same unfocused way that he had the previous night. Even so, he was drawn back to Hypnos, being unable to keep away from it, shaking when seeing that another hour had gone.

Just before lunch, Ethan realised with a horror that only made sense in his neurotic state that he had forgotten to reply to Aislin's message of two days earlier. He rang her twice, going to answerphone, before laboriously typing his response:

> Sorry sweetie phone had run out of battery. hope your well call when you can.

He opened his sent folder and read his message. *Will she believe me?* He had not used that excuse for a while so perhaps she would. Needless to say, he had already broken his commitment to treat her better. He had taken the opportunity of her absence to behave as if she did not exist.

I've not even spoken to her since she's been away. I need to sort everything out before she gets back – both Hypnos and this other stuff. His pledge to himself was all the more vehement given that he did not quite believe it.

That afternoon, he abandoned any pretence of doing anything other than waiting. He planned to stay in the office until the appointed time. Having thought about little else all day, Ethan had decided that that was the best way to avoid suspicion. *It's hardly unusual for me to still be here after everyone else has gone.* He was so tired that he could not have concentrated even if he had wanted to. *This is nothing short of disgraceful.*

To his surprise, only a few people left at the end of their shifts. He had planned to leave at seven, having thought through his actions in such detail that he seemed to have already left many times.

At ten past, Ethan thought that his watch had to be wrong, and at quarter past that they might be finishing files. At twenty past, he became suspicious and stood on tiptoe to watch the others over the dividers. They were just… working. He had evidently been excluded from the office, as there had to be a glut of breaches for this to happen. Even Alfie was still there. In normal circumstances, he knew the tiniest details about what everyone was doing, meaning that people often asked him for advice. Since he had become busy with Hypnos and strung out the rest of the time, he had stopped paying attention. *I don't know the first fucking thing about what's going on.*

They left one by one rather than en-masse, as they usually did, until he was alone with Mo. Ethan realised that it must seem suspicious that he was sitting there doing nothing, so he opened one of his old files and wrote up some notes with the utmost reluctance.

"When are you staying till?" Mohammed asked.

"Just a few more minutes. Until I get to the end of this section."

"I don't know why you cover for them all the time. With all this shit going on with the contractors and with dweeb, you should just do your bit then go home."

"I suppose you're right. It's made me fall out with Ash a few times recently. I'm taking the opportunity to finish things up now so we can concentrate on looking for a house when she gets back."

"Do you want to go down the promotion route?"

"I don't know. I might do."

"Then you need to be careful of Dan. The problem is that if you're making everything work here, he doesn't have to do anything and he'll take you for granted. Why should he promote you if you're doing the job for nothing already?"

"I know what you're saying."

"Okay, well, that's what I think."

"Yeah… yeah… thanks…"

"Right, I'll see you tomorrow."

"See you later."

Ethan had the impression that Mo had stayed late specifically to warn him. He looked out of the security glass but could not see him; no light ever entered or escaped the SDMA. He remained there for several minutes, waiting for he knew not what.

After clearing his desk to comply with policy, Ethan wondered how lying his head on it could have seemed so attractive the previous day. It felt like some perverse whim now, like an out-of-body experience. *This is why the Icks are so dangerous, they're like odourless gas.*

As he left the building, he felt the same childish thrill of that morning, knowing that not only was he doing something radically out of his routine, but that it was dangerous in a way he could not imagine.

Ethan made his way to a fast food place and waited in a queue of bored-looking commuters, all of whom carried either a briefcase or a backpack, and regularly looked at their watches. Ethan was the only one who did not hop from one foot to the other and who examined the menu above the counter with a more than cursory glance.

Flickering holograms showed shiny coloured food, elongating then contracting every few seconds, and there was something offensive in the lack of care shown in the images, the confidence that the crudest splodges would be enough to sell the muck. It worked though, of course. The area seemed to capture the sighs of the queuing bored, which reverberated around the room before becoming trapped in the walls.

When it was eventually his turn, Ethan ordered – it was all much the same – then sat on a high chair near a window. His stomach grumbled after he had eaten; the food had been the same colours as depicted. He had enough time that he even bought dessert, which could not have been differentiated from the main course had they been placed side by side. He took a perverse pleasure out of guessing what Aislin's response would have been if she had seen him eating there.

However, that place was not designed for reflection; after a few minutes, a man came over to clear away his rubbish, rubbing the table perfunctorily with a cloth and sighing when their shoulders made contact.

Ethan thought that it would be better to go early than to continue wandering around. *I must have been caught on security cameras hundreds of times by now. Anyway, what's the worse that can happen?* He didn't want to think about that, but whatever it was, being early wouldn't make a difference. *Are the Iklonians any bigger on timekeeping than the SDMA? They probably don't have a time book.* Ethan sniggered at the idea, making a woman push a buggy to one side as she passed him.

He had never been to the street the Iklonians had given him but knew the general area, having been given a tour of it by his predecessor as an example of an SC breach hotspot. They had not got out of their car the entire time, she having frightened him with stories about how many police officers, postmen, social workers, and other officials had gone missing in that part of Central Zone.

Apparently, the estate had the highest number of missing persons reports in the country. It was also subject to high rates of crime, disease, fires, and everything else that was recorded. Most famously, it had been the location of a notorious triple murder when a known Iklonian had stabbed a mother and her two children after deliberately going ten days without sleep. His interview with the police was later made public, in which he had babbled for hours with slurred speech about his clothes being made out of animals and the 'red between the cracks'.

Although Ethan had recognised the initiation rite for what it was after he had worked at the SDMA for a few years and seen the same thing done to other rookies, the aimless fear he had felt about the place had remained with him; the statistics his predecessor had quoted were true, after all. He switched off his personal mobile in his pocket, knowing that its expense would expose him if anyone saw it.

There were graffiti tags sprayed around the area in no pattern that he could discern. In some streets, there was one on every house, whereas others had none. As he walked, Ethan saw that somehow, someone had daubed the top of a lamppost with fluorescent colours. He thought he recognised symbols from DIA reports but could not be sure. Around the corner from his destination was a derelict warehouse entirely covered with the marks, although a single slogan, written in bubble letters, dominated the wall facing the road: 'Being woken by an alarm clock is always the first humiliation of the day.'

The address was a block of flats that stretched to the sky, of the type that Ethan had only ever seen in documentaries about post Second World War poverty. None of the windows were lit, and the concrete looked black in the darkness, giving the building the impression of being abandoned. Ethan went inside into a cramped lobby, at the back of which was a set of narrow stone steps that spiralled upwards. The walls were covered with posters advertising the PSH. As he moved forward, brown leaves crunched underfoot, sounding like boots squelching in water.

There was a panel of what must have been doorbells near the entrance, and by standing on tiptoe, Ethan saw that the highest number was 155. The note had not given a flat number. *Surely they can't want me to knock every door?* He could only guess how many floors there were. *Shit, they're as disorganised as us.* He heard something moving on the stairwell above him and felt the same lurch in his stomach as when he had set out. A small rat-like man appeared at the top of the stairs, his head covered by a hoody. He stared at the floor as resolutely as a socially awkward child.

"Are you…?"

"Come on."

He turned and slouched away, never lifting his eyes. He spoke with a dull regional accent, making Ethan think how rough he sounded. Ethan was taken aback by his impression, as he had always thought that he had the most common accent of anyone who worked for the SDMA. He had never before listened to someone with the recognition that he was of a higher social class.

The man led him up a series of stairwells, each of which had a window the size of his hand. He noticed the varying states of decay in the frames as he passed them. Most were opaque with dirt and he shivered at the draft every time.

At first, he was annoyed by how slowly the man walked and stepped closely behind him, trying to pressure him into speeding up. However, as they climbed ever higher and exhaustion tightened around his ankles as if they were being compressed, Ethan was glad of his lethargy. He concentrated on the echoes of their footsteps with a strong sense that his actions were not real.

He regretted not counting the stairwells from the start. *With three sets of stairs making up one floor, that's been… at least ten.* He tried, futilely, to work out how many floors there were by estimating the number of doors on each one. Just as it seemed that they would walk through a skylight then fall through endless cloud, never reaching the ground, Ethan realised that there was a man waiting at the top of their current set of stairs, his arms folded. The guide stopped a few paces in front of him and said, "Okay…" then turned and walked past Ethan with the same slow, stubborn pace with which he had gone up, making him step aside.

"Hello, you must be Ethan…" the man said. He scratched the back of his ear before holding out a hand. Ethan shook it, crushing his clammy fingers. *Is this how they initiate people into the cult? With a handshake?* His vision wavered before him, and for a moment, he thought that he was going to faint.

"Yeah."

"Come in, it's cold out." The man's voice was hesitant, making Ethan uncertain. The man wore a purple shirt with the top button undone, which gave his double chin space to wobble. There was a large mole on his neck that Ethan at first assumed was a scar because of its size. The buckle on the belt of his trousers seemed too big, given how tight they were. After a few seconds of looking at him, Ethan saw that his hair was thinning without there being any actual bald spots.

The lounge immediately beyond the door seemed huge at first, and as his eyes grew used to the gloom, he saw that it was because there was very little in it. The only lighting emanated from lanterns in each corner, which were covered with drapes the same colour as the man's shirt. There were two sofas pushed against the far wall, also the same colour. Ethan saw a couple lying entwined on one of them, whereas on the other sat a man in his early twenties dressed all in black, his pale skin evident even in the haze. His hair stood up and he was very thin, giving him an impoverished, aggressive look. He stared at Ethan petulantly.

"Move out the way, Max," the man said to him. 'Max' remained still for just long enough to make his irritation evident, before sidling into a back room.

After he had gone, Ethan felt that he was being swept along by events. Max's aggression passed into him like an infection and he turned to the man and said, "I've had enough of this, I want to know what's going on. Now. Why did you manipulate me into coming here?"

"I'm sorry… I know they can all be… It must seem like there's some kind of… *conspiracy* against you, I'm sorry things have happened like they have…" The man held his arms out with an ambiguous gesture, and was so reasonable sounding and apologetic that Ethan felt soothed.

"Who the hell are you anyway?"

"Well… it's a bit embarrassing. They call me the Professor. I used to work at a university, you see. You wouldn't believe how funny everyone thought that was when I first mentioned it. Anyway, I'll tell you about it later. Have a seat."

Ethan did as he was told, bewildered. It seemed as if the only way he could disregard his instructions was by being absurdly perverse. The moment he was seated, he felt so drowsy that he had to concentrate to speak. He felt as if he were being massaged, and it was so easy to go with the flow…

"What's… all this about…?"

"We don't need to go through that stuff now. The main thing is to help you with your problem."

"You're going to help me?" Ethan could not keep the sneer from his voice. The Professor looked away.

"Sorry… yes… I know it sounds strange but… your problem is that you've been shoehorned into an unnatural sleep pattern. Humans aren't meant to have all their sleep in one go like you've been forced to do. Like we've all been forced to do."

"Oh?"

"Before the studies were suppressed, research showed that when people don't know what time it is, most will sleep in two four and a half hour blocks a day, with a few naps in between. Electricity has proved to be the invention that's caused more disruption to sleep patterns than any other in history. Before electric lights were invented, people would sleep as long as it was dark. They'd sleep longer in the winter and only get out of bed when it was light outside."

When giving his speech, the Professor seemed confident for the first time since he had met him, not looking away or touching his face. Ethan felt unequipped to respond, his knowledge of the investigative and administrative procedures of the SDMA now seeming startling parochial and inadequate. He jumped when feeling someone stroking his arm. He looked around to see the couple hugging in the corner, too far away for it to have been them.

"But what's any of this got to do with me? Why did you have to threaten Aislin to get me here?"

"People go… overboard. But let's not discuss that now, just lie down."

Ethan's initial reaction was to resist what the Professor was saying by any and all means. However, the urge to rest his head, to free himself of exhaustion in an environment where he would not get punished, was overwhelming. *I suppose I've got to see what it's like if I'm going to go properly undercover...* He stretched his legs on a purple sofa.

Ethan was soothed by the warmth and heavy ambience of the room. He thought he heard music but could not be sure whether it was only part of his drowsiness. He closed his eyes and let his mind drift, as if he were floating towards an embracing heaven...

Ethan slept so deeply that he was reluctant to wake, and when he did, he pressed his face into the sofa. After remembering where he was, he heard the soft rhythmical sound of sleep breathing. The room was almost completely dark. From what he could hear, there had to be a dozen people around him. The communal nature of dreaming in a crowd felt shocking in a way that he could not understand.

A moment after he had managed to sit up, he felt a gentle touch on his shoulder, obviously from a woman's hand. Ethan wanted to throw it off, acutely aware of his vulnerability. He could not bring himself to move. Suddenly, he felt a piercing pain in his arm, as if he had been injected with a needle. His legs jolted and he rasped. He clutched the air desperately. He fell and felt himself twitch before falling unconscious...

Ethan was next woken by a low hum. The room was light and there was no one else there. The sound increased almost imperceptibly, such that it made him concentrate to convince himself that he was not imagining it. It seemed to seek him out as inevitably as water pouring into a container will find any holes. He sat up and the sound stopped. Ethan stretched and yawned, shaking the last dregs of weariness from his limbs as concretely as if he were wiping dirt from his shoes. There was a knock at the door.

"Come in," he said, feeling ridiculous.

The Professor stepped inside, his head lowered and a hand over his eyes. "Are you… decent?"

He said the word 'decent' tentatively, as if it were obscene.

"Yeah."

Ethan felt embarrassed, as the man's every gesture suggested that he was worried that something could go wrong, as if he were talking to a violent criminal.

"I thought you'd need to get up soon. Did you hear the tone?"

"Yeah."

"Research has shown that the body responds better to being woken gradually, by stimuli that gently rouses one from REM to stage one, then consciousness. Harsh sounds, like those made by modern alarm clocks, disturb sleep too rapidly and lead to a groggy sensation that—"

"What time is it?"

The Professor had been gazing dreamily into a corner of the room and reddened when interrupted. "Well… it's seven o'clock."

"In the morning?"

The Professor nodded.

"Shit."

Ethan paced around the room before sitting back on the sofa and rubbing his eyes. *This is it then.* Despite knowing that he could not go on forever, he had never thought about when it would actually happen.

"Ethan, I hope you don't mind… I took the liberty of getting you a new shirt. Sorry, I know how strange this must be for you…"

"For the last time, why the fuck am I here?"

"It's difficult to explain everything. Let me just say this. With what's happened while you've been here, you'll be able to function on six hours' sleep a night without any impact on your performance for… probably a week. Not that that's ideal of course, but… If I can say, the most important thing is for you to get yourself to work. I've left everything you need in the bathroom, so if you get moving, you can be there well before eight."

The Professor had become confident again, speaking as if reading from a script. Ethan was infuriated by his evasion and wanted to argue further, to put an end to this once and for all. Given how weedy he was, with his thick glasses and paunch, there was nothing he could do if Ethan grabbed and shook him, even if his associates were waiting nearby, as he suspected. Nevertheless, he knew that what he said about getting to work on time was right. *Am I really going to walk into the SDMA headquarters straight from an Iklonian safe house?* Then again, was it any worse than the SC breaches, the deterioration in his work, and everything else? Without replying to the Professor, Ethan went through the door behind him into a bathroom.

The flat was much more prosaic than he remembered from the previous night, to the extent that he thought they must have changed things while he slept. The lounge was definitely less purple. He obsessed about what had happened so intently that he did not notice the clothes hung over a bath rail until after he had brushed his teeth.

When he had dressed, he thought there might be listening devices hidden in them. He patted himself down but could find nothing obviously out of place. He knew that he should search them properly, but when he checked his mobile, he saw that it was half seven. Ethan felt as if he had been transformed into an animal, that he no longer thought through his actions but only moved from one set of stimuli to the next, blown between different scenarios without control.

He suddenly remembered the pain in his arm from previous night and his fingers tensed as if he had just heard a piercing scream. He peeled the shirt back to check himself. There was a slight discolouration on his skin. *What does that mean? Was it a drug to knock me out? Or a hallucination? A dream?* He was unsure of his memories and tentatively explored his back as if expecting to find a new limb growing there…

When he returned to the lounge, the Professor was sitting on the floor eating toast. He stood hurriedly and wiped his mouth, leaving most of the crumbs in place.

"You should have something before you go."

"I'm fine."

"Okay, okay. So… you'd better be getting off then. Erm… try not to, you know… worry about anything."

"Right."

"Someone might be in touch at some point, but…"

Ethan again felt tempted to hit the man. However, the need to get away was still more pressing.

"Never contact me again."

"Here, get yourself something to eat on the way. You can't go twelve hours without eating."

"Are you taking the piss?"

Nevertheless, when the Professor stepped forward and pressed some coins into his hand, Ethan remembered the importance of time and did not want to argue.

As he walked down the endless stairs, which were as dark as the night before, he thought about throwing the money away out of principle. However, no one would ever know what he had done, making his stand futile. *What difference does a few quid make?*

Walking to work from that part of the city felt surreal, as if he were watching video footage of himself. Several times, he thought that he should sneak through alleys rather than take the quickest route, but there were so few people around that there seemed no point. *Anyway, it would look more suspicious if I did. And I don't have time.* He moved as confidently as he could but his legs were tense.

When he reached the lobby of the SDMA building, Ethan felt as he had many times in recent weeks: that one of the guards would be sure to think that there was something suspicious about him and draw him to one side for questioning. He could not help but glance at the supervisor behind the counter and the plethora of cameras surrounding him, which flickered between people walking along corridors and the concrete vista surrounding the building. When their eyes met, he nodded and Ethan returned the gesture, before hurrying to put his identity card against the lip-shaped security barrier. Dots of light danced frantically across his back.

"All right?" he said to Mohammed when reaching their office.
"Hi ya, how you doin'?"
"Good. You?"
"Can't complain."
Ethan switched on his computer. He stretched while waiting for it to load, and it was only then that he realised what a difference his long sleep had made. The weariness in his limbs and the heavy feeling behind his eyes had gone, but more than that, his perception had sharpened. He could hear his computer humming beneath his feet and the tone of Jo's voice as she whispered at the other side of the office. Colours seemed more vivid than before, as if he had ignored the world his whole life. Now, he saw a fuller truth and was taken aback by the variegated greys of his desk and the unevenness of its texture.

When he opened his report and started writing, Ethan swum through the words like an eel wriggling around rocks. Previously, he could only concentrate by willing himself to focus on a few relevant facts in the great sea; now, he could look at everything around him and write while barely conscious of what he was doing, simultaneously arranging the next paragraph in his mind. It was as if the barriers that surrounded him had suddenly become soft, allowing him to move at will.

Life was so much easier when he was rested and Ethan wondered whether this was why people were willing to risk associating with the Iklonians. The common response from an SDMA agent investigating a professional was astonishment that anyone would risk their career and everything they had for the sake of a few hours of illicit sleep. Ethan realised that the creative potential it unlocked had to be part of the draw. *Perhaps everyone who's successful is secretly an Iklonian, or at least uses their techniques. Of course, when you get rich, you're not monitored as much and can get a decent lawyer, so you're above the law.* That had to be be how people got on. It was certainly the case for Ethan, as by eleven, he had finished the draft presentation that Daniel needed for the next day, and had started planning the next section of Hypnos.

When Aislin rang, Ethan grabbed his mobile with a compulsive movement.

"Morning! All well?"

"Good thanks. Sorry for not ringing earlier, I wasn't ignoring your message. It's been mad here. Dad's hard work, I'll tell you that for nothing. I don't know how mum puts up with him. I'd have grey hair by now if I were her. In fact, I'd probably not have much of anything left, my teeth would've fallen out by the time I was twenty-five."

"Why, what's been going on?"

"Nothing really, it's just how… intense he is all the time. He can't just do something, he's got to do it to death. Like the other day, when we were in Tipperary. He grew up near Lake Derg, and he got it into his head that he wanted to walk round it. Well, it's miles all the way, so we had to get a tent and some boots. Actually, I'm not going to go through it all now, suffice it to say that it involved lots of mud, lots of walking, and getting knackered. I thought I was going to fall off the end of the world by the evening. It's good exercise though. I've not had time to do much running lately so it's got me back into the swing of things."

"Are you okay, you sound out of breath?"

"Yeah, I'm just… it's just the memory of it all, probably."

She laughed in a somewhat manic way, making Ethan shift in his seat.

"Ash… this is the last time this is going to happen. He sounds like he's getting… strange. We can't have our lives disrupted like this. I know where you're coming from, but… we need to sort something out."

"I know, I know…" Aislin sounded deferential in a way that surprised him. "Anyway, have you had chance to look at any houses?"

"Erm… yeah, I've gone through a few websites and just had a basic look so far. What we need to do is to find out how much we can borrow. You can go on a site to estimate it but we'll have to do it properly. When you get back, you can look at the houses I've found."

"What areas have you been researching?"

"Within ten miles of my house, for a starter. There's loads on the market at the moment so it'll take a while to go through them all. Look, are you sure you're all right with all this, with your dad, I mean? I'll be honest, I've never known a situation like it. It's pretty unusual you know."

"You've told me this. This is the last time it'll happen. It's just… well, what he needed to do, I suppose."

"Right, okay."

"Anything else been happening then, what you been up to?"

"Just the usual really. Work work work. I'm going to have most of this finished by the time you get back so we can concentrate on houses."

"It sounds like you'll have got some lined up soon so that's no problem."

"Yeah, yeah. Talk more about this later then. Love you."

"Love you. Bye, bye."

Ethan made a note to himself to do some property searches when he got home that night. The prospect of taking action to actually move in with Aislin, as opposed to accepting to do so in principle, made his stomach churn such that he could not sit still.

"How's she getting on?"

"It's all very odd. You know what her dad's like, it's like having to look after a child. It's hard to say anything 'cos what can you do? Tell Aislin not to listen to her dad? But I'm going to have to think about it. We can't go on like this when we're living together. Do you think I'm being unreasonable?"

"No… no…"

"You see, the problem is, I've never really said anything to her. I didn't know how to go about it, you know what I mean? Now though, I think I'm gonna have to, but I don't know how to start the conversation. It's different when you're going to live together, isn't it?"

"Yeah, yeah. It's just how you phrase yourself. You need to wait for the right moment then say it like you're not having a go at her."

"I suppose. I don't think it's gonna go down well though, however I put it. I still think it's a very funny situation. I don't know anyone else who suddenly decides that his twenty-eight year old daughter has to go on a pilgrimage to his home town with him."

Mohammed smiled wryly. "I don't know about that, mate. There's always something weird going on with any woman."

"Sometimes, I wish I had one of those jobs where you don't carry things over from one day to the next. With us, there's no end to anything, is there? The more you do the more there is."

"Yeah right, you wouldn't last five minutes living any other way."

"Maybe." Ethan rested his head in his hands, for a moment wishing that he could have a view of something other than the partitions that divided them from the neighbouring workspaces.

"Hasna's just as bad you know, sometimes…"

"Oh?"

He looked around his computer at Mo. Ethan's ears suddenly felt red and he realised that he might have compromised himself by talking about personal matters at such length.

"It's all stuff about the baby. She's having a hard time of it, and making sure that my life's a misery as well. I mean… it's getting hard to talk to her at the moment. She's said a few times now about getting fat, then she has a go at whatever I say. So when she was on about it the other day, I just listened. Then she called me a whole load of names, saying that I looked like an idiot sitting there nodding at her."

"What do you think's the matter?"

"It's hard to know what she's thinking. I reckon she's just worried about things in general. The problem is, you know she believes in the religion and all that…" Mohammed rolled his eyes. "Well, it makes her funny about going to the doctor too often. Don't ask why, I can't explain it. Her mum and dad don't help either. She usually just humours them about their ideas of things, but now, it's like they've drugged her or something, she takes it all in. They're on the phone giving advice everyday, they're loving it."

"Sounds like a nightmare."

"It is, mate, I'm glad to come here to get away from it sometimes."

"It's probably just a phase she's going through."

Mohammed nodded then looked at his screen.

"Maybe. But before all this, she'd speak to you normal, almost like we're talking now. You know, I had to apply three times to get into the job. When I got it, I thought that meant that I was out of the shit. But if it's not them at work who are after your soul, then it's the fuckers at home. You need a stick to keep them all away sometimes."

Ethan felt his collar stick to his neck and knew that he needed to end the conversation. "You couldn't, I don't know, take her out somewhere, use up some leave? Perhaps if she gets out the way of her parents a while, she'll be able to relax."

"I'm not sure about that 'cos she's been obsessing about leave, working out a schedule about how long it's going to take to do the decorating and whether we can fit everything in before she goes on maternity."

"Well, why don't you have a few days off on flexi? Then you can have some time together without having to do anything."

"Problem is, I'm not like you, I don't do hundreds of hours over every month. I always go home at four."

"The policy says that you can go ten hours under as long as you clear the deficit in a month. Tell you what, I'm having a meeting with dweeb tomorrow, why don't I tell him that you've had a family emergency and you won't be back till Wednesday? He'll never be brave enough to ask what's happened, never mind check your hours."

"You think?"

"Well, let's have a look. How many hours have you got?"

"Hang on… okay, I'm eight hours over."

"I don't know what you're complaining about then. That falls within the parameters. I think you should do it. You'll be able to take her out somewhere, all that blah."

"All right then. You'll sort it with dweeb for me?"

"Yeah, I'll mention it last thing tomorrow. No problem."

"Okay, cheers, mate. I'll do it."

Ethan made a note to remind himself. Needless to say, he had no doubt that he would be able to order Peter to do what he said.

Despite having wasted half an hour chatting, by the end of the afternoon, Ethan had not only finished the presentation for the next day but also sketched out the framework for the remaining Hypnos sections. He had made such progress that he was actually able to estimate an end to the project. He thought that if he worked at the same pace, it would be finished in a month. That would mean that he would be able to use Aislin's goodwill when she returned by staying late for a week or so, before surprising her by being true to his word and concentrating on looking for houses. That was when she would understand the importance of overtime payments.

Ethan saw that it was four o'clock. He heard Mo packing his

bag and thought that as he had little to do on his remaining cases, having completed all initial enquiries on the outstanding low priorities, he may as well leave on time.

"Hang on a minute, I'll walk with ya."

"What?"

"I said wait there and I'll walk out with ya."

He concentrated on locking his paperwork in his cabinet so that he would not have to look at his incredulous face.

"Come on then."

As they walked across the office, Alfie shouted "Oi", making Ethan's heart skip a beat, although fortunately, he did not jump, otherwise he would never have heard the end of it. Alfie held still a moment to watch him before laughing and banging his head against the desk.

"All right, calm down. Very good."

"The end is nigh, that's what this means. There'll be an earthquake tomorrow now, you just watch. We're doomed, we're all doomed!" Alfie jumped to his feet and waved his arms around, causing laughter to ripple around the office.

"When you going to start looking at houses?" Mohammed asked when they were out of the room.

"I'll do it when I can. There's other things I've got to sort out first."

"What do you mean? You've seemed very distracted lately."

"Bits and pieces, nothing much…" Mo looked at him but he resisted the temptation to say any more.

"I've warned you about Dan, it won't do you any good in the long run to do his stuff instead of sorting out your life."

"We've all got to do our duty. There's no choice about it."

"It's a choice everyone else makes."

"I only have to justify my own choices, not everyone else's."

The direction the conversation had taken made Ethan wish that he had started the next section after all. He was half inclined to go back out of principle. *This is the last time I leave early. There's always more to do. There are always ways to improve.*

"So where are you looking to move to?"

"We haven't discussed it properly yet."

They walked outside and Mohammed slapped him on the back, almost knocking him over. "Have a good 'un."

"Bye."

When Ethan got home, he opened a letter from the organisation to read that they were changing the pensions again. A booklet was enclosed but he could not be bothered to read it as the general situation was plain. 'Reform' and 'change' always meant that things were about to get worse.

He ate dinner while watching the MV. An eerie sense of normality hung over the house; he could not remember the last time he had eaten that early.

He spent an hour researching properties on a website, feeling that he was doing a chore. Ethan saved some of the descriptions on his MV so that he had proof of what he had done. He then watched a film, but by the time it finished, it was only half eight and time seemed to stretch endlessly before him, as if he were looking along a motorway. He rang Aislin but her mobile went to answerphone.

He wanted to stay up all night, to see whether he could go without sleep at all. It was as if he wanted to punish himself for still being rested from the previous night, as if he wanted to be exhausted, that he could not exist in any other state. Like a sleep bulimic, he had to hurt himself in an ever more damaging cycle for reasons he could not explain.

He eventually went to bed at twelve after doing every odd job he could think of and wasting hours messing around on the Internet, thinking how ridiculous he was the entire time,

As he lay in bed that night, he worried about what would happen when they moved in together. Whenever Aislin had stayed over, they were like excitable children taking pleasure in each other's company. What would she do when she realised how disordered his sleep patterns were? *I don't know whether I'll be able to change just like that.* The subject was too painful to think about.

Ethan categorised what he had left to do for Hypnos, and how he was going to carry out his presentation the following day. Needless to say, Daniel would do most of the talking, but there would be questions to answer, there always were, and he would have to spend the morning preparing.

By the time he stopped worrying, Ethan was exhausted and was able to sleep with a clear conscience.

Ten

WHEN HE GOT INTO WORK the following morning, Daniel was sitting at his desk.

"Oh, hi Dan… I wasn't expecting you first thing."

"Ethan. Good to see you…" he twirled to his feet and shook his hand, "… I popped over early to let you know the running order for today and to ask for a few changes."

"Right, okay."

"Let's go through to the conference room."

Ethan followed him there, wondering whether there was a meeting he did not know about, as there was no one else in the office.

"Firstly, thanks again for all your hard work. What you've found has got the DIA interested and I've heard they're going to send over one of their regional directors. He calls himself Jones but I doubt that's his real name. It's all very secret with them, you understand, he's probably got a five barrelled name…" Ethan smiled. "Anyway, I asked for a few facilities from the top floor – a bigger screen and a faster computer, so we can show your work to its best advantage. Can I just ask please, and I apologise for not asking sooner, can you put the main points on some slides, so we can put them up while going through the draft?"

"Well… I've already done it. I guessed that you'd want that."

"Why did I bother asking? I mentioned your name to our director the other day, as he's following the progress of Hypnos as well now. It's not going to be long before you move seats, Ethan. It's a good team here, but there's some things I want changing. Start having a think about how we could improve."

"Okay."

"On this subject, when was the last time you saw Simon?"

"Simon? It must be, I don't know, at least four months, well before I last went on leave. Isn't he on long-term sick?"

"That's a good question, Ethan. Our excellent financial contractors tell me that he's been paid overtime for the last six months although they only decided to let me know yesterday. He's not put a sick note in so it looks like he's stopped coming to work and no one's done anything. This is why I need someone to get a grip of the department."

Ethan looked at the table. Daniel never told anyone anything, let alone confidential information, without some purpose.

"So… how are we going to go through the stuff then? Are you going to read the slides…?"

"I'll go through the headline points. We're not going into the detail today, they just want to start getting their heads around what you've found. They might have some questions though so I want you to come to the meeting."

"No problem, I'll go and get it ready."

"Thanks."

They went back to the office, which had filled up since they had left, and Ethan e-mailed the presentation to himself so that he could open it in the conference room, while Daniel chatted with the others. Ethan thought that what he had said about the SDMA director was almost certainly untrue, and wondered why Daniel imagined that he would have been impressed by the lie.

Little work was done that morning, Daniel's presence giving everyone except Ethan the opportunity to chat about everything and nothing. At one point, Peter came out, and when seeing Daniel talking to Jo, he rested against a partition and smiled. Ethan watched him a moment with pleasurable scorn before re-checking the presentation.

Needless to say, the meeting started late. Senior management and DIA officials were never on time, and as the morning went on, Ethan thought that bringing them together might prove impossible. Eventually, Daniel came over to his desk and said, "They're on their way, Eth. Can you set up the computer?"

"It's ready to go. You just have to enter the password I sent you this morning."

"Okay, great, let's go and see how it works."

He smiled and rolled his eyes self-deprecatingly. Ethan knew that he had a comprehensive knowledge of computers and only wanted to check that everything was set up correctly.

They went into the conference room and Daniel asked to use Ethan's account, which meant that he had to give a blood sample for the fourth time that morning. The others arrived a few minutes later. The DIA Regional Director was the highest ranking official Ethan had ever met, and he wasn't sure what the proper protocol was or how he should address him.

"Sir," Daniel said, and Ethan nodded at the man who had come last time. The new figure with him had to be Regional Director Jones, whose sharp, angular features were amplified by his suit. His slicked back black hair made him look like a stereotypical DIA agent.

"Good to meet at last, Mr Lee."

"This is Ethan, who's done all the research around the report."

"Pleasure," Jones said, his handshake cool.

They sat around the conference room table, Ethan by the computer, at which point, the purpose of his presence became clear to him. Peter burst in, clutching a notepad to his chest. All the seats at the table were taken, so he sat in one of the corners. Daniel looked at him with blank faced disapproval that was all the more obvious for being suppressed. No one else marked his appearance in any way.

"The Iklonian threat increases as it becomes less visible, not least because its lower profile weakens public support for counter subversion measures…" Jones said, slowly casting his eyes around the room with the indifferent confidence of someone used to being listened to. He seemed to focus on everything at once. "Strategic planning must be built into our daily work, whether as part of regional projects such as this one, or as synergised stratagems that employ lean prioritisation for maximising potentiality. As the Italians say: 'At the end of a game of chess, both the king and the pawns go back in the same box'."

He raised his eyebrows at Daniel, who in turn nodded at Ethan. He clicked on the first slide. Listening to Jones had made him worry that he would be asked a question he did not understand, which would undermine everything Daniel had said about him.

Although he had summarised the draft of his report as much as he could, it still encompassed over a hundred slides, and no one seemed in any hurry. Daniel read the material and Jones asked him questions; the other DIA agents took notes on everything that was said, even when they told a joke. Ethan moved to the next slide when prompted.

When they reached the section on the links between attacks on energy companies and SC breaches, Jones said, "What's the position regarding the Strategic Management Board?"

Daniel looked at him a moment then said, "Ethan?"

Ethan shifted on his seat. He had resigned himself to sitting and listening for a few hours and had hardly registered the question. "Sorry… in what sense?"

"I'm afraid that it's not acceptable to carry out research in isolation. The SMB develops policy using the data sources you've looked at, and some others. It can't simply be ignored."

Ethan nodded, feeling himself go red.

"We'd best move on."

The subordinates scribbled furiously. Ethan noted the point, feeling unsure of himself when seeing how much the others were writing; one of DIA officials started a new notebook, slickly moving from one to the other with deft flicks of his fingers without wasting a motion. They were evidently recording more than was being spoken, as they could not have written that much if they had transcribed the meeting verbatim. Peter looked on like a child who had been excluded from a game, and when Ethan saw him crossing and uncrossing his legs, he felt humiliated that Peter had heard what Jones had said.

In one of the following sections, Ethan had conducted an analysis of the amounts of different types of SC breaches recorded over the timeframe of the report. Daniel was reading one of the bullet points when Jones said, "That is *not* a recognised definition of subversion. This is intolerable. We've got to use our own terms correctly, otherwise how can we expect anyone else to?"

"Yep," Daniel said, making a quick note. Ethan only stopped himself from speaking with extreme effort. It was obvious that the description he had given in that slide related to section one breaches, not to subversion in general! *Dan must know that too. He'd highlighted the point in bold, for fuck sake. What's the matter with everyone?*

They continued relentlessly, testing what Ethan had thought were his unlimited powers of concentration and ability to push through boredom. He heard his stomach rumble several times, although only realised how hungry he was when Daniel motioned for him to move to the next page and the screen went blank.

"That's it then, sir."

"When are we expecting to finish the final draft?"

"We're still talking with our partners for access to some of the information. I'd estimate about a month."

Ethan was amused that no one had asked him that question, given that he was the only one who knew the answer. Jones chewed the inside of his cheeks before saying, "Good, that will fit in with the timeline around the Strategic Impasse and Review meeting at the end of October."

Daniel nodded and everyone was silent, waiting for the great man to conclude the meeting.

"Gentlemen, there are clearly a few matters to clear up. I appreciate your time here today."

He made a circular gesture as if about to start another speech, before standing and patting Daniel's shoulder then shaking Ethan's hand without looking at him. Jones and his retinue left the room.

Ethan switched off the computer. It was only when he was not looking at the glare of the screen that he realised how dark the room was. "How do you think that went?" he asked tentatively.

"As good as it could have done. I've been in meetings with DIA Directors before and you know it when they don't like something. You know it then you know it again. We've just got to make sure that we do those few extra bits he was talking about and we'll be in credit with the DIA for a good long time."

"Are you sure? He didn't sound too pleased."

"Ignore that. If he were too complimentary he'd make his own people look bad."

"Dan, is it all right if I get off? I was supposed to be picking Jan up from swimming tonight," Peter asked.

"Yep."

"Oh, Pete, before you go, Mo said that he was going to book Monday and Tuesday off on flexi. He said sorry for sending an e-mail so late but he had some family stuff that he needed to sort out."

"Right, yeah… erm… yep."

Pete left the office and Daniel smiled at Ethan.

"I'm going to be off. There are a few other matters I've got to deal with tonight. Thanks again for all your help, I'll be in contact to see where we are with the deadline. Are you still okay with your other work?"

"Yeah yeah, I've sorted it."

"Good. I'll see you later then, Eth."

"See you later."

Ethan was left alone with the quiet hum of the projector. After listening to it for a few minutes, he went back to his desk and checked the points Jones had made. As he knew would be the case, the SMB notes published on the secure intranet did not contain any relevant material. In fact, that talking shop had a much narrower, and inferior, methodology to that he had used for Hypnos. When he checked the slides, he was happy that his definition of subversion was correct. *Cheeky bastard.* As he looked over at the empty chair opposite, he thought with surprise that perhaps Mo had a point about Daniel after all.

He felt flat on his way home. Ethan knew that now the bosses had taken hold of the project, the investigative and creative aspects of it were over.

Although it was late by the time he had washed and eaten, he was at a loose end that evening. He was so habituated to running around, doing everything as quickly as possible, that being able to relax threw him out of synch.

Ethan lay on a sofa, watching the MV ill at ease, until the screen flashed with a call. He stirred with the darting movements of a disturbed insect, seeing from a wall clock that it was midnight. He was unsure whether he had been asleep; the images he remembered before being interrupted did not seem quite real, and his head movement had been too sharp to be natural. He watched the display before answering, seeing that the call was from a withheld number.

"Hello?"

"Hello Ethan, I hope I didn't wake you."

It was the Professor. His voice was smarmy and sarcastic, much more confident than he had been when they'd last spoken.

"What do you mean, what are you talking about?"

"Just a turn of phrase."

"What do you want?"

"Ethan, I'm sorry, but—"

"I want to know how you've got my number."

"Okay, well… Ethan, don't forget that if you get a large enough group of people together then they can find out pretty much anything. I mean… how do journalists find things out? People talk. It's as simple as that."

Ethan felt at a loss. Whenever he found himself in this situation, he tried to be angry but was foiled by their phoney reasonableness. He was tempted to hang up but knew that that would only invite further intrusions into his privacy by whatever techniques they had at their disposal.

"You don't want to tell me, that's fine. But what do you want? We agreed last time that you wouldn't contact me again but you've not left it a week before you ring my number, my *personal* number, in the middle of the night."

"I need to see you tomorrow to go through a few things. Nothing serious, just a few bits and pieces."

"Are you mad? Why would I want to do that? You want me to meet you on the weekend? It was bad enough on a work night, but at least then there was a reason for me to be in town. What would I say if I got caught with you when I've no reason to be there?"

"Yeah, I know, I know… You're right, Ethan, but you don't have to worry about any of that. I wouldn't want you going back to the same place you went before, we'd never do that to you. It'll be somewhere completely different, somewhere out of the way. You won't even be met by the same person, so there's nothing to worry about there either."

"I'm not going. And if you threaten Aislin again then I'll call the police."

"Yeah… erm… you see… I don't… It's not as simple as you think it might be, Ethan. And you know… the other thing is… well, if you call the police, don't forget what you've already done. And you've been paid for it, you see, so… it's not a one-way street…"

"Five quid for a sandwich? What are you talking about?"

"It's difficult to say, Ethan, but… the amount doesn't really make a difference. You've accepted money and that's the end of it. As I said, it's not a one-way street."

His hand was cold against his cheek and it took Ethan a few seconds to realise that he was blushing. The Professor was right, of course, and although Ethan wanted to argue further, the prospect of being confronted by that unalterable fact for a second time stopped his tongue.

"What's a good time for you? Six in the evening?"

"Make it seven."

"Okay, seven is fine. Have you got a pen?"

"I'll save it into my phone, hang on."

"Even better."

Ethan got his mobile and typed the address that the Professor gave him into it, in addition to a series of gnomic directions. If his assurances were to be believed, it would take him an hour to get there on a Saturday.

"… That's good… good. Right, okay… I'll see you later then. See you tomorrow."

Ethan hung up without saying goodbye, the only resistance he could think to make in the circumstances.

Although he knew that he was playing into their hands, his actions that night were inevitable. He watched the MV mindlessly, flicking the channel every so often to little purpose before playing computer games, repeatedly telling himself that he would switch it off when reaching a certain point, then carrying on. He only managed to drag himself away when realising how light the room was, and seeing from a wall clock that it was four in the morning. He had stayed up from light until light. It seemed so absurd that he stared at the clock hands then turned away before looking back. *This is the worst night I've ever had.* He unplugged his alarm. He had never gone to bed that late in his whole life; the illegal interference with the alarm (section three, subsection one), when considered with all the aggravating circumstances, was certainly a level-one SC breach.

Ethan yawned. After having denied himself sleep for so long, he needed more and more. *If I'd gone to bed on time I would have missed their call. Perhaps I should sleep the whole day tomorrow as an excuse for not going. They might accept that. Isn't that what they want, to turn me into a criminal?*

He woke at three the following afternoon and wandered around, dazed grogginess adding to his confusion. It was dark and cloudy outside and he was at first excited that he had woken early, before realising the truth. *It can't be good for you to sleep like this. God knows what it'll do long term.* A few years earlier, an SDMA video had been made in which sleep disorders were compared to smoking in the way they progressively damaged the body. He seemed to be personally proving every deleterious effect of SC breaches.

Ethan ate toast for 'breakfast' then paced backwards and forwards in the lounge, marvelling each time he saw the clock. The fact that shadows were encroaching across the floor struck him as ridiculous. *Hasn't the day gone fast?* He would have to go to the Iklonians soon. Despite the threats the Professor had made, Ethan hoped without allowing himself to dwell on the idea that he might be able to help him. As he logged into the MV to search for the address, he thought that sleep had taken over his life, that it dominated his thoughts in the same way that food does for anorexics. Today would consist of nothing other than sleep and Iklonians. And the only thing that would change his routine was going to work on Monday when he would research the same things.

As he peered out of a window, he wondered what his neighbours thought. *They must know I'm still here because my car hasn't moved since I came back yesterday, but they'll have seen that the blinds were closed until an hour ago. Are they going to report me? Have they already reported me?* Now that he was associating with subversives, the whole world was hostile and he thought with bitter irony about how often he had rued the inefficiency of the SDMA's reporting protocols. Now, they were the only thing protecting him. *The only reason I'm going is to gather information. I can't let them give me the slip like last time.*

The safe house was in the countryside and he imagined a ramshackle old house on a hill, beams of light from fading sun cascading through the windows. The Professor had lied about how long it would take to get there, and the prospect of being on the road for hours felt to Ethan as bad as the destination. The distance meant that there was little chance he would be able to get back that night.

Ethan's stomach rumbled and he thought that he had only had two slices of toast to eat in the last twenty-two hours. He went to the kitchen and ate all the biscuits in the house. Then, feeling bloated and ashamed, he checked out of a window for passers-by before going to his car.

The journey was unlike any he had ever taken before, with the roads almost deserted once he had got out of the suburbs. The radio became crackly and his feet tingled when they touched the pedals. Market principles had caused the countryside to become uneconomic over the last twenty years; the lack of infrastructure resulted in poor radio coverage, and the disproportionate granting of shift sleep licences in rural areas had emptied the roads during the day, meaning that there was nothing inherently sinister about his experience. Still, his mind continually reverted to thoughts of vengeful spirits, and the omnipresent sense that he was being watched and assessed.

The directions were simple; when he reached the motorway that led out of his zone, he had only to stay on it for forty miles before following a country lane to the village. The drudgery of the journey was such that he did not notice the gradual disintegration of the road as he went further from the city, until he was ten miles away and was jolted from his seat as he went over a pothole.

It was frightening that the Iklonians had safe houses in the countryside. He could understand what he had seen in Central Zone, with its sprawling developments and too many SC breaches for there to be any logic in trying to enforce the law in any but the most egregious circumstances. However, experience had taught him that there would be no strategic value for the Iklonians to establish a presence in depopulated rural areas, where their activities would be more likely to be detected, and there was little infrastructure to attack and fewer influential people to corrupt. *It just shows how much we know. Fuck all.*

The safe house was in a village called Caville. He followed the country lane for several miles, during which there were no turnoffs and nothing around that would identify where he was. Ethan pressed on despite worrying that he had taken a wrong turn. There was abandoned scrub in every direction as far as he could see, with patchy grass giving way to mud in places as if a series of bonfires had been lit there.

Eventually, he came to a sign marked 'Caville' in white letters on a green background. He relaxed before becoming anxious again after driving through the wasteland for another mile. He slowed down when seeing something in the distance, and when it loomed larger, he saw that it was a billboard from one of the first SDMA public information campaigns. Most of the space was taken up by a menacing black and white figure looking over his shoulder. The PSH was printed beside it, together with the SDMA clouds. He knew how old it was because some of the sponsor logos were from firms no longer associated with the organisation. The fact that it was still there seemed vaguely sinister, as if it were an ironic sign of defiance, or else a signifier that he was entering a forgotten place.

Finally, to his relief, he saw a building that looked like a granary in the distance. He looked at the directions on his mobile to see that he had to take a left into 'Green Lane', but there were still no turnoffs, so he carried on, slowing down and hunching over the steering wheel.

He passed the building and the road went up a slope and ended in a ramshackle car park. Vehicles were abandoned at different angles across the bays. They were much bigger than those he was used to in Central Zone, meaning that they were more than twenty years old. Gouges in the road formed barriers that broke up the space. Ethan parked at the edge of one of them.

Wind chipped his cheeks as he looked around. *Could I have taken a wrong turn?* There had seemed to be only one path and the sign had been clear. *Perhaps there's another Caville?* It seemed very implausible. Or maybe the instructions were out of date. Green Lane could have been abandoned and slowly reclaimed by the elements, grass and water pulling it apart piece by piece. Ethan rubbed his hands, suddenly aware of how cold he was.

He decided to walk to the building, thinking that it was not far away and that he would block the road if he took the car. *I'll have to look for a hotel after I've finished tonight. Shit.*

As he walked along the side of the road, Ethan saw himself as if through binoculars, his sight panning out to show more and more empty space. He could see all the way to the motorway in the far distance. His shoes squelched in the mud until he could feel it between his toes.

The distance was greater than he had thought, and he did not know whether his feet were tingling because of tiredness or because he was unfit. His mobile rang and he saw that it was Aislin.

"Hi Ash, how are you sweetie?"

"Good thanks, I just thought I'd ring to see how you're doing."

The signal was crackly.

"Yeah, fine. Sorry for not ringing you back. I wasn't sure what you'd be doing after what you'd said before."

"That's okay. What you been up to then?"

"Just bits and pieces really, nothing special. We had that big presentation I was telling you about, you know, with Dan and everyone."

"Oh yeah, how did that go?"

"Fine. Boring really, in the end. It took ages to set up and there was a massive meeting that went on the whole day. I'm hoping to finish that project soon."

"Oh right."

"Apart from that, just gone out a few times with Mo, that kind of stuff. I've got some more houses, by the way. You can have a look when you get back."

"Why don't you e-mail me, then I can have a quick look now?"

"Erm… okay. I'll do it later 'cos I'm doing the shopping at the moment."

"No problem."

"And how are things with you, has it been going any better?"

"It has actually, he's calmed down a lot. For the first few days he was really emotional, like I was saying before, but now, we've just been doin' a lot of walking, going to places that he used to go to when he was younger, stuff like that. I think he's realised how awkward he's been 'cos he's started saying thank you a lot when we've got back to the hotel. Yesterday, he told me that no one's got a better daughter than he has."

"Well, he's right isn't he?"

The sky suddenly darkened and Ethan hoped beyond hope that it would not rain.

"I didn't know what to say. He's really sweet when he says things like that. It's easy to only remember the mad things he does but he's not always like it. He threw me last night. I was touched."

"Yeah, yeah."

"So that's it really."

"I'm glad you've said that, it sounds like you're enjoying yourself now. What's the best time to ring tomorrow?"

"We try to get back to the hotel about nine."

"Okay, I'll ring you about half nine?"

"Okay."

"And I'll send you that stuff as well. The properties I mean. Ash… I'm really looking forward to you coming back. I've missed you. I love you. I want us to get the house sorted as soon as we can. Perhaps you can move in here while we look 'cos who knows how long it'll all take."

"I'd like that."

He listened to his steps for a few seconds.

"That was everything then, I just wanted to tell you how it was all going."

"Yeah. I'll call you tomorrow. At half nine."

"Love you."

"Love you, bye, bye."

"Bye."

The conversation emptied his mind until he reached the building.

It was a squat, stone structure with sloping walls. He paused as he stood outside it, forced back into the immediacy of reality after his interlude with Aislin. *I wish I'd gone with her.* Now that he thought about it, he was sure that she had wanted him to. She had made enough hints about how difficult the situation was going to be, and his presence would have undoubtedly tempered her father's behaviour. And they needed the time together. Ethan thought that she was still not convinced of his sincerity about the house situation.

He stepped inside into a small lobby, with winding stairs to his left and right that twisted out of his vision. Immediately before him were shelves filled with ornaments with a door between them. Of course, the other advantage to having gone with her would have been that none of this would have happened. Even with how powerful the Iklonians were, there was no way that he was important enough for them to follow him out the country.

"Do you need anything?"

A man had come through the door so quietly that Ethan did not register his presence until he had spoken. He wore a blue shirt and tie and had a moustache that filled a third of the distance between his lip and nose. His smile was very false and Ethan was immediately suspicious of him.

"Oh… yeah… hi. I was looking for a turnoff but I think I might have missed it. I was after… Green Lane?"

Ethan became more tentative the longer he spoke, imagining that he was giving something away by telling him where he was going.

"In Caville, is that?"

"Yeah."

"You'll need a map. We've got plenty here."

Ethan glanced around but could not see anything; all the merchandise in the shop, if it was a shop, had to be hidden from view. The man produced a crumpled A-Z from behind his back.

"Thank you…" Ethan took it from him and was looking through the index when the man cleared his throat. "Oh, sorry, how much is it?"

"Fifteen pounds sixty please."

The man's grin seemed to broaden and Ethan felt a hatred towards him that was out of all proportion to anything he had done.

"Right…"

He reached for his wallet, and fortunately, he had a twenty-pound note. He handed it to the man, who made it disappear with a skilful sleight of hand.

Ethan opened the relevant page and sat on the floor to read it. Caville looked much larger than it had seemed on the Internet. When he found the square that Green Lane was supposed to be in, he could not find it despite squinting at every road on the page. He checked over everything again before saying, "Excuse me, you can't help me with where Green Lane is can you? Is says here it's supposed to be in E5 but it doesn't seem to be there. Is it a new road?"

"No no no, that's the most comprehensive map there is. Let's have a look…" The man turned it around and traced out a series of lines with his finger, "… here it is, there's an abbreviation just above it."

He had an air of weary wisdom, as if nothing could surprise him. Ethan looked at where he had pointed to see the letters 'GL' written above a tiny road leading into the village.

"Do you know how I get there from here?" Ethan spoke tentatively and had the impression that the man was going to charge him for the additional information.

"When you walk out, turn left and carry on for about ten minutes. Right at the end of the road you'll come to a big car park. There's a stile at the far end. If you climb over then that's Green Lane. It runs parallel to a farm down that way."

"Climb over a stile? Isn't there a way you can drive into the village?"

"Nah. It's all been pedestrianised around here for ages. It was 'cos of all the accidents you see, 'cos of the state the roads were in. A few years ago, the council decided that the maintenance costs were too high, so everything was shut down. Once things are gone they never come back, so here we are."

"Oh right. Well, thanks for that."

The man smiled beneficently and looked at him with silent expectation, like a waiter expecting a tip. Ethan walked out of the shop, if that was what it was. He walked back the way he had come. The road was silent.

When he reached the car park, he followed the instructions the man had given him, and as if by magic, he saw the farm and stile as described.

As he walked along Green Lane, Ethan could hardly believe that it had once been a road. It had become little more than a dirt track, broken up in places into scrub. Not that the 'farm' was any more accurately described, as after he had walked a few steps from the stile, he saw that the neighbouring field was filled with weeds of all shapes and sizes. They had even knocked the fence over in places and spilled into the path.

When he reached the end of the trail, the ground before him dipped in a steep incline and his vantage point offered him a view of the village. For a moment, he thought that he had gone back in time, matchbox houses and half-tilled fields shimmering under a sea blue sky. Beggars lay in doorways of abandoned houses. It was only the ubiquity of jeans and earphones that gave away the true date. Ethan followed the route to the address he had been given.

The roads had disintegrated even further in Caville itself, with the concrete pitted in places with bits sticking up, making it look like a pastiche of cobblestones, which must have been what the man from the 'shop' had meant when he had said that it had been pedestrianised.

Given the Arcadian nature of the village, Ethan expected the people there to be inquisitive about a stranger, but happily, Caville was as anonymous as the city. No one paid him the slightest attention, even when he could not find one of the streets and had wandered the length of a lane several times, before finding a signpost on a front garden and working out that what the map designated as a road was now an alleyway between a cottage and an abandoned building.

After half an hour, he found the Iklonian safe house. It was a detached rundown building; when seeing it, he immediately identified it for what it was by the way it had been extended so that its back half stuck out much further than any other house on the street. One of the windows had three wavy lines on its frame that he recognised from the DIA report he had read when starting

Hypnos. It was supposed to mean 'welcome'. Ethan knocked at the door and looked through a window but could see only shadows inside, as if they had torn themselves from their owners and were dancing in celebration.

Eventually, he heard fumbling and the Professor answered.

"Oh... good... you're here... excellent, excellent, come in." He smiled like a kindly uncle and pressed himself ostentatiously against the wall to allow Ethan past, before locking the door. "Did you find your way okay? I mean, obviously you got here, but... some people find it a little... out of the way."

Ethan nodded. The Professor always sounded false when speaking about inconsequential things.

"Anyway, come through, come through..."

Ethan followed him into a room where people lounged on or against sofas, resting their heads on each other's shoulders. There was a MV in one corner with the news on, although no one seemed to pay any attention to it.

"Can I get you anything?"

"No."

"You sure?"

"Why have you got a safe house in a place like this? How many people can you have out here in the middle of nowhere?"

The Professor cleared his throat. From the corner of his eye, Ethan saw a man sit up on the far side of the room.

"The safe houses are more about coverage than convenience. The aim is to have one within a twenty-minute drive of anywhere in the country."

"If you've got that many then how come I've had to drive all the way out here?"

"Well..." The Professor drew in his breath as if about to speak then looked at his shoelaces. "You're a bit of a special case. But we're not going to talk about that today." He bit his lips.

"Are you going to tell me what you want then or carry on messing about? You've got me by the balls, haven't you?"

"Well…" The Professor looked away and did not speak for an uncomfortable length of time.

Someone sat next to Ethan, cutting into his space, his legs crossed and his arms folded. It was the bad tempered youth from the last safe house.

"I need to talk to you," he said to the Professor, staring at him sullenly.

"Erm… okay… yes… right. Is it really so urgent that we need to go through this now?"

"Yeah." His voice rose with obnoxious pleasure from the discomfort he was causing. He wore a black leather jacket with a white t-shirt underneath. The Professor turned to Ethan and said, "This is Max, he's one of our… students here. Excuse me for a moment. Erm… how are things then?"

"I've filled in all them papers. But I've got more important things to talk about. I need money. I told you it was never gonna be enough and it's not been."

"Right… okay… this probably needs to be something to talk about another time. The money is an important matter, certainly, and with the—"

"You're not getting the papers if I don't get my money, simple as."

"Yes. Of course… you may say that, but… well, there's no nice way to put it… you see, if we don't see the results, you won't be paid for any future projects or have access to our networks. That will be the ultimate sanction, I'm afraid."

"I want my money."

"Of course. Let me think about it. Do you want… a drink?"

"Beer."

"Fine. Ethan, are you sure you don't want anything?" Ethan shook his head. "My apologies, let me sort this out, it won't take long."

"Take your time."

Ethan smiled, making the Professor's glance wilt. He muttered

"Yes", looked back to see them both staring at him, then moved away.

Ethan wondered whether Max was going to say anything now that they had established a fraternity of sorts in their mutual antagonism towards the Professor, but after he had left, Max turned away.

As he looked around the room, Ethan thought that Max looked more out of place than he did. Although a few of the people had long hair and wore homemade clothes, most were entirely unprepossessing. One man even clutched a suitcase as if expecting it to be snatched from him. Ethan felt disappointed, as he had expected there to be a more evident hierarchy. When he had forwarded case files identifying Iklonian links for the attention of the DIA, he had often said that the guilty party appeared to be a senior operative. Now that he understood them a little better, he was unsure whether they were structured at all.

Ethan looked at his watch several times but the Professor was nowhere to be seen and no one in the room stirred. Ethan started fidgeting. *He's doing it on purpose, it's some kind of trick. Everything about this place is designed to confuse me.* He uncrossed then re-crossed his legs, touching Max in the process.

"Watch yourself."

"Sorry." Ethan felt annoyed that he had apologised automatically. He stretched, kicking him harder than before.

"So you think you're pretty clever, eh?"

"What are you on about?"

"You've forgot about how you get *your* money, have you?"

"What's that got to do with anything? And what's it got to do with you?"

Ethan felt the condescension in his voice but could not stop himself. *What's this little brat's problem?*

"You're a Sam."

"What's that supposed to mean?"

"You've never even heard of that before?" Max sneered. "You're not very 'street', are ya? You know, 'Sam', one of the 'SDMA', the secret police."

"Not very secret though, are we? Do secret police forces normally have buildings with their name on them? Do secret police normally advertise on *The Guardian* website? Come on, do you really believe that crap?"

Max jumped up and knelt on his knees, and for a moment, Ethan's heart leapt when he thought that he was going to swing a punch. As he looked down at Max's reedy features, he wished that he would do so. That would make things so much easier.

"No no no, that's not what it's like these days. It's *normalised*, that's why, the secret police have all been *normalised*. The secret police can't go completely secret now like they did in the old days 'cos of the Internet, and you can't keep everything hidden anymore. So you have to make it sound reasonable, to give out snippets of what you're doing so that people will accept it. It's worse than ever now because everyone knows what's going on – by making it more reasonable, you make more people accept it, that's all…"

He stopped, out of breath, his speech so rushed that it must have been something he had been waiting to say since he had first seen Ethan.

"Right, so it would be better if we were like the Stasi? So that if we were more 'unreasonable' then people might reject us? We were set up by the government, who were elected. How do you think it all happened, that we dropped out the sky? We came about because most people wanted it to happen."

"No no no, that's the really *obvious* way to look at it, you're not looking at the *reality*. The government doesn't just do things, it's controlled by *interests*. People don't know what they want anyway."

"And you're in the pimply vanguard are you?"

"Okay okay okay, well… how many people voted for your alarm clocks then? All the surveys show that they would be got rid of tomorrow if anyone were ever asked."

"How many people voted *against* alarm clocks and specified waking times? Nowadays, people only vote if you hold knives to their throats, and some don't even then." Ethan saw the Professor watching them nervously with a beer in his hand.

"People will wake up eventually, then you'll see. Don't get too comfortable at your desk." He made an explosion sound and gestured with both hands. "It won't be long before we get to you. Them spikes at the front won't protect you forever."

"Now we're getting to the truth about what you're interested in."

The Professor stepped between them and gave the beer to Max. Ethan realised that everyone in the room was staring at him with blank, doll-like faces. His limbs felt weak, as if he had lost a lot of blood.

"Everyone knows… I'm ruined…"

"No no… that's not true… I should say that I didn't tell Max, or anyone. It's just… how can I put it… it's very difficult to keep things like that a secret. And, well, your background is quite… obvious, I'm afraid, without anyone saying anything."

"I don't look any different from anyone else in here." Ethan sounded whiny, like a child. He realised that it would be easy for them to kill him without anyone ever knowing what had happened. Only the Iklonians' eyes moved. He felt as if he were surrounded by wax statues.

"It's not your appearance I'm referring to Ethan, rather, your manner, the words you use, your… views on things. They're all quite explicit I'm afraid."

"Why did you bring him here?" Max asked. "You've compromised us. You've polluted us. He's seen my face. You've told him my name."

The Professor looked down on him and made a sweeping gesture, like a priest granting an absolution. Max sneered then stood and elbowed his way through the crowd. As if on a signal, the other Iklonians starting moving again, talking to each other in low voices.

"Don't let him wind you up, Ethan. Max is very… tetchy at the moment. He's going through a… a radical stage where he's looking for confrontation. His views are marginal. Nowadays, at any rate. That's why I assigned him to the natural sleep patterns experiment. Our tests have confirmed the historical research about the unnaturalness of sleeping in a single block a day.

"After two weeks of a natural cycle, most subjects see a decrease in anxiety and an increase in all positive indicators of health, not to mention concentration and mental abilities. Our current obsession with trying to get all our sleep at a set time is quite unnatural, I'm afraid. It goes against our circadian body clock. I was hoping Max would calm down the same as the others, but apparently… well, I didn't factor in the pecuniary issues, if I can put it that way…"

Ethan nodded, feeling numb. Everything the Professor was saying went against what Ethan had understood and lived throughout his life, but the fight had gone out of him after his depressing loss of control. Suddenly, he remembered that he was there to gather intelligence. He moved closer so that the others would not hear.

"Why was he upset that you told me his name? Doesn't everyone he speaks to know it?"

The Professor laughed distractedly. "You would think so, wouldn't you? He prefers to go by the 'revolutionary name' he gave himself. He likes to be called 'Morpheus', or 'M'." The Professor rolled his eyes. "I'm afraid he's not quite understood that the organisation has changed from when it was an underground movement. We don't have assumed names anymore. There are too many of us, apart from anything, there wouldn't be enough to go around."

"Except for you."

"Well… that's a slightly different matter. I think that it's… too late for Max. He's not understood that ultimately, everyone is an Iklonian now. But anyway… I think we need a little more privacy."

Ethan nodded then followed him, stepping over those lying on the floor. As he left the room, he heard a bang and turned to see pictures of yet another bombing on the MV. A woman shook her braid and Ethan's throat felt blocked as if he were about to be sick when he saw the side of her red face. She looked like Daisy. *She's always hated us. It has to be her.* The bloody images on the screen felt like a threat. He hurried his steps.

The Professor led him into a side room with cream coloured walls with almost indistinguishable patterns on them. When Ethan looked closer, he saw that they were clouds. There was a table and two chairs in one corner, whereas on the other side of the room was a bed with linen the same colour as the wallpaper. Above it hung a crib mobile, comprising figures of animals.

"I know this is difficult for you… it would be hard for anyone. We brought you here today to help us with a simple matter. I'm sure you'll be able to do it in a few minutes. I just want you to tell me the layout of the floor you're working on."

Ethan nodded and thought over his request, trying to work out why they would want the information and what harm there would be in providing it. There was nothing apparent, which made him suspicious.

"Right."

"Ethan… you know… we've explained what will happen if…"

The Professor looked away and Ethan despised him for the weakness of his veiled threats. He seemed to want to intimidate him without being rude. The possibility of his death was no longer outlandish, and the utter fear it had first engendered had faded. What he could still hardly bear to think about was what might happen to Aislin. His realisation of how little he knew told him that the danger was real.

"What do you mean, the layout? As in, how many rooms there are? Or are you asking me about the security of the building and what's in the files?"

The Professor blinked rapidly as if outraged at the suggestion.

"No, no. No. Nothing like that. Only the general plans of the building, as in, what it would look like if the roof was taken off."

"So, where the offices are in relation to the toilets, stuff like that?"

"Yes, more or less."

Ethan weighed up his options. Put in that way, the request seemed reasonable, even banal. "I can tell you everything I know now, then there's no need for me to come back."

"Okay… just a minute…" The Professor fidgeted on his seat, searching through his pockets before eventually finding a pencil and a piece of crumpled paper.

Ethan thought that he could easily lose something as small as that. "How are we going to do this?"

"I'll draw it. You explain it to me and I'll put it down."

"Right… I only know about my floor 'cos it's against regulations for me to go to the other floors without permission."

"Oh. What's the regulation?"

Ethan froze. "It's just that, I have to have permission from a supervisor to go to another floor."

"So no one can go on a floor they don't work on?"

Ethan nodded slowly. The Professor looked at him with more penetration than usual, making no notes about that part of the conversation.

"Okay, so you work on the…"

"The tenth floor."

"Yes, the tenth floor. Let's start with how you get there from the lobby."

The Professor proceeded to ask him very detailed questions about every aspect of the tenth floor, from the lip-shaped security barriers to the length of the main corridor. "Just give me your best guess," the Professor said when he struggled to estimate it. Ethan told him how many offices he had been in and their dimensions.

The Professor's usual hesitancy had gone and he had become sharp, to the extent that Ethan wondered whether his mannerisms were part of an act. Once they had started, he no longer vacillated when answering his questions, even elaborating on occasion to give information that the Professor had not asked for.

When the interrogation had finished, the Professor sketched the tenth floor on the scrap paper in such a confusing manner that Ethan thought that it would be more a hindrance than a help to them. When explaining the layout, he had realised that he had only been into a small number of offices on his own floor, and had been to other floors so rarely that he could remember his visits as vividly as holidays. (He had made it a point of honour to say nothing about the other floors.) During the last few years, he had felt on top of his work and had become highly aware of his understanding. The interrogation had shown him the boundaries of his knowledge, and he had been embarrassed when having to admit that he did not know the answers to some of the Professor's questions. *I don't know much even about my own side.*

"Okay, well, I think that's about it then. That's good. Good." The Professor surreptitiously slipped the paper into his pocket, as if stealing it. "You can... well... you're free to stay here. Of course, it may be a good idea, with the—"

"With what, what do you mean?"

"Well, it *is* past twelve, Ethan. As you know, there are SC patrols at this time..."

"It's past twelve? Shit." He checked his watch and saw that the Professor was telling the truth.

"I'll leave you to decide. The room is lockable. Thanks again for... all your, you know..."

The Professor stood to leave, but before he did so, Ethan grabbed his shoulder, making him shudder.

"I want to know what's going to happen next. After I've left here, I mean. I'm tired of having mysterious contacts, telephone calls out the blue, and the rest of it. I'm done with this. I can't... well, I may as well say it 'cos you seem to know everything about me already. I can't have anything to do with you after next month 'cos I'll be moving in with Aislin, and she's got nothing to do with this. Is that clear?"

"Moving in next month? But that won't happen straight away, will it? It takes time for mortgages to clear, for—"

"It's finished. Anyway, you don't think this can carry on, do you? I'm surprised we've got away with it for as long as we have."

The Professor put his bottom lip over his top lip and puffed his cheeks out several times before answering. "All I'll say, Ethan, is that concerning important matters, the only things that come to light are those that need to. I can't give you any... promises about what might happen, but I'll be... sensitive to your personal situation. If we have to talk again, I'll make sure it doesn't impact on your relationship. Don't worry, if we do meet, it'll only be to tie up a few loose ends, nothing more."

"Before you go, let me ask you something. What does a black rose mean?"

"You people are obsessed with symbols."

"A black rose was put into a letter that was sent to me."

"I've never heard anyone mention one. Just someone being dramatic, I should imagine. Anyway, I'll let you get on with what you need to do."

He nodded and left the room. Ethan knew that he would have to stay the night, as he could not risk the SC patrols. He felt dread in his heart as he thought that he would always be under their power. He wished he could feel angry like he used to. He did not know what had sapped his energy.

Ethan paced the room until his legs were sore. After the Professor had left, he committed to memory what he had learnt about the Iklonians, such as the fact that most of them no longer used assumed names. He thought that he should go to bed, but could not stop thinking about the answers he had given about the layout of the tenth floor. *It's worked out about equal: they've learnt something about us, and we've learnt something about them. In fact, what I've found out is probably more important, because their agents would already know about the floors they worked on.* He sat on the bed and thought through everything he had said.

After he had convinced himself, Ethan was exhausted, but the thought that Daisy was in the same building was like a reed stuck between his toes. He walked around the room before holding still. Silence. Ethan slipped to the door, opened it a slither, and looked out. Nothing. He walked along the corridor on his tiptoes.

Light trapped under his eyelids transformed into spirits that flew towards him, making him pause and hold his breath until they had passed. The roof of the corridor had become curved after the lights had been switched off. After long, tortuous steps, the way before him opened up and he realised that he had come to the lounge. The only light emanated from the MV, which pulsated a series of dots one after the other against a black background, first white, then purple. The Iklonians slept over each other on the floor, like lions. Ethan slowly scanned his eyes over them until seeing one sitting on the sofa. They looked at him with eyes all white. His breath caught in his throat and he froze.

Eventually, he managed to tear himself away and softly stepped back, feeling that he was going to fall over any second. Daisy wasn't there. Ethan went in the other direction, feeling recklessly bold now that he walked at normal speed. He could not remember where his room was. It was definitely on the right, meaning that he felt a stab of excitement when seeing a door to his left. He turned the handle.

The room was the same size as his own, although a large window with no curtains faced the door, so that the darkness of the room mingled with the darkness outside. Daisy sat at a desk looking out and up, her braid almost touching the floor. His hand brushed the bed and she spun around, baring her teeth. She was on him in a moment, tearing at him with her hands, twisted into claws. He could somehow see himself being ripped to pieces, his flesh bouncing across the floor…

Eleven

WHEN HE WAS WOKEN BY the alarm on his mobile, Ethan's eyes felt sore and he clutched the sheets with both hands. He looked down and tentatively touched his legs, to find that he was unharmed. He had to consciously control his breathing. *Bastards*, he thought.

As he walked through the silent house, Ethan started when seeing the Professor. He seemed to never sleep.

"I'd hoped you'd want to take part in our natural sleep experiment. You're about two hours short of what you need now, which according to my research would set you up for another… about ten hours. You don't want to be run down for work, do you?"

"This has got nothing to do with what we agreed. I only stayed because it was too late to risk driving back."

"Ethan…" The Professor held his arms out before withdrawing them, "…you've got the wrong impression of what's going on here. You're a fanatic, like Max. You've created images for yourself of… I think you're setting yourself up for a disappointment…"

His weary manner suggested a level of understanding that worried Ethan.

"Are you going to stop me from leaving?"

"Well… no. Are you at least going to have something to eat before you go? Unless there are any regulations against that?"

"Goodbye." Ethan brushed past him.

Ethan's stomach rumbled as he left the house, making the journey ahead seem very long and onerous.

The village was preternaturally quiet given that the legal sleeping time was over, making him imagine that it was being used in its entirety by the Iklonians as part of their experiments. He hurried along Green Lane, past the abandoned farm, and when he drove off and reached the motorway, there were enough cars to provide a mirage of normality.

Ethan felt relieved when arriving home and opening the blinds. However, although his mind had been blank when he was driving, he was now consumed by awareness of how flimsy his agreement with the Professor was. In fact, it meant nothing at all, and he thought that he would inevitably call him again in a few weeks. *Why wouldn't he? He's not risking anything and has a lot to gain.* Ethan felt angry at the sly methods he had used to force his co-operation. *How can it be my fault when I had no choice?* He stalked backwards and forwards as if searching for answers in the lounge.

He only stopped when his mobile went off. He jumped on it to read an automated message from the SDMA.

Contacting the Public Safety Hotline is free from any number. YOU are part of the jigsaw. Report anything suspicious today. Why take a chance?

The solution was obvious now he had thought about it but none the less dangerous for that. He could ring the PSH and tell them about the two safe houses. The first problem was that the information was too closely associated with him. *What would they do if they knew I'd informed on them? Tell the SDMA? Something worse?*

The better way would be to only say about one of them. *This must happen all the time so it wouldn't be obvious that it was from me.* The one in the city was the more conspicuous of the two locations, as there were numerous people who might have seen something suspicious about it. The only people who knew about the one in Caville were the people who lived there and the Iklonians themselves, if any distinction could be drawn between them.

Ethan felt his lack of knowledge, as he had no idea how the DIA would deal with the information. Surely, after raiding the flat, they would examine it forensically and get fingerprints from everyone they found there? *Would they be able to identify that I had visited?* Ethan was not sure but his desire to convince himself of the merit of his plan was such that he dismissed the dangers. Presumably, they'd look into who rented or owned the flat, and the Professor had to be associated with it somehow. *Then again, is he my biggest problem, or just their representative? Assuming they'd do anything with the report.* He forced himself not to think about that possibility.

As he looked at his MV, he felt as if he had eaten too much. He knew the number off by heart but whispered it to himself several times before picking up the controller.

The number rang for a long time, creating grey ripples across the screen, such that Ethan wondered whether he had made a mistake, as government departments usually place the caller on hold. However, eventually, a computerised voice said, "Thank you for calling the…" There was a burst of static then the next few words were spoken in a higher tone. "… *Public Safety Hotline.* Your call will be answered within a maximum time of… *five minutes.* Please do not hang up. Your call is vital to us. An operator will be with you shortly."

It was a strange feeling to be at the inputting stage of the process. His call was answered after precisely five minutes by a bored sounding man, who said, "Public Safety Hotline, how can I help you?"

"Hi. I'd like to give some information about something I've heard, please."

"One moment, let me start a new record. Okay, what's the information about?"

"It's about somewhere where I know a lot of Icks go…"

Ethan proceeded to give the address of the city-based safe house and to describe some of the characters he had seen there. The man said 'uh-huh' every so often and occasionally asked him to repeat himself. Ethan tested him by giving a very weak description of Max; he only said 'uh-huh' again without asking any questions. Ethan now knew why so many DIA reports were of such poor quality.

The trickiest subject was, of course, the Professor, and Ethan provided extraneous details about the flat to give him time to think of how to phrase himself.

When he finally started talking about the Professor, Ethan gave a more detailed description than he had of the others to make him stand out, adding that "He's always on a mobile when he comes out and he looks like he's organising things". When the man made no comment, his instinct was to add more details, but he decided against it because he thought that it might make the information sound unreliable.

When he ran out of steam, he hung up, not wanting to hear the script they used to end the conversation. He felt flat, as he wanted instant results, and was tempted to ring again to give other information and hurry the situation along, but persuaded himself not to. Although the line was supposed to be confidential, some alert system would undoubtedly activate if multiple calls were made from the same number. It would be best to allow the system to take its course. Its long, meandering, inefficient course.

Ethan looked at the screen for a few minutes before the

memory of Daisy hit him like a slap to the face. He rang Aislin on his mobile.

"Hi Eth. I wasn't expecting you yet."

"I needed to speak with you. Are you free for a few minutes?"

"Erm… yeah, what's up?"

"I'm going to tell you something and I need you to trust me. I know it's… I just need you to trust me."

"Sounds serious… go on."

"I need you to promise me that you'll never contact Daisy again. Not in any way, meeting her, ringing her, being in contact at all."

"What? Are you being serious?"

"I need you to promise me."

"Ethan… you're not going to tell me not to contact my friend. Who do you think you are?"

"Aislin, I'm not joking, this is important. I've never asked you anything like this before and I'll never do it again. Please."

"Has she rung you while I've been away? You didn't start up that stupid argument about the news again, did you?"

"I've not seen her since she last came over. Have you seen her?"

"I've had my phone off most of the time I've been here, not that I have to tell you when I call my friends. Ethan, are you drunk? What's this about?"

"You know that in our jobs we can't always tell each other the details about what we get up to day to day. Please, Ash, please."

His voice cracked and she paused before replying in a more emollient tone. "I'll promise that I won't ring her until I get back. But Ethan, I'm not cutting off a friend just because you tell me to. You're scaring me."

"No no, it's not like that… I'm sorry to ring out the blue like this… I don't want to put you under any extra pressure… I'm sorry…"

"I've got to go, I'll ring you later."

"Okay… I'm sorry… I'm sorry…"

He sat on the sofa and felt like crying, although no tears would come. He sent her a message apologising for how abrupt he had been and waited for a reply. None came.

After all the events of the last few days, Ethan felt as if he was catching his breath after running a marathon and could not stand the prospect of spending the day by himself. He flicked through the contacts in his mobile and could not be bothered to call any of his university friends. He stopped on Mo's number and thought that he had not seen him outside work for a few weeks. He rang it without any expectation that he would be free.

"Hi Eth, what's up?"

"All right, how are you? All well?"

"Yeah fine, just the usual shit, you know. The whole weekend meet and greet the family blah. Better than work though, eh?"

"Tell me about it. I was just wondering on the off-chance, are you free for a drink later?"

"Erm… yeah, why not? Hasna's gone to her mum and dad's for the day so I'm pretty much free. What time were you thinking?"

"Let's say, three?"

"That's good for me. I've got to do a few bits round the house but I'll be done by then. Usual place?"

"Course. Cool, see you later."

"Okay, see ya."

Ethan felt a sense of relief.

The afternoon before he went out seemed like dead time. The knowledge that he could easily sleep for a few hours, that no one would know the difference, prayed on his mind. He watched the MV mindlessly, making time slip away until he noticed with a start that he had to go.

Mohammed grinned when seeing him, making Ethan copy his expression.

"Pleased to see me, are ya?"

"Mate, you know that I can't stand to be away from you. I only go on leave to keep up appearances."

"You're not lying either."

"You know I'm not."

Ethan laughed.

"Come on, get inside, I don't want you standing here staring at me all day. It's embarrassing."

"That's what you say now."

They went into the fac and bantered and drank for a few minutes until Ethan said, "Pete was funny with Hugo after you left Friday."

"Go on."

"He stood by him for ages, waiting for him to say somethin'. You know what Hugh's like, he just carried on looking out the window. Pete could have stood there all day and he wouldn't have moved. After probably half an hour, Pete said, 'Can I talk to you a minute?' and Hugh tapped his watch and said, 'On me lunch'. Dweeb said, 'Why you not eating anything then?' and he shrugged and goes 'Not hungry'. Do you know when you have one of those moments when you want to laugh but you know you shouldn't? It was seriously good." Mohammed smiled and shook his head.

Ethan tried to return to the subject of Peter a few minutes later, but Mo only rolled his eyes.

"How's the house hunting going?"

"Yeah, I've done some searches. I haven't gone mad with it yet. The problem is, like I said before, without speaking properly to Ash, I don't know what area she wants or how much she wants to spend. We'll start it properly when she gets back."

"Is she excited about it, do you think?"

"Dunno. Yeah, I think she is. I'm pretty sure she is. I suppose the details are not as exciting as when we agreed to do it."

"Wait until you're buying furniture, then she'll perk up. I can guarantee that. You want another drink?"

"Go on then."

"Same again?"

"Yeah. You know… there was a… one of her friends—"

"Hang on, mate, you can't talk without a drink in front of ya."

Ethan nodded and Mo went to the bar. As he watched his back, Ethan thought that he could not tell him anything. *We've always got on and he's been my partner for years, but ultimately… no one can be trusted unconditionally.*

When Mohammed came back, he placed the drinks on the table and grinned.

"Go on, what were you saying?"

"Nothing… just that I was looking forward to moving and everything."

"Yeah, it'll be good…" Mohammed sipped his drink and stretched his arms, "… It's been hard work with Hasna lately."

"With her mum and dad?"

Mohammed spoke very quickly. "No. Well, a bit, they've not been helping. She's gone off on one again, she's been… all kind of… distracted. Like yesterday, she said that she wouldn't know what she would have done if it were a boy because she wouldn't know how to talk to a boy. Then when I asked her what she meant, she burst out crying and had a go at me. I think she might have depression or something."

"Oh? How long's she been like that?"

"This lot started up in the last few weeks. I said to her the other day that maybe she should see a doctor, but she screamed at me until I said to forget about it. That's what she does now when I say something she doesn't like, she screams until I give up…"

Ethan nodded and looked at the table.

"I'm fed up at the moment. No one tells you about this stuff. Maybe it happens with loads of couples, God knows. It's got to the point where I wish we were back to how things were before sometimes."

He looked at Ethan until he felt that he had to say something.

"Maybe you should talk to her about seeing the doctor again."

"She'd never go for that. Not with her mum blaring in her ear. She'll come up with some blar about why it's forbidden. Isn't it funny that everything that's forbidden is the same as everything she doesn't want to do?"

Ethan nodded.

"I just… I don't know what to do these days. I dreaded going home last week. How sad is that? Can you imagine – I'd rather sit around listening to Hugo all day."

Ethan waited until the silence became awkward before saying, "If you ever want to talk about it then just give me a ring or whatever…"

"Cheers… anyway, enough of that drama. It's all a load of rubbish, isn't it? You have to do this and say the other just because someone decided it was a good idea once. If only people would let everyone do their own thing, we wouldn't have half the shit that goes on."

"Yeah… yeah…"

As he drove, Ethan gritted his teeth at the thought that he always listened to other people without ever receiving anything in return. *Everyone takes advantage of the fact that I'm the only one who can sort things out.*

He felt wistful by the time he got home. *Why wouldn't I want to live with my girlfriend? It's normal, it's what everyone does.* He switched on the MV.

He had been worried that he would fall asleep in the evening then lie awake all night and set the week off on a disastrous course. However, he found that concentrating on the screen enabled him to stay awake, despite the heavy feeling behind his eyes, until ten to eleven, when he brushed his teeth with a strange relish. *If only I could spend my whole life in front of the MV then I'd be fine, probably.*

When he got to bed, he felt so exhausted that he was surprised he had not collapsed before putting his pyjamas on. He worked out how many hours sleep he would have that night, and how many more hours that would be than he had been used to recently. It felt as if he had entered a promised land. When he realised how long he had been thinking about the situation, he felt alarmed, as he must have cut into his sleep by at least half an hour. He wanted to get up and check the time but decided that that would only make him more tense. Worse, thinking that deeply meant that he did not feel tired anymore. Ethan folded his arms and did his utmost to clear his mind.

He made good progress with Hypnos the following week and only worked a few hours over, which meant that he went to bed earlier than usual, adding to his virtuous cycle. Keeping regular hours enabled him to contact Aislin daily. She did not mention their conversation about Daisy, and one night, she said that she was glad she had gone to Ireland, as her father had not been as 'focused' for years. Ethan was unconvinced but told her how pleased he was and agreed to set up a meeting with a mortgage adviser for the week she was back.

He went to bed at eleven that Sunday too, and when he got up refreshed on the Monday morning, he felt that he had established a new routine that meant he could live sensibly again. Aislin would be back in two weeks, which seemed to mark the end of an era in his life, giving his final time by himself a somewhat baroque feel. The coming events seemed large and frightening, like when he had moved from little school to big school as a child. Nevertheless, no matter what his feelings were, he had committed to his path and had to follow it.

When Ethan opened his e-mails that morning, he read a message from Security Support, telling him that he needed to fill in the attached document to accompany his security access form before he would be able to view the restricted record. It took him a moment to remember what they were talking about, before the fear he had felt re-emerged. He at first thought that perhaps he could send an edited version of his investigation report, but the policy was that no one but him should see that until it was complete, as multiple versions of reports cause confusion. In normal circumstances, he would have rung the relevant manager and ordered them to do what he wanted.

After thinking about the situation for some time, he filled in the document with his details and the relevant reference numbers, before giving the reason as: 'following up an identified enquiry on a medium priority SC case'. *If they want more than that then they'll have to ring me.*

Ethan thought that the policeman had never got back to him. He went on the Internet to get the switchboard number then booked half an hour in the interview room so that he could speak to him using voice distortion. He muttered to himself as he walked to it. "No fucker can do anything right." He rang the number and a woman answered, asking if he knew who he wanted to speak to.

"This is the SDMA. I need to speak to DS Tomalin."

"One moment please…" There was silence and Ethan enjoyed the tinge of fear in her voice. "Can I check the name please?"

"DS Tomalin."

"Can you spell that?"

He did so, elongating the letters sarcastically.

"I'm sorry. No one of that name works here."

"What? That isn't right. Could he have retired? I need you to check your personnel files."

"I'm sorry, sir. I have done. We don't have an officer of that name."

Ethan hung up. He sat still in the darkness. *What the fuck is going on?* He'd got a police e-mail address and it was a recorded case. He had a sudden hope that he might have made a mistake with the name or department, and was about to jump up before thinking that he knew they were right. Who would be able to pull off this kind of stunt? And why? In normal circumstances, Ethan would have immediately reported the possible security breach. But now, he felt that he would only be exposing himself. He held his head in his hands. *Fuck.*

That lunchtime, Ethan went to the shops for food, contrary to his usual routine. Nodding at the security guard on his way out gave him an unpleasant reminder of the time he had fallen asleep at his desk.

When in a supermarket picking out pears, someone pushed into Ethan with enough force to make him double over. It felt like something was stuck in his back. He brushed his hands over it and was relieved to find that there was nothing there. He turned around to see a thin, reedy man in a dirty coat leaning against a shelf on the other side of the aisle, glaring at him ostentatiously. Ethan looked away then looked back to see him still staring. The blood drained from Ethan's face. He clutched his fruit to his chest and hurried to the counter.

His every movement seemed significant, and he ignored the shop assistant who served him to look around for the man, making her loudly repeat the amount he had to pay. Ethan left the shop and made his way back to the SDMA building at barely less than a run. He had a strong impression that he was being followed.

When he realised that he was outside the jewellery shop, his heart froze. He could no longer tell whether or not he was moving. It was no surprise when someone pushed into him with enough force to knock him over. As he was sprawled in the doorway, Ethan glimpsed a cloak before a flash of pain made him put his hands over his eyes. When he looked up, people were hurrying their steps to walk around him.

Before the latest incident, the city had seemed flat and existed on a single plain; now, spaces between apparently solid structures opened up to him, each containing another world. Ethan felt something scratching his neck and realised that he was lying on a carrier bag containing a wedge of papers. He stood and stumbled along the road before slipping into another supermarket. He went into a toilet and locked the stall door.

The first pages of the report comprised a series of grainy pictures of the Professor taken from various angles that had to be surveillance photographs. The remaining pages were filled with small script with no space between the lines. His first thought was to flush it away, before thinking that to do so before reading it was even more dangerous. He tried to fold the papers but there were too many of them. After a moment's reflection, fatalism overtook him and he put them back in the bag.

As he walked to the SDMA building, Ethan thought that he should have skim-read the report, berating himself for his stupidity. *If I lose it now then I'll never know. Whenever something like this happens, I lose my head and act like an idiot. Nothing I do makes the slightest fucking sense.* He debated with himself as to whether he should hide somewhere to study it. *They'd only have given papers to me like that if there was some urgency.* However, it would look too suspicious not to return to his desk.

When he got there, he nodded at Mo and said "all right?" in what Ethan hoped was a natural voice. Yet again, reality had been undone and he felt like a soldier in a foreign country, not knowing which of the smiling natives would be the one to slide a blade in his back. Or through his ribs.

"How you getting on?"

"What?" Ethan sounded very weak, as if he were being strangled.

"Secret squirrel project number one. You know, whatever it is you've been doing for God knows how long?"

"Oh, yeah, right, sorry, I was miles away then. Erm… not too long now, I think. A few of the sections need expanding to cover what the bosses were asking about when they came down the other week, otherwise, it's just a matter of sorting out a load of bits and pieces. You know what it's like, whenever you do something like this, you spend the most time on the tiniest details that no one ever reads and no one except you cares about."

"You won't know what to do with yourself when it's over. You've been hobnobbing with the people who go to meetings for too long to go back to investigating what time an HGV driver fell asleep outside a warehouse. You won't look at anything other than a one now. In fact, you've probably got a special category of zero designed just for you."

"Shut up."

"You will, I'm not joking. It's all set out for you now. New house. Girlfriend moving in. Starting to look at rings I bet. Going to lots of meetings. You know what all this means, don't ya?"

"What?"

Mohammed leant over his desk and looked at him portentously. "You're a dickhead." He laughed with childish simplicity.

Ethan smiled, hardly recognising his words. He wrote for some time until reaching the end of a sentence and remembering the papers at his feet with a sickening feeling. He surreptitiously nudged the carrier bag further under his desk. The papers crinkled, the sound seeming to echo around the office, and he froze like a cat in a flashlight, holding his breath.

For the rest of the day, Ethan alternated between concentrating on his work then suddenly remembering the papers. Whenever it happened, it took all his mental strength to force himself not to look down, after which he would imagine them being blown around the office by the air conditioning then being traced back to him. He could not leave them so did not go to the toilet for the entire afternoon, the pressure against his groin amplifying his discomfort.

Ethan left at the end of his scheduled shift. In addition to needing as much time as he could to look through the papers, the timing would hopefully throw off anyone following him. His world was now dominated by minute fears.

The train was unusually busy and he did not get a seat. Ethan stood in the middle of a carriage, clutching a bar. His legs felt as if they were going to crumple any moment and he constantly put his spare hand in the bag, checking the papers as if reading them in Braille. His discomfort was so severe that he felt his eyes start to close several times and had to pinch the backs of his legs and squeeze the bar to remain upright.

He broke down the journey into five-minute sections but even then, each one was horribly long and he was so exhausted that only his fingernails held him in place.

When he got home, Ethan looked out the window, listening to cars drive past, his feet throbbing like a heartbeat. Eventually, he closed the blinds and spread the papers over the floor before lying beside a radiator. He read the first line of the first page without the slightest recognition of the words before falling asleep.

He woke five hours later. When he lifted his head, Ethan felt the same sluggish indifference as after his last bout of illegal sleep. He lay back down and drifted off again for a short time before standing. He was amazed to see that it was past eleven. Despite how irregular his recent lifestyle had been, sleeping the day away still amazed him. He stumbled around awhile, weary and hungry. He did not know whether or not to eat, as if he did then he would not sleep again that night, but on the other hand, how could he go to work the next day on only his breakfast?

He cooked some soup, keeping the papers nearby as if following some arcane superstition. He switched on the MV and flicked through the channels compulsively. Eventually, his awareness of the papers became too great. It was madness to have left them scattered around like that – what if someone had knocked on the door? Still, it was hardly the worst thing he had done lately.

He spent several minutes putting them in the right order and tapping their edges against the floor to ensure that they were perfectly lined up. The night had opened to him after his illicit sleep. He read the report by the light of his mobile.

The photographs of the Professor showed him leaving various buildings, followed by a series of close-ups in which he looked directly at the camera. He was much thinner then, making Ethan think that they must have been taken long ago. No other figures were present. Only the DIA could have that kind of interest. The word 'Secret' was written at the top and bottom of every page.

After the pictures followed a page comprising a detailed physical description below the heading 'Subject H-Alpha'. Ethan only knew that it related to the Professor by the reference to the mole on his neck, as it was impossible to believe that he once weighed ten stone.

The remainder of the document was written in very closely typed script, in a thick blurry font, like that produced by a typewriter. Ethan read greedily, so willing to get to the end that he skipped ahead several times, only to lose the meaning of a sentence and have to go back.

Subject H-Alpha

Subject H-Alpha was introduced following his arrest in September 2030 under the Subversion Act. Significant evidence was gathered prior to that arrest to justify charge in security court five. However, the charges were later held on file. Associated case REM13/T1205/30 was also held on file. A summary of the material gathered during those cases is included as an appendix.

Ethan paused at the reference to an SDMA case number. Typically, when a person was charged with other criminal offences that implicitly involved SC breaches, the main offences would take precedence and the SC breaches ignored, as the mainstream judiciary had reached the widely publicised conclusion that two prosecutions would result in double jeopardy, as the same act would be punished twice. However, in a subversion case, DIA courts were not bound by those judgements.

Ethan went to his bedroom for a piece of scrap paper to copy the reference number onto. The report continued:

> Subsequent to the above mentioned events, the following risk assessments were carried out:

The rest of the page, and three subsequent pages, comprised a series of tables filled with arrows, letters, and numbers. Ethan's eyes slid over them and he read the next few sentences before thinking that he would not understand the rest of the report if he didn't work them out. He flicked back to the first table and forced himself to concentrate, picking his nails until they bled.

The letters at the top of the columns cross-referenced with a key at the end of the tables, which went on for a page. However, it did not make the meaning any clearer, as the words the letters represented had nothing to do with anything Ethan knew about the Professor or the DIA. For example, several columns were headed with the letter 'O', below and to the side of which were a series of numbers and other letters. The key defined 'O' as meaning 'Octave' in most circumstances, although 'Orange' when followed by one-five, except four.

After several minutes, he sighed and moved on.

> The subject demonstrates some considerable intelligence and was able to speak knowledgably on a number of sleep related security matters. The subject's reliability is confirmed by their lack of…

Ethan turned the page to see a series of short paragraphs, each starting with a reference number, the format of which he did not recognise, followed by place names with some of the letters mixed up. After a moment's thought, he realised that they had to relate to the pictures. He wanted to know what the subject 'lacked', but the next paragraph did not follow on. He skim read the report but could not find the end of the sentence.

To his surprise, Ethan suddenly felt tired. *Perhaps it's reading that does it.* He clasped the papers to his chest and added the idea to his canon of superstition about exhaustion. The MV staves it off, reading increases it. He was about to go to bed when he thought that he needed to hide the report. The easiest and safest thing would be to destroy it, of course, but he could not deny himself. Vague impressions of conspiracies swirled around the edges of his thoughts; menacing figures looking out of windows from offices far away. He could only imagine what was happening as generalised evil, the elusiveness of the feeling making it all the more real.

Ethan slept sporadically for several hours and when he woke in the night, he was alert for what seemed a long time, his senses crisp. He could hear the pitch of wind outside and discerned which direction it blew from the impact it made on the windows; his eyes were attuned to the slightest change in the shadows and how they leapt between the blinds.

Eventually, he drifted into hazy semi-consciousness in which he had a strong impression of himself but did not know where he was.

When Ethan realised that he was underwater, he screamed and salty water filled his mouth. The pain was so real that he felt both the sensation of drowning and his body jolting in his bed. His vision was bleary and he could sense the water dissolving his eyes. Darkness was worse when he closed them. He thrashed his arms to move in tiny increments.

He was there for years, for lifetimes. Everything went dull, then his senses were acute again. He saw the pink tendril. He forced himself towards it, swallowing more water. His vision reduced to mere impressions of colours. The orbs stung his hands as he climbed, digging into his flesh like a series of tiny drills. He gripped tighter the worse it got.

When he came to the surface, water poured from his eyes. He rubbed them ineffectually against his shoulders. He opened his mouth and air tasted acrid in the back of his throat. He pulled the tendril, which continued boundlessly into the air, and the world rocked, the sea shifting places with the sky, crashing against his back. Ethan was a creature of pure instinct and continued to pull himself along, deeper into the ocean…

He jumped when woken by his alarm clock and was surprised to find that his room was light. Nagging exhaustion kept his legs fastened to the bed. Ethan imagined that if he slept for another twenty minutes, he would be perfectly rested. However, that missing twenty minutes was like a jigsaw puzzle with a single lost piece – the absence enough to ruin the image in a horribly obvious way.

Twelve

AFTER STRUGGLING THROUGH THAT MORNING, working as hard as he was able, Ethan ate his sandwiches at his desk.

"Have you even been to the basement?" he asked Mohammed.

"I've never been on any other floor, except on my first day when I was getting my pass and everything. Why?"

"I need a few references for some of the things I'm saying in the report."

"It'll say what you've got to do on the intranet."

"I know. I'll have to get dweeb to sign a form, that won't be a problem. It's just the hassle, that's all."

After having spoken, Ethan thought that Mo might volunteer to get the information for him.

"When do you need it?"

"As soon as possible really."

"There must be a fast-track process, what does it say you have to do?"

"Hang on, let me just check something." Ethan went to the relevant section on the intranet and did not mention the subject again.

Later that afternoon, he printed the form, filled it in, then went into Peter's office.

"Hi. I need you to sign this, it's for access to stuff in the basement. It needs your authority."

"Yes, I, yes… I was going to speak to you in the next few days. It's good that you've come in, you've reminded me. I think we need to review what's going on to make sure that… The workload is affecting the rest of the office, you see…"

"Yeah, fine, it's almost done now anyway. Can you sign this then so I can do what I need to do?"

"Yes, the… Why do you need to do this exactly? What's the—?"

"If you remember, Dan said that Hypnos was going to have priority over everything else. Are you going to sign this or do you want me to ring him?"

Ethan realised that he had raised his voice. However, his awareness of how unreasonable he was being only further irritated him.

"Ethan… give it here but I will need to speak to you next week. I'll arrange a meeting with Dan to go over what I think the issues are."

He signed the form and gave it back to him. Ethan checked it, feeling chastened. He had hoped that he had signed in the wrong place or ticked the wrong box, but he had no justification to do anything other than mumble 'thanks' before leaving the office ill at ease.

He went through his report and compiled a list of the information he needed from archived material. The next step was to arrange for a porter to escort him.

There was a section on the intranet where the contact details of SDMA and some DIA workers could be searched by name or job type. Ethan searched for porter and was surprised when only two records came up. *They must never leave the building.* Entries for most members of staff gave their name, floor, office designation, a landline, and a job title, but the entries for the porters only gave a mobile and a title of 'one' and 'two'. Ethan did not know whether that represented a rank or was only a way to differentiate them. In case it was the former, he copied out the mobile for 'two'.

He worked late that night, not wanting anyone to overhear his call. There was no logical reason for his fear, as now he had the signed form, he had a legitimate reason for what he was doing and no one listening would be able to tell any different. However, even so, he was not prepared to take any chances where the porters were concerned.

He read his checklist many times. When Mohammed stood to leave, Ethan was about to make a joke about him working part time before seeing that it was six o'clock.

"Don't stay too late." Mo smiled wryly.

"All right, see you tomorrow."

"Bye."

His concentration was broken and he waited for the overhead lights to flicker off. However, two sets of desks were still illuminated twenty minutes later, and Ethan was first annoyed then suspicious, as it was rare for more than one team to stay late.

Ethan typed as if attacking his keyboard.

He worked until his stomach rumbled, then saw that it was eight o'clock. The other lights were still on. He stood in the walkway, where he heard whispering and pages being turned. There was nothing wrong with the lights; his colleagues were still there. He decided to go home.

When he went through the security lips on his floor, he thought that he did not know how big the building was. Of course, he had looked up at it before entering many times, but had never even seen it from the back. With the amount of paperwork they stored, never mind the amount of staff who worked there, it seemed impossible that it was only fifteen storeys tall. The other floors seemed like enchanted forests, containing the wild magic of the organisation. There had to be unique colours and machines hidden within secret passages, which were only stumbled upon occasionally, perhaps once a lifetime, yet were very real.

When the train arrived, he sat in a group of four seats. A man wearing a Stetson sat opposite him and opened a broadsheet newspaper. A moment later, he peered at him over the top of it. Ethan stood and sat as far away from other passengers as he could.

He jolted when hearing his stop being called and looked around in alarm, unsure whether he had been asleep. The train was almost empty. There was no one close enough who would have been able to see what he was doing. After he had obsessed over the situation, Ethan felt sure that he had been daydreaming. *I would've known, I'd have slumped on the seat. I definitely wasn't asleep. Definitely not.*

When he got home, Ethan thought that his life had been paused; the only important thing now was to follow up the lead he had been given. Feeling refreshed after his journey back, he read the remainder of the file while eating biscuits for dinner:

> Subject H-Alpha has an unexpected ability for leadership and organisation, as illustrated by their involvement in the REM/125T41/24 incident. The inability of subversive groups to commit to a sustained strategic plan has long proven problematic; by example, and by the evidence of their success, Subject H-Alpha has the ability to change this.
>
> Subject H-Alpha has also shown a distinct aptitude to instil discipline within section five through decisive action. Most notably, the removal of M-Alpha has ensured that all actions undertaken by section five go through agreed channels. Furthermore, alternative, more radical sources of leadership in the section have been seriously weakened (REM/126Z53/26 refers).

The following list identifies all other cases that Subject H-Alpha has been involved with since being initialised:

REM/125T41/24
REM/126S41/24
REM/128T41/24
REM/129A41/24
REM/131C41/24
REM/134H41/24
REM/135I41/24
REM/135JT41/24

The organisational cascade following the introduction of disciplined methods has led to SC breaches increasing by 35% in Subject H-Alpha's sector since their introduction and 3% nationally. Other subversion events increased by 10% in Subject H-Alpha's sector and 2% nationally.

There is further significance in the research carried out by Subject H-Alpha beyond its correlation to the level of subversion events. This will be summarised here – full details are available in the archive under reference D50034A/24.

There followed a series of abstracts written in italics, describing experiments to determine the effects of various scenarios on sleep patterns, including manipulation of temperature, levels of sunlight and artificial light, the type and amount of food consumed over different periods of time, and many others.

Ethan struggled to understand them, as much of the language was highly technical, with several words that he could not find the meaning of on the Internet. Also, some of the report was given over to statistical analysis that was poorly presented and difficult to interpret. He found his attention wandering and only read on because he thought he should, his eyes flicking over the words without recognition.

After he had finished, he went to his bedroom, stretched, then meandered to the kitchen and poured himself a glass of water. The sense that he should be doing something remained very strong in him; he thought that he should have found a way to ring the porter, even risking using his personal mobile. Although it was late, he did not feel tired, and it was only by supreme effort that he forced himself to return the file to its hiding place in the airing cupboard.

His mobile rang and Ethan was surprised to see that it was Terry, as it seemed so long since they had last met that he had assumed their friendship had run its natural course. "Hi. How are you?"

"Listen, I've got no time for small talk. Listen…" he paused until Ethan said "okay", "… there's something gone wrong, *badly* wrong. I've upset some seriously bad people and I don't know what to do.

"Right, listen to this. I've started doing my photography again, I've got pictures in magazines and everything, it was going really well. The problem is, I was doing some landscapes in this place I know round the corner and some dodgy people were in the shots. I went back the next day and they were doing the same thing. They were plotting something, definitely. So now, it's not landscapes, it's… action pictures, you know, *action*. I don't know what they were up to. They must have been burying things…"

"Right, erm—"

"I've got to go, I'm going to lock the door. I'll call you back in a few days. Think about it. I need some advice on what to do next."

He hung up and Ethan looked at his mobile before switching it off. Terry sounded as if he had been drinking. He hoped that he would not ring back. Ethan realised that the SDMA had changed him too much for him to be friends with Terry anymore. Perhaps too much to be friends with anyone.

He was hardly aware of what he was doing the following day, as he thought about nothing other than calling porter two. He heard different combinations of his colleagues going to meetings at various times, although maddeningly, there was never a point when they were all away at the same time.

At five, Mohammed asked, "How long do you think you've got left on that thing?"

"What?"

"That thing you've been working on since just after you were born."

"Oh right… I don't know."

"Well… don't forget all that trouble you had with Ash about your hours. You don't want to start an argument with her as soon as she gets back."

Ethan looked up in surprise. "Yeah, yeah, I know what you're saying."

"Anyway… I'll see you tomorrow."

"Yeah, have a good one. See you later."

After Mohammed had left the room, Ethan raised himself just enough that he could see over the dividers, to discover that the same two spaces from the previous day were again illuminated.

He knew what information he needed off by heart by now. Ethan was considering whether his colleagues would be able to hear him from where they sat when he heard shuffling. They said goodbye to him a few minutes later.

Now that he was on his own, Ethan thought over what he was going to say, and the awareness that he was scripting a telephone call made him feel awkward. He picked up the receiver and his thumb slid off the end, slick with sweat. It took him three attempts to give his blood sample. He rang the number from the note he had taken the previous day. It was answered with silence after a single ring.

"Hello? Hello, is that porter two?"

"Who is this please?"

"Hi. This is agent Ethan Thomas, from the tenth floor? I needed some help with a floor visit."

"This might be a wrong number. What's your number please and I'll call you back."

Ethan gave him his landline, feeling confused, then hung up. He looked at his screen and after a few minutes, he checked the number he had called, first on his notes then on the intranet. It was definitely the right one. He was about to try it again when his landline rang.

"Hello, tenth floor, Ethan speaking."

"Can you state your full name and designation please?"

It was the same man he had spoken to before.

"Ethan Thomas, tenth floor. Sleep investigator. Office 12 slash 91T."

"And your reference?"

"202154T."

"Are you in your office now?"

"Yeah."

"Hello Ethan, this is Two, how can I help you?"

"Thanks for ringing me back. What it was… well, like I said before, I need to arrange a floor visit to the basement to look through some files. Is that something you can help me with?"

"You have, of course, got the necessary security clearance?"

"Yeah."

"Good. As a matter of fact, a gap in the schedule has arisen in three hours' time. Is that convenient?"

"That'll be great."

"Excellent. You were fortunate; the next gap is in five weeks and two days. You will be picked up from your office, by One, of course. You have been allotted one hour, including the time it will take to move between floors."

"Thanks, that'll be plenty."

"Good."

He hung up and Ethan thought about how disapproving he had sounded when saying that One would escort him, as if he had discerned the reason why he had contacted Two. Nowhere in the policy had it stated which porter needed to oversee a visit, but listening to him for a few seconds had convinced Ethan that he would see through any attempt to explain himself.

Ethan spent ten minutes reading through the authorisation form, double checking Peter's signature, before standing and looking along the line of desks. The movement made several lights flicker on, and wall shadows scattered like disturbed insects.

He went back to Hypnos until realising that a man was standing at the back of Mohammed's chair, watching Ethan unblinking. He jumped as if a slug had dropped on his flesh.

"Mr Thomas, can I see your identity pass please?"

The man raised his eyebrows as if having identified a misdeed. Wrinkles hid his features like a mask and he remained still as Ethan looked through his pockets and under piles of paper for it.

"Are you One?"

Ethan handed the man his pass, who examined it for a few seconds before looking at him, then inspected it again.

"I am. Can I see your authorisation, Mr Thomas? We have less than an hour now."

"Yep."

Ethan handed him the form, and he examined it in the same way as he had his identity pass.

"Follow me please, Mr Thomas."

Ethan took his notepad and locked his computer.

"Wait there please. What did you just pick up?"

"A list of the reference numbers of files I need to access. And some paper so that I can make notes for my report."

"Paper and a pen will be provided. Let me see that please, Mr Thomas."

The act had quickly become exasperating and Ethan had to suppress a sigh when giving One his notebook, which he examined with the same thoroughness as everything else, reading every page several times then shaking it over his desk. One put it in his pocket.

"This will be returned to you. Please empty your pockets of any items, including handkerchiefs. You may not take any items of any kind to another floor. This is your last chance to remove any items you may be carrying. Carrying any unauthorised items after this point may result in disciplinary, criminal, or extraordinary action. Do you understand the caution, Mr Thomas?"

"Yes. I'm not carrying anything."

Despite having told the truth, Ethan checked his pockets as he spoke, an action that One noted with a flick of his eyes.

"Follow me please, Mr Thomas."

The room lit up in sections as they walked, as if One could command electricity, illuminating him for the first time since Ethan had seen him. He wore an extremely smart loosely fitting suit that hid the outline of his body. When they reached the lift, One pressed the button to call it then stood at the other side of the door. He adjusted his tie, revealing for a moment a red sash that ran diagonally across his spotless white shirt.

The lift seemed to take a long time to arrive and the wait was awkward, as whenever Ethan caught One's eyes, he looked back with disinterested attention, as if watching a neighbour's dog.

When the lift opened, they went inside and One said, "Your identity card, please."

Ethan gave it to him and One scanned it over a wand-shaped device, which he then inserted into a hole in the wall, under the buttons for the different floors. He pressed the '0' button, which stuck out further from the wall than the rest.

Ethan's stomach flipped when the lift lurched down. He shifted from one leg to the other before putting his hands in his pockets and leaning against the wall. *There must be something wrong. We could have gone from the top of the building and back again by now.* One seemed entirely relaxed, which, given what Ethan had seen of him, did not mean much. He gave the impression that he would barely bring himself to raise an eyebrow if he was robbed at gunpoint.

"Did I follow policy by contacting Two first? I wasn't sure which of you I should have rung."

One turned by pivoting on his heels, looking at him as if having decided to fulfil his curiosity. The lift jumped before opening and One stepped out.

Immediately beyond the door was a small square room, one side of which was filled with a series of panels containing brightly coloured, twinkling buttons. The wall opposite was featureless grey except for a monitor in its centre. One pushed his pass into the bottom of it, making a hidden section extend. He touched it first with the index finger of his right hand, then the thumb of his left. He typed something into a miniature keyboard and a door opened. "This way please."

Ethan followed him.

"Stop."

Ethan did as he was instructed and there was a flash powerful enough to make him rub his eyes. When he opened them, red circles danced around his vision.

"Raise your arms please, Mr Thomas."

Ethan did so and there was another flash, this time hurting his eyes enough to make his head jerk back violently.

"Turn out your pockets please, Mr Thomas."

Ethan did so and One stepped forward to squeeze them.

"Follow me please."

Ethan stood still, taken aback for a few seconds, before putting

269

his pockets back in. He had had the same feeling when meeting the DIA Regional Director, of a divide born out of an unbridgeable difference in rank. Not wanting to be left behind, Ethan hurried to follow him.

Beyond the square room was a corridor that did not seem quite straight, making him feel as if he were leaning to one side as he walked through it. Grey lumps stuck out of the walls in places, which, together with the cool air, gave him the impression that he was passing a rock face. There were doors at regular intervals either side but One only stopped when reaching one fastened shut by a circular metal sheet with square teeth around its edges. There was a monitor in its centre like the one in the previous room.

"Wait there please, Mr Thomas."

One positioned himself to the side so that he could operate the computer while watching Ethan. One pressed combinations of his fingers into a slot on the keyboard before typing.

After he had finished, the door swung back. Ethan was confused for a moment, as given its shape, he had expected it to roll to one side. The teeth had to be fake. One looked at him and Ethan followed, grimacing when thinking that he was about to be called 'Mr Thomas' again. *I've not been called that since I got detention at school.*

The room beyond was featureless sky blue and stretched so far that Ethan could not tell where it ended. The walls were covered with barely perceivable cracks.

"You have thirty six minutes, Mr Thomas."

"Right... What am I supposed to... Where are the files?"

"May I refer to your notes, Mr Thomas?"

"Go on."

The formality was now entirely tiresome. One took the notebook from his pocket with an elaborate gesture then pressed the nearest crack. A panel opened and he typed something into what had to be a computer inside. In that moment, Ethan's irritation fell away and he was as excited as a little boy. He stood on tiptoe to tantalise himself with a glimpse of flashing colours. It was as if he had stepped into a spaceship.

"Mr Thomas, you have high enough access to view all the files referred to in your notes. They're stored in two different areas. Follow me please."

Ethan felt a sense of danger, as the 'two different areas' must refer to the information he genuinely needed, and the information about the Professor. He hoped beyond hope that One would take him to the files relevant to Hypnos first, as that would mean that he could spend however much time he needed on his legitimate enquiries and consider the rest a bonus.

They walked for what seemed several minutes before One stopped and tapped the wall above a crack. A panel jutted out and he pulled it forward.

"The files are in reference order, Mr Thomas. You can read them on the monitor there; some have been transferred to the electronic system, but I'm afraid no guarantee can be made that all of them were."

There were a series of dividers and files inside the cabinet, with a computer panel built into one side of it. One gave him a pen and a square of notepaper with narrowly spaced blue lines.

The cabinet was so large that Ethan could not reach across it and thought that he could fit inside. He felt an incipient smile on his lips before quelling the expression, feeling One's dead eyes on him. He pulled the cabinet out as far as it would go. The papers were so neatly ordered that he soon found the source details for the cases that demonstrated the links between Iklonian activity and the degradation of infrastructure. The files displayed a perfection of organisation that made him feel that he was looking into the nature of things.

Whenever he took out a file, Ethan sensed One taking a mental deep breath, his psychic peace disturbed by the possibility of it being put back in the wrong place. The efficiency of the basement contrasted sharply with the chaos of the rest of the organisation, and that it was apparently maintained by two men gave it an otherworldly, archaic air.

Ethan made notes of details that were not on Mirror. He wrote as small as he could, not wanting to ask One for more paper, as there would certainly be another procedure for doing so that would take him over his time limit.

When he had looked at most of the files he needed for Hypnos, Ethan started to dawdle, thinking that he did not want to mark out the file relating to the Professor as special by spending a noticeably longer time on it than the others. After taking an age to read the last file he legitimately needed to view, he slid the drawer back into the wall. "Thank you."

One slipped beside him and locked the drawer with a click.

"Do we have time to look at the other file I was interested in?"

One slowly turned to look at him with an inscrutable expression, as if he were made out of brass.

"There are seventeen minutes remaining, Mr Thomas, ten of which must be spent returning to your floor. Whether that's enough time, only you can say."

Ethan did not want to reply and initiate conversation, which with One always took longer than necessary; Ethan was driven to distraction by his stare and the lumbering way in which he eventually started to move. It was like watching a statue coming to life. Eventually, he examined Ethan's notes in his ponderous way, displaying no recognition, as if they were written in a foreign language, before moving deeper into the basement.

One opened a drawer that was as long as the other one, although there was only a single folder inside. Ethan expected him to say something but he only withdrew to just outside his vision like he had before.

Ethan checked the file number before weighing it in his hands as if it were a Christmas present. It was very light. After the first divider was a single page, on which was written:

> All files relating to Project Samson have been classified
> as TOP SECRET by Senior Agent Daniel Lee, reference
> 102x/15.

There was an illegible signature underneath those words, followed
by a black rectangle that covered the remainder of the page. The
paper had a grainy quality and was clearly photocopied. Ethan
put the file away and was about to say that he was finished when
he remembered the computer built into the drawer. He switched
it on and in a few seconds it went to a main menu, where there
were two options. The first was for a contents page for the selected
file. When he clicked on that, a message appeared stating that
the information was unavailable. Ethan went back to the main
menu and moved the cursor over the second option – 'Audit – for
security personnel only'.

"Your time's up, Mr Thomas."

Ethan felt his hand on his shoulder, the grip such that it would
crush him should he clench his fingers. One had to be able to
defend himself, otherwise he would not have come down here
alone with him.

Leaving the basement was like the experience one has after
waking in the night after a vivid dream. The impression is so
strong that reality seems unsatisfactory, and one looks around,
to be confronted by the disappointing blandness of one's
surroundings. Sleep seems only an escape from what one has
seen, such that it is with great reluctance that one is subsumed
into the night. The dream repeats in fragments without the
narrative of before. The story cannot progress and one wakes
tired the following morning with a sense of longing, the sound
of the alarm clock lashing one's back. The feeling of loss is vague
and soon fades into a sad absence.

When they reached his floor, One told him that his notes would be examined for security purposes before being returned to him in the internal post. Ethan nodded, feeling a sudden lack of energy, and went to his desk.

He remained still until the lights went off. There was no reason for him to be there and he wanted more than anything to go home. However, in the same way that he would stay up all night watching the MV and wake exhausted rather than going to bed, Ethan could not be bothered to stand and walk to the train station.

He flicked through the contacts on his mobile. Aislin was near the top of the list and he rang her from the landline. *I may as well use the free phone.*

"Hello?"

"Hi Ash, it's me. How are you?"

"Yeah, good thanks."

Her voice was heavy with sleep, making her sound as if she were underwater.

"Sorry, are you okay to talk? I know it's late."

"Yeah yeah, go on. What's happening?"

"Busy day today, you know how it is."

"Yeah…"

"Sorry, Ash. I'll ring you back tomorrow – you sound knackered."

"No I'm okay, go on, tell me what you're doing."

"This and that. It's hard to say really. When I'm busiest it seems like I get nothing done. I'm really looking forward to seeing you. I've got loads of houses saved on the MV. Some of them have been put on again in the last few weeks at a lower price. That's good for us, isn't it? I don't think it'll take long to pick somewhere."

"We've got to sell ours though, don't forget. It's not good if they're not being sold."

She was fully awake now, and that she showed less than blind optimism filled him with alarm.

"Nah, it'll be no problem."

"Yeah, yeah…"

"Sorry for ringing late, Ash. I just wanted to say that I miss you. I've been thinking about things while you've been away and I've realised that I never make myself clear to you. So that's what I was ringing about, I suppose, to say how much I miss you and that I… I love you…"

"That's really sweet. I'm glad you called. You can call anytime."

"Look, I won't keep you up any more, sorry for ringing when you're so tired. It sounds like you're worn out."

She yawned. "I'm okay."

"I'll speak to you tomorrow then."

"Okay, love you, bye, bye, bye."

She hung up and Ethan held the receiver by his ear. The feeling of not being bothered to move returned the instant their conversation was over and he wished Aislin was with him. He felt desperate in his love for her. He imagined holding her waist in the way she liked until the sensation was almost real.

He did not look at the time before leaving, not wanting to put pressure on himself, as he was aware that such a disruption to his already irregular routine would mean that his alternation between sleepless night and soulless day would continue until the weekend, when he would sleep until the afternoon.

Little happened during the rest of the week, until Friday afternoon, when he realised that he had finished Hypnos. He had sighed when checking the final section, not wanting to start the next part so late in the week. However, when he looked through his notes, there were no revisions left.

It took him a moment to update the contents page, a few minutes to check that the formatting was correct, then he looked at the document in 'print preview' to see that it appeared very professional: full of graphs, charts, headings, all immaculately presented. He security locked the file then flicked through it one final time with no evident purpose other than to delay the moment, before e-mailing it to Dan.

Hi Dan,

Please find attached the completed version of the report, including the amendments and the extra sections, as requested at the meeting on the 25th. If you want to make any other changes then let me know, but I think this is about it…

Thanks,

Ethan

He sat back and closed the file. The idea that he would go back to his usual job on Monday seemed surreal.

"I'm done then," he said to Mo.

"What was that?"

"I said I'm done, that monster job is finished. I've sent it off to Dan."

"Is that everything now then?"

"I think so. He might come back with something else, you know what he's like. And there'll be meetings and the rest of it. But basically, yeah, that's it."

"Crumbs. Well then, mate, you won't be a one-job charlie anymore. How will you manage? Will you be able to cope? Do you need any counselling?"

Ethan smiled. He thought that he should tell Peter, before deciding that he would organise his own workload for a few days. *It's not like the wheel's come off up until now.* He browsed the Internet until he grew bored, then checked his e-mails to see that Dan had replied:

Cheers, Ethan,

Will review this and be in contact soon.

Thanks,

Dan

Ethan looked out of the security glass, contemplating that rarest of situations – leaving early.

"Have a good weekend then, enjoy yourself," he said to Mo.

"Cheers, mate. See you later."

Ethan nodded and smiled at his other colleagues on his way out, hurrying his steps so as not to have to explain himself to anyone.

He was at a loose end when he got home as it was too early to have dinner. At the back of his mind was the thought that if he slept for an hour, he would be refreshed for the weekend. Ethan put on the MV and forced himself to watch until he had forgotten his boredom.

Thirteen

THAT WEEKEND, ETHAN FELT VAGUE anxiety about what would happen when he returned to work, combined with the sense that when Aislin came back, their relationship would finally run its natural course. His fear about the late night with the porter disrupting his sleep patterns did not come to pass, except on the Sunday morning when he switched off his alarm clock then dozed for half an hour. A situation that would have horrified him two months earlier now counted as success.

He felt well enough that he was able to drive to work on Monday, experiencing a strange mix of new and old as he travelled his familiar journey. Several shops had been boarded up since the previous week, and after he had parked, his feet tingled on his every step.

As he walked, he thought that he was still adjusting to the fact that he had lost indefinable parts of himself to exhaustion. His eyes were simultaneously sharp and dull, and the dragons of his dreams looked down at him, kept from swooping by radiant energy from his sandpapered nerves.

When he reached the SDMA building, Ethan felt some satisfaction when checking his watch to see that he had arrived at precisely the time he always had before his problems had started.

There were black-suited guards at the entrance. He nodded at one when he was a few steps away and was taken by surprise when the man stepped forward and grabbed his arm, twisting it so that Ethan doubled over. Someone unseen controlled his other arm.

"What are you doing? I work here."

"We know who you are."

Efficient hands emptied his pockets. His coat was noticeably lighter after his security pass had been removed. There was a pause then they dragged him away with his head held down. Ethan could not hear anyone else, giving him a strange sense of relief that no one would see what had happened. He wondered whether the guards were solely intended for him.

They took him to a white van at the rear of the building. It was smeared with mud and there was an advertisement on its side for window cleaning that he did not have time to read before he was pushed into the back. He sat on a bar then the men went out and appeared in the front a few moments later. There was a divider between them that looked like plexiglas, and when they started talking, Ethan realised that it was soundproof.

As they drove off, he was jolted into the air; there were no seatbelts or anything else to hold him in position. It seemed as if they were driving very quickly, and whenever they stopped or turned, he bounced off the sides like a pinball. He felt pain at random points around his body as if his clothes were filled with biting insects, and after it had happened a few times, he waited for the next jerk with the pensive air of a dog that knows it is about to be kicked. He looked to his right to see whether the men were doing it deliberately, but they were both watching the road, ignoring him.

They can't know much about what's gone on or this would have happened ages ago. At first, Ethan thought about explanations he could give. *They definitely won't know about anything that's happened in my house so it must be something from the jewellery shop that gave me away. I'll just have to say that I was too scared to tell anyone. Perhaps that I didn't trust Peter to deal with anything, that would be believable.* The van swerved and Ethan was propelled into the other side. He felt his nose compress and liquid drip from it. There was no pain, and in his bewilderment, he looked up to see whether rain was leaking from the roof. It was only when he held his nose between his fingers that he realised it was blood.

He could not bring himself to move back, so slouched against the wall, watching blood drip on his trousers. *I'll never get out*, he thought. Ethan stared at the side of the van. *Everyone will know. Aislin will know. Mum and Dad will know. Mo will know. Alfie and Jo will know. That I'm a traitor.*

He tentatively traced the sore spots with a finger. There was a space on his back where he felt a burning pain, a feeling that continued when he wrapped his arms around his knees. *It's all over.* He cried, making the places where he had been struck pulsate.

He felt better when he had finished and thought that they had to be going a long way, given how fast they were travelling and how long it was taking.

Some time later, the van stopped abruptly, making him fall off the bar. He felt no enmity, as he could understand their anger. They must have reached their destination. He shuffled away from the door, thinking that it would not be wise to surprise them by being too close when they opened it. Ethan was shocked by the amount of his blood on the floor. His sodden trousers were very uncomfortable and he lifted the material so that it did not press against his skin. It looked as if he had been stabbed and he was suddenly aware of the coppery smell, which made him queasy and light-headed.

When the door finally opened, he did not dare to look up for several seconds, when he saw the two men looking into the van but not catching his eyes. One of them stepped forward and banged the side. Ethan's knees cracked when he stood and he squinted as he stepped into the light. They led him with hands on his shoulders.

They were in the countryside. They took him along a dirt path with lush greenery either side, as if they were walking through the garden of an old aristocratic home. There were apple trees at regular intervals, the fruit hanging just above them. Ethan stumbled over divots several times and was dragged for a few steps on the tops of his feet, the men pinching him painfully in their grip.

After they had followed the line of trees for a while, Ethan saw a portentously ugly building in the distance, a flattened grey block that looked like a smaller version of the SDMA headquarters. He was reminded of how conspicuous the Iklonian safe house in Caville had been. *They both rely more on power than secrecy; they've reached a point where they can operate in the open and defy anyone to point them out. They can be secret by virtue of being omnipresent.*

The path widened into a vast lawn that surrounded the building on all sides, a startling bright green that made Ethan wonder whether it was artificial. It made sense, of course. Their security staff would never allow a DIA building to be surrounded by trees. Open space enabled them to see who was coming and monitor nearby paths to determine whether there were any patterns in the amount of people who used them, the time they walked past, and whether the same person or combination of people recurred. That would allow a series of reports to be written to assess whether any of the activity was suspicious, then meetings would follow to discuss the findings. *It's what I would do.*

After going through a set of revolving doors, they stopped in a square space before a lip-shaped security barrier that looked to be the same design as those used by the SDMA. One of the men shouted "all right". They waited a moment until the barrier opened and someone handed them a security pass, which they put around his neck. They then scanned themselves in and one of them pulled Ethan's pass to the machine, making the cord cut into his neck. He wanted to laugh, as their amateurishness was as painfully obvious as that of the SDMA.

They took him into a lobby that was filled by a semi-circular reception with gaps at each end, which were blocked by security barriers. People sat behind the counter at regular intervals facing outwards, typing and ignoring them. All but one of them were men in expensive-looking black or grey suits, with a single woman sitting incongruously amongst them wearing a shiny blue dress, her hair tied back. She had a black rose in her hair and thick red lips. It was Daisy. They dragged him before one of the men.

"It's for this," one of the men holding him said.

"Oh, right. Go on through."

The man behind the counter frowned at him in such a way that Ethan thought that he must know what he was accused of. They moved him towards one of the barriers and he glimpsed a walkway behind the reception that was dominated by what looked like a huge piston. The striking nature of the image made it remain in his mind for several seconds.

The corridor behind the barrier was sterile white, with panels at regular intervals either side that were almost indistinguishable from the walls; he only became aware of them after having been dragged a considerable distance.

Eventually, they stopped before one and the men scanned their identity cards then pulled Ethan's towards it. A door opened and they pushed him through. As he heard it closing, Ethan twisted and put a foot in the way. One of the men stood before him.

"When am I going to be able to see a solicitor?"

"You're not under arrest, you dumb fuck."

The man stepped forward and punched his stomach. Ethan

stumbled back. The door closed and he did not try to breathe for several seconds.

Ethan was no longer afraid and did not berate himself like he had when he had been taken. His mind was blank. He was like the drug and sleep addicts who lined the city streets, gazing at passing commuters with the indifference of those with nothing to lose, almost revelling in disproving the idea that law can be enforced, free in their way, knowing that no restraint or punishment can touch them. He felt so lethargic that nothing was worth thinking about for more than a moment. He would not have thought that anything was out of place if Daisy had had three arms.

There was a constant level of light in the room and no windows, meaning that Ethan did not know the time. It had to be late morning or early afternoon, although it seemed like he had lain on the floor for a very long time.

When he finally got to his feet, he saw that the room hardly seemed like a cell at all. There was a double bed with clean linen that was more comfortable than those of many hotels he had stayed in. An MV monitor faced it, built into the wall so that nothing protruded, with a plastic covering over the glass. Beside the bed was a wardrobe bolted to the floor with a variety of clothes inside. There was even an exercise bar attached to the top of the door.

Ethan ran his fingers over the walls to find that they were uniformly smooth, like marble, and he could smell soap wherever he stood. Above the bed hung a picture of a stormy horizon. It was cool to the touch, making him imagine that it was covered with some kind of protective film.

The only aspect of the room that reminded him that he was in a DIA prison was the hatch on the door, which opened soon after he had finished looking around. A tray was pushed through that contained soup, a chocolate bar, and a packet of crisps. Ethan sat on the bed and sniffed them suspiciously, but there seemed no reason to poison him now that they could do whatever they wanted.

There was an en-suite bathroom that he did not see for some time after he had entered the room, as the door to it was hidden by the angle of the wardrobe. He would not be able to fit into the bath, the towels were only slightly larger than his hand, and the ceiling seemed very low. However, given everything that had happened, Ethan was amazed that they had allowed him such comfort.

After he had finished eating, there was little to do other than watch the MV. When he switched it on, he saw that all options other than two-dimensional television had been disabled. There was a list of channels to choose from, although when he selected some of the options, he saw that the descriptions of the programmes were available but the channel had been blocked. Those included film channels and pornography.

The other oddity was that when he watched the news, the space in the bottom right corner of the screen where the time was usually displayed was blacked out, and the contrast was such that he could not tell whether it was day or night. He flicked the channels to find that the options must have been set that way. Furthermore, at certain points, presenters' voices were muffled by static. After watching awhile, Ethan realised that it had to be whenever they were mentioning the date or time.

Having no pressure and nothing to do was an unusual, and very pleasant experience. As he watched a summary of the sport over the weekend, Ethan at first struggled to pay attention. However, after going over his situation until his mind felt numb, he realised the futility of worrying. *If I could predict what they were going to do then I wouldn't be here.*

Instead, he fell into a drowsy stupor, and when the sport had finished, he flicked through the channels until he found something vaguely diverting. He wondered what would have happened if he had lived this way. Although he was not rich, he had earned a good salary working for the SDMA, and could have done a passable job, gone home on time, and led a life of domesticity and mild dissipation, like everyone else.

Would I have been happy? It was difficult to say whether Aislin would have approved. On the one hand, she would definitely have appreciated more time together and the ability to go out whenever they wanted, rather than when it was convenient for the organisation. However, she had signed up for the same lifestyle and must have known that if the SDMA had not gone to hell after the recent changes and she had got her promotion, she would have been in the same situation as him. There was no answer.

At some point, Ethan dozed off, waking with a jump after a loud noise on the MV. He felt alarmed, as there were bound to be hidden cameras recording his every movement and sound, which would be constantly analysed. For a moment, he tried to convince himself that it might easily be night; after all the programmes he had watched, a day could have passed. But when he was honest with himself, Ethan knew that it was not true. He knew the hazy feeling very well by now, the sense that sleep was like a thief that would sneak up on him the moment he lost concentration, after which he would be lost in a fog of constant napping.

He looked at the door, imagining that they were monitoring his thoughts and would break in after hearing his mental confession. But time, whatever it was, only drifted on.

Ethan continued watching the MV until he guessed that it was late by the amount of times the headlines had been repeated. There were no pyjamas in the wardrobe so he stripped to his underwear and got under the sheets, which were thick enough that he felt swaddled.

When he woke, he remembered where he was and thought that there was no point being conscious for long in that place. He turned over and fell into a deep sleep in which he seemed to chase fragments of dreams. That happened several times until every last drop of sleep had been squeezed out of him.

The absence of clocks meant that Ethan was confused as to whether he should feel tired and hungry or not, and whether he should feel guilty or not. His captors gave him no indication of what he should be doing. He switched on the MV and watched some cartoons before getting dressed.

There was a tray of food by the door, but before he ate, Ethan tried the exercise bar. He could not lift himself parallel to it and was surprised by how much his arms ached at the attempt. After stretching them, he tried again and did a small number of reps, lifting himself to a lower height. He felt a vague sense of excitement at the idea that he could bulk up like people in normal prisons. When he was a child, he had been able to run around the playground for hours at a time; he would likely fall over if he tried the same thing now. *I don't know when I got so unfit. Just snuck up on me, I suppose.*

The lack of recorded time made Ethan learn a new routine. He soon abandoned any attempt to placate his unseen guards by sleeping lawfully; not only did his inferences about time based on what he saw on the MV become increasingly tenuous, but he thought that he might well be viewing a series of recordings set up to test him. In any case, he soon felt blasé, thinking that he could not commit worse crimes than he already had. *What are they going to do, put me in a cell with worse wallpaper?*

He alternated between watching the MV, daydreaming, trying to exercise, and napping. Despite his initial enthusiasm, he still could not lift himself to chin height after numerous attempts.

After he had exhausted his limited set of activities, he would climb into bed and wrap himself tightly in the sheets, rolling around until he felt tired then thinking about how he would be fading in the world; his work being taken over a piece at a time, Aislin and his parents worrying about him before gradually accepting his disappearance, his friends first perplexed then irritated at his failure to return their calls, before he turned from a talking point into an unmarked absence. Few care profoundly; loved ones will continue to eat while grieving and most live on, despite their protestations about the impossibility of doing so. After imagining that process, Ethan was happy to watch the MV again.

His meals tended to be provided while he slept, although occasionally, he heard the flap slap shut when he was daydreaming. After a time, Ethan decided to leave some washing by the door, as there were too many dirty towels for them to be stored anywhere. To his surprise, he found clean replacements when he woke. If only there had been alcohol and a selection of consumer goods available, the room would have been many people's idea of paradise.

Soon, Ethan ceased to have any cognizance of being watched, or even where he was. He adapted entirely to his new life, as if it were natural to live in two rooms and for food and clothes to appear and disappear while he was not looking. Once, he wondered how much longer this would go on before whatever process they had set up for him came into effect. *They must be preparing their case and gathering more evidence against me.*

One of the men who had brought him here had said that he was not under arrest, which meant that he would be tried in a DIA court. *I must have a deeper understanding of the Sleep Code than anyone, because I know it from both sides.* Ethan knew that the only conceivable punishment was death. He switched on the MV.

He was embarrassed and ashamed that he did not miss Aislin and his family as much as he should. His sleep problems had taken over his life to such an extent that now they had been alleviated, the mental space they had colonised was a void. The subject was too painful for him to focus on for long, and when it intruded into his thoughts, he winced as if remembering childhood pain.

It seemed as if he had been forgotten, that he was subject to automated processes that would continue long after civilisation had crumbled. As such, it was a considerable shock when his cell door opened and a man in a black jacket stepped in.

"Come on," he said, barely opening his mouth. Ethan switched off the MV and began making the bed before realising that the man was staring at him. Ethan paused and looked over the room with a sense of regret before going outside.

To Ethan's surprise, the man did not take hold of him but rather turned his back to shut and lock the door, giving Ethan every opportunity to run, if he had had any inclination to do so. The spotless corridor was as foreign to his imagination as if he had never seen it before. The man made his way along the route they had taken to get there without looking at him, leaving Ethan to follow of his own volition. His actions were so strange that he thought it was a trick. *Could they be putting me in a situation where they could say that I was about to escape, to allow them to do something?*

There was a different set of secretaries on the front desk, one of whom glanced up as he passed, only to look away the instant their eyes met, the movement as instinctive as when one pulls one's fingers from a naked flame.

It was dark outside, which was a shock to Ethan's senses. He had only recently slept, meaning that he had become nocturnal during his isolation.

When they reached the edge of the field where they were hidden from view by trees, the man slowed and Ethan thought that he was about to be killed. But they continued walking until they reached the van that had been used to bring him there.

He walked to the back of it, remembering the previous journey with equanimity. He did not feel upset about the prospect of being battered again. It seemed an apt punishment, and not humiliating in the way that being beaten would be, when he would be faced by his triumphant attacker.

"Round here."

Ethan had been deep in thought about what was going to happen next, meaning that the man's voice surprised him and Ethan did not move for several seconds, when he realised that he was telling him to get into the passenger seat. He did not say anything further and Ethan could feel his dislike. The vehicle had no safety monitor or other standard security equipment.

It was difficult to tell where they were going in the darkness and he only started to recognise some of the landmarks when they had almost reached their destination. They stopped outside the SDMA building. Someone had stuck an advertising poster on the side of it, which showed a bulldozer clearing away a slum. The words 'Our Development, Our Future' were printed underneath it, but over them had been written 'FUCK YOU' in black marker pen.

"Inside."

He was about to say 'thanks', but when seeing the man's expression, Ethan thought that it was best not to reply. He got out and slowly walked towards the building before resting against the side of a security spike. He gazed at it for some time before suddenly coming to himself when realising that the van was still there. He hurried to the door, and as soon as he was in sight of the guard at the front counter, he heard it drive away.

"Wait there."

The guard picked up a telephone and spoke into it in a low voice while keeping his eyes on him. Ethan had never seen him before. He heard him say "okay" before putting down the receiver.

"Have a seat."

"I'm all right as I am."

Coloured dots flickered perfunctorily across his body.

His legs ached by the time the lip-shaped security barrier opened and Daniel walked through.

"Thanks," he said to the security guard, nodding dismissively before turning to Ethan, "Come on."

"I've not got my ID with me."

"Privilege of rank," Daniel said, waving his pass, then waited until Ethan stood parallel to him before opening the barrier.

After they had entered the lift, Daniel pressed the button for the top floor and Ethan did not know what to say as they ascended. He should not be there, he should not even be in the building, but it seemed patronising to state that fact to his superior. He felt entirely under his power.

When the door opened, Daniel let him through another security barrier.

The fifteenth floor was designed the same as the tenth, with a bare corridor followed by a noticeboard, making Ethan feel disappointed. Daniel led him into the first office they encountered, and he thought that it was not so big, until he realised that it was for a single person. There was a bookcase filled with regulation manuals in one corner, which he paused to look at before Daniel sat behind his desk and gestured for Ethan to sit opposite him.

"I've never been on this floor. It's not what I was expecting."

"What were you expecting?"

"I don't know really. Bigger desks?"

Daniel smiled. "What am I going to do with you?"

"Did you get me out of there?"

After being reduced to desperation, Ethan felt a wild sense of freedom.

"You know that you're our best agent, don't you? Don't answer, you do know. Apart from your talent and how hard you work, what makes you effective is your discretion. It's hard to believe that so many people lack that quality in an organisation like this one. Accepting the parameters of the possible leads to success."

Daniel sighed and leant back in his chair.

"The Strategic Review Board met last week to discuss your document. You took over the entire agenda. I've sat on it on and off for a year and it's a talking shop. They've got a handful of subjects they waffle on about every month, and every month, they set the same actions, none of which ever go anywhere. Last week, they agreed a set of actions that the DIA wants implemented in ten days. I've nominated you for commendation, first class."

"Thank you... I appreciate that, sir."

Ethan felt uncomfortable, as he was unsure what was happening.

"I'll see that it goes through. There'll be no issues. The problem with our organisation is that performance questions are never addressed as they should be. We should reward these kind of achievements, and discipline those who waste our time."

Dan rested his head in his hands, as if having forgotten that Ethan was there. "What have you got to say?"

"I don't know, sir. It's hard to say what happened. It just got out of control one day and... I didn't know what to do. Do you need the details?"

Dan waved a hand. "No. Your problem, Ethan, is that you've become a fanatic. You don't see that there are occasions when we share interests with our enemies. There are fanatics on the other side too and what all fanatics don't understand is that to destroy one's enemy is to destroy oneself. Our purpose, Ethan, is to curb excess, it is not to change the nature of things. That's why you're here, because you haven't understood that. Our leaders want efficiency, but only within the proper limits. Too much efficiency will destroy the system. You don't want to end up like Max. Of course, you'll not have read the papers recently..." Daniel shook his head. "The thing that's saved you is that you're an organisational man. There are few people today who'll put the organisation before their self-interest, and you're one of them. Loyalty is an old-fashioned virtue. I'm returning the favour."

"Was it you or the Iklonians who gave me the file about the Professor?"

"Only fanatics draw too strong a distinction between us and the Iklonians. Ultimately, everyone is DIA. Everyone. You haven't made a habit of asking dangerous questions before. Don't start now. I'm not going to allow our more... short-sighted colleagues to take advantage of the situation."

His voice had become sharp and Ethan looked at the floor.

"Dan... I'm grateful for how you've helped me... not just now but before as well..."

"Next week, Peter is going to be offered a redundancy package based on certain medical evidence that has recently come to light. He'll accept what's offered then you will apply for the vacancy. The following month, you'll be interviewed, then you'll become the Chief Agent of the Investigative Section. There's no need for me to say this but I'll tell you what I'd tell anyone: that I expect you to maintain the high standards that you've shown throughout your career hitherto. I'll be your line manager, so when you get news of your promotion, please report to me for further instructions."

Ethan nodded.

"Go home now, it's late."

"Sir, what day is it?"

"Friday. Don't worry about tonight, you'll be able to have four hours and revert to your proper pattern tomorrow..." Daniel gave him a significant look, "... Aislin went into a panic about you, she rang everyone she could think of and wouldn't stop until I arranged for someone to give her a limited explanation. She broke two security guard's noses. God, that was a long day. The organisation values stable relationships, Ethan. The organisation values those who take what it provides."

Daniel stood and it was obvious from his tone that he wanted Ethan to leave.

"How can I go back to the office when I've been away for so long? What will I say to everyone?"

"You've been away three weeks. You'll say that you've been away. This conversation is over. There's one final thing you've got to learn, Ethan, which is that in the running of an organisation, there are no conversations. Information is always implicit, never imparted. That's it, here are your things, go."

While he was talking, Daniel had placed the items that were taken from Ethan by the DIA agents on his desk, including his security pass. Ethan put them in his pockets and hurried away, turning back after a few steps to see Daniel giving his computer a blood sample.

He paused with trepidation when hovering his pass over the lip-shaped security barrier near the lift, but it opened. When inside, he switched on his mobile to see that he had had two hundred and thirteen missed calls, and when he unlocked it, most of them were from Aislin, with a few from his parents and Terry. There were also five automated messages from the SDMA, detailing the jail terms handed out to a gang who had manufactured fake alarm clocks, shift licences, and SDMA identity cards. Fifteen years each. It was only seven o'clock, so there was no excuse not to see her that evening. He waited until getting outside the building before calling her.

"Ethan, is that you?"

"Ash, I've got to see you tonight to tell you what's going on."

"What the hell's happened? You disappear for weeks then call me out the blue? Why the fuck couldn't you ring before?"

"They took my phone away. Will you see me so I can explain?"

The phone went silent.

"Where are you?"

"I'm outside work. It'll take me a few hours to get to you."

"I'll drive to your house, it'll be quicker. Whatever you've got, it'd better be good."

"I'll see you there."

293

Ethan walked to the car park, and as he went, he saw that the jewellery shop was open, despite it being outside the opening times printed on the door.

As he turned a corner, a swarm of coppery butterflies arose from a nearby wall and fluttered in the direction of the field leading to the train station. He paused for a moment to watch, unsure whether he was more real than them.

As he drove home, the night had a new meaning for him. When previously looking into the darkness, Ethan had seen the smallness of the world and it had made him weary and frustrated. Now, he saw the unchanging nature of things.

When he got home, he parked beside Aislin's car and clutched the steering wheel tightly, steeling himself.

He unlocked the door and Aislin was standing in the hallway, looking at him. She looked very beautiful in her blue dress and did not say anything. She folded her arms.

"Aislin, listen to me. I'm going to tell you everything that's happened, but first, I want you to know how much I love you. I've made a lot of mistakes but I know what's important now. That's why before anything else, I'm going to ask you this."

He bent on one knee and presented her with the ring he had been given at the jewellery shop. "Will you marry me?"